MW01622007

John Paul Jones, Jr.

Cold Before Morning

A heart-warming novel about
a Florida pioneer family.

10—09—08—07—06—05

Illustrations by Oscar Rayneri

Dedicated to
Marion Pecot Jones

PUBLISHING, INC.

4909 North Monroe Street • Tallahassee, FL 32303

800–741–2712

www.fatherson.com

Preface

As I walked through the musty, empty rooms of the "old McCredie House," almost hidden from view by live oaks and tall weeds, at the south end of the shady lane that in my youth we called "McCredie Lane," I somehow felt thrust backward in time.

I was born in this Micanopy, Florida, house on March 3, 1912, only thirteen years after it had been built as an exact duplicate of the original James McCredie home that was destroyed by fire in 1899.

My footsteps stirred the dust and sent little shining stars scurrying after one another up a beam of late afternoon sunlight that flooded through a vacant window. I felt the still–satiny smoothness of the newel post at the foot of the stair and ran my hand slowly along the carved mantle of heart pine that my grandfather had cut and sanded and shaped with great care for the new home.

COLD BEFORE MORNING

The bay window that ran from floor to ceiling in the living room, facing the sandy lane was still there and I pictured Lorna Doone McCredie, age three, her face and arms spotted with measles, standing there watching with envy her brothers and sisters playing in the snow during the great February freeze of 1895.

Time now had me in its clutches and I felt a great need to tell the story of this house and its people, all dead now, including Lorna Doone, the last of the original McCredie line to go.

I've lived with the story for more than sixty–five years, gathering it piece meal from winter night tales around the open fireplace, from old letters, from newspaper clippings, from family Bibles. It's a story of personal and economic disasters, of wars, separation from loved ones, diseases, death, romance and love, attempted murder and suicide.

It's all here, within the echoing walls of this two–story Victorian house with its rusting tin roof, its old–fashioned lightning rods that point skyward like stern, parental fingers, and the two gable windows that held lamps at night to guide family members back to their fireside.

As though from a great distance I can hear two of my grandchildren who came with me this afternoon "to see where Papa was born."

They are running through the house jumping up and down on the sturdy pine floors. I can barely hear one say "Listen it must be a million years old, and it doesn't even squeak!"

"Not a million years old, grandson," I said to myself, softly, "but merely a hundred—and what a hundred!"

Actually, Lorna Doone McCredie's story began more than a hundred years ago in Glasgow, Scotland.

1

Journey To America

1854

David McCredie, fifty–one, shivered slightly as he peered from the door of his cobbler's shop into the heavy fog that swirled and danced over the narrow cobblestone street that curved around his business and then straightened out toward the waterfront. The year was 1854 and the place was Whithorn, Scotland, near Wigtown Bay, an arm of Solway Firth that opened into the Irish Sea.

The cobbler already was an old man with white hair, hanging to his shoulders and matted against his creased forehead from the dampness of the fog. As he stood there, the fog, like wisps of grey smoke, stole past him into the shop.

"A night for thieves," he thought as he closed and double–barred the door, and then checked the two windows to see that their thick, wooden shutters were closed and bolted.

COLD BEFORE MORNING

David thought of his youth in Glasgow, where he was born and of his marriage to Janet Milwain, as pert a highland lass as you'd find in all of Scotland. The simple wedding took place in 1827, and then the bairns began to arrive. First there was Helen, born in 1828, and then John Stewart, a husky lad, in 1829. Another daughter, Janet, came in 1831. Tragedy struck in 1834, when the "first" Margaret, who was born in November of 1833, died at age four months.

The next child was a daughter, born in 1835, also named Margaret. David and Janet wanted a "Margaret," so they named this daughter "Margaret" and called her "Maggie," a name she carried all her life of ninety–five years.

David remembered his wife's warning, as she repeated an old superstition that only evil would follow the naming of a new child for one that had died.

The next two children were boys, James, in 1837, and David in 1839. During these years the shoe business was good in Glasgow and the McCredie family, with leather for tanning plentiful and cheap, fared well as the family grew.

The eighth child, a lass they named Susan, was born in 1841, and then there was William, born in 1849, the year of the great famine that drove the McCredie family out of Glasgow to Whithorn on the southwest coast where it was hoped the family would prosper. The last child born in Glasgow was Thomas, who arrived in 1846.

The McCredie's eleventh child was born in Whithorn in 1850, a lad also named William, for his brother who had died at age five. Again the cobbler and his wife defied the old superstition.

David thought about the superstition as he snuffed out the candles in his shop and started slowly up the worn stairs to his living quarters above the shop, where Janet and his children were waiting for him to appear for the evening meal.

This Scotsman was a stubborn man with a bent frame and calloused hands who had worked hard all his life and who believed that honesty and honest toil would be rewarded. He refused to believe in the old superstitions shared by many of his countrymen, but, even so, he couldn't quite shake the feeling of despair that gripped him this night.

He brushed his hand almost angrily across his face as though to wipe away some kind of dark shadow.

He thought of the famine, the deaths of four of his little ones, and the lack of food at times to feed his family. On the morrow he and Janet would lose their two eldest sons, John and James, and it was their own doing.

"They eat like a pair of highland wolves," David had said when it was decided after many sleepless nights that the two boys would be sent to America to David's brother, John Stewart McCredie, who lived at Orange Springs in Florida on some river with a strange–sounding name.

"They'll learn a trade," David said, "and we'll have food to go around."

Janet had cried often at the thought of losing her second and sixth child. She was sure in her heart that she would never see them again. For her, it was like sending them to their graves.

"James is just a lad," she pleaded, "and so far a way from home. There must be another way."

David would not be moved. "He's seventeen and a stout lad. And John is twenty–five. He's due a family of his own. We were married before I was twenty–five. The nest is too full. They must go to America."

That ended the subject.

There was no laughter around the supper table that night, but secretly, in their hearts, John and James were exuberant. They had dreamed for days of the moment of departure on the greatest adventure of their lives and longed for the hour of sunrise when they would leave by coach for Liverpool to sail to America.

James lay on his narrow bed, trying to force sleep, but it would not come. His head was a tangled mass of thoughts that seemed to move in several directions at once, leaving his mind filled with uncertainty, with fear, with sadness and yet, above all with a sense of high adventure. He feared to leave the warmth and love of his home but at the same time he was eager to go.

Then he heard a slight rustling in the dark room and a trembling hand brushed his cheek.

"You'll take care of yourself, my son?"

It was the voice of his mother, Janet, whispering next to his ear. She was kneeling beside his bed.

"Aw, Mama," James said, "don't you be worryin' about me. John and me will be fine at Uncle John's."

"But it's a big ocean you'll be crossin' and there are still storms this time of year." Her voice indicated the fear and turmoil she suffered.

James sat up in bed and put his arms around Janet, leaning his face against hers. He felt the tears on her cheek and suddenly shed his youth. He felt like a man, with a need to comfort his mother. For the first time in his life he–sensed her age, her frailty, her fear.

"No need to fret," he said, as though he were soothing a child. "You've always told me not to fear anything. What is to be will be?"

"Take this," she whispered, pressing a round, hard object into his hand.

"It's a coin," James said. "You had best keep it. Times are hard. You'll be needin' it for the family."

"No, keep it," she insisted. "I've saved it for a long time. We'll get along."

There was a candle glow at the door. It was David.

"Come to bed lass," he said softly.

"The lads will be needing their rest. It's a long journey they go tomorrow."

As the flickering light of the candle faded from his room, James settled down in his bed and soon joined his brother in deep, untroubled sleep.

But there was little rest for Janet McCredie.

She had been afraid of the sea all her life and tales of horrible sea monsters that devoured ships and their crews kept flashing before her eyes as she rolled and tossed. When she was small, her eldest brother delighted in tormenting her with tales of these fire–breathing monsters that could come up out of the sea without a moment's warning and spout flames, that burned the sails of the largest ships, leaving the ship and the crew to their mercy.

Her brother had run away from home at age fourteen to sail around the world and somewhere off the coast of Africa his ship had disappeared and was never heard of again. She knew deep in her heart, even at that moment when her sons were sleeping their last night at home in their beloved Scotland, that one of his monsters had put an end to her brother's stories.

David fared not much better. His fears were not of stormy seas or sea monsters, however. He thought about these strapping young men, his sons, and the void that would be left in his heart and at the family table. These were sons meant to comfort his old age.

He could feel the bed tremble as Janet moved restlessly.

"Poor lass," he thought. "Tis a horrible thing I've done to her."

After David and Janet McCredie had reluctantly decided to send their eldest sons to America, they had to find a way to accomplish this within their financial means. They sought the help of the *London Times*. David scanned the shipping news, seeking a cheap, safe passage across the Atlantic.

The *Times* had announcements of sailings each week of the new fangled "mail steamships," but, alas, the fare was thirty pounds for first class, twenty pounds for second class and eight pounds for steerage.

One day David saw this special announcement, "Notice to Emigrants. The undersigned dispatch first class ships from Liverpool to New York weekly by American Line of Packets; to New Orleans weekly and to St. Johns, N.B. on the fifth and twentieth of each month by Liverpool Line of Packets. Luggage of passengers stored and put onboard free of expense. Berths for first and second class and steerage passengers secured by remitting a deposit of one pound for each passenger to Babel and Cortis, three Clarence Dock, Liverpool."

A later notice indicated that the *Patrick Henry* would be sailing on April 15th with J. R. Hurlbert, commanding. Steerage fare was eight guineas. The decision was made, and David went into the family trunk for the deposit money.

The *Patrick Henry* was a clipper of one thousand–two tons register and when the McCredie boys saw it for the first time on the morning of April 15th, 1854 they thought it was the most beautiful thing they had ever seen, a judgment that was destined to be altered in the weeks ahead.

The departure before daylight from Whithorn had been sad. Janet was in tears and David busied himself with their luggage, his face lined and unhappy.

The advertisement for the *Patrick Henry* had said that the space between decks was well ventilated and the passengers "would be quite comfortable," but John and James were dismayed when they saw their berths, two shelves not more that twenty–four–inches wide and not enough head room between the bunks to turn over without getting out.

"*Patrick Henry*," James read on the side of the vessel. "He wasn't a Scotsman, was he John?"

"American patriot," John replied. "This is an American line. We couldn't get passage on the *Glasgow*. Cost too much."

Captain Hurlbert, a New Englander, was brusk and all business when they went aboard. "You boys watch yer provisions," he advised. "Some of these folks'll run out before we reach New York an' they'll take anything they can get their hands on."

Food had been a problem. Steerage passengers had to provide their own and that meant enough dried fish, biscuits, pickled herring, chocolate and some smoked ham to last six weeks. "You kin use the ship's water barrel," the captain said.

The McCredie boys stowed their gear and then went on deck to watch the preparations for departure. Captain Hurlbert had said they would sail with the tide in about two hours. That would be about sunset except there was no sun to see. Already the day was dank and dark and the April air was anything but spring like. The harbor at Liverpool was a confusing mass of ships of all sizes, some coming in but most getting ready to depart for unknown destinations.

The departure of the *Patrick Henry* promised to be exciting.

The wind had almost reached thirty knots, and even the sheltered cove was dotted with white caps. "It's like Mama's old calico apron, the grey one with the white dots," James thought.

He was worried about the voyage to America and this whistling wind, the ship rolling and tugging at its lines like a huge, hungry dog, didn't make him any less fearful. "When we are outside of the harbor, I wonder how it'll be," he thought "Hope I don't get sick."

As one of the sailors passed him, a lad who appeared to be about his own age, James asked,"Will we be leaving in this kind of weather?"

"Hah! This is nothing," the young sailor said, and went about his duties.

The departure from Liverpool was more then exciting. It was almost a disaster. Once the ship's lines had been cast free, even though the Patrick Henry had raised only a small amount of sail it bounded forward into the bay, scraping the wharf as it went and only expert seamanship at the helm kept them from colliding with a number of ships, having similar difficulties with the wind and waves.

Salt spray across the deck, driven by a mean–tempered wind, soon drove the passengers below decks, and as it turned out, that's where they remained

most of the first week at sea as an April storm swept down from the North Sea and gathered strength as it drove the small ship out of the Irish Sea and through St. George's Channel, between England and Ireland.

There were only a half dozen passengers traveling steerage on this sailing. Besides James and John there was a young English husband and wife, the John Andersons, bound for Baltimore, Maryland, where they would live with Mr. Anderson's brother and John would assist his brother in a mercantile establishment; then there were two men, a Londoner who had recently been released from debtor's prison; a Ben Smoot, who was going to California to prospect for gold, and lastly, Mr. Anthony J. McClure from Glasgow, Scotland, a cabinet maker who hoped to make his fortune plying his trade in Boston.

The small steerage compartment was crowded with six occupants and the boys were embarrassed to use the "necessary," a bucket behind a square of canvas in one corner of the compartment, particularly with a young and attractive woman in their midst. Ben Smoot, accustomed to this lack of privacy, made matters worse by always announcing in a loud voice when he had to use the facility. "I'm about to do my business, begging pardon, ma'am. Yew kin close yer eyes or hold yer noses as ye sees fit."

This happened a number of times and finally John Anderson, approached Smoot and said quietly, "Sir, my wife is not accustomed to such language and if you keep doing this I will take up the matter with the captain."

This challenge set Smoot afire. He drew a long, thin knife from his boot. "Ye just do that, laddie," he snorted, "an I'll slit yer throat and throw ye to the sharks."

Now, John McCredie, though still a mild–mannered young man, was no coward, and, in addition he was all of six feet tall and weighed one hundred eighty pounds, all muscle and bone. He moved between Smoot and John Anderson, his jaw squared and his eyes glinting. "Mr. Smoot," he said "you put that knife back in your boot or I'll be obliged to push it down your throat."

Ben Smoot was a coward, the kind that strikes in the night and then slinks back into the shadows. He sized up the situation, for all four of the men were on their feet and he could see he was outnumbered, even if he did have a knife.

"No offense meant," he said, and put his knife away.

But the atmosphere in the compartment was no longer comfortable. All of the passengers felt compelled to keep an eye on Smoot.

There were other discomforts. Most of that first week the hatch to the compartment had to be battened shut because of the wind and heavy seas. James felt like he was in prison, a prison that pitched and rolled and threatened to split apart from the pounding of the waves. He marveled at how this wooden hull with its human cargo could keep plunging deep into the ocean's bosom and then rise again as though shot from a cannon and then drop like a wounded bird. Over and over, hour after hour, day and night, it rose on the crest of a mountainous wave, plunged into a watery canyon, and then bounded back up again.

During that week, there was no communication with Captain Hurlbert or any member of his crew, and for all the passengers knew those topside might have been swept overboard and left them imprisoned in a derelict. It was a very real and haunting fear for people who had lived all of their lives on the land.

Added to the fear was the sickness.

The "necessary" was overfilled and the stench was almost unbearable. Ordinarily it would have been emptied each day, but the weather did not permit such activity.

But on the seventh day, April 22nd, came some relief. During the night, the savage movement of the ship changed to a gentle roll and in the morning a crew member opened the hatches and shouted for the passengers to come on deck if they wished.

They were greeted by the sweet smell of the sea, sunshine and the dark blue water slipping quickly by as the *Patrick Henry* plowed southwest toward the Azores, under full sail.

Captain Hurlbert mingled with his passengers, expressing regret that the voyage had begun under such "cruel circumstances," as he expressed it. He assured them that the ship had never been in danger and that the trip to America would be completed within another five weeks. To further reassure them about the hospitality of the shipping company he invited all passengers, including those traveling steerage, to be his guests in the captain's quarters at sunset for a round of spirits.

James McCredie was accustomed to his mother's eggnog at Christmas, a delightful foamy, milk and egg drink, only flavored with a touch of Scotch whiskey. John, being older, was allowed to drink with his father on festive occasions that called for some kind of family celebration. They decided after due consideration to accept the captain's invitation to celebrate the end of their first storm at sea.

They gathered in Captain Hurlbert's tiny cabin, along with a dozen or more passengers and ship's officers to receive a "hot toddy," of Irish whiskey. The late afternoon air had a sharp bite to it and the hot drink was satisfying. They had to line up to go into the cabin and then returned to the deck to consume their cups of refreshments.

After a sip, John turned to his brother and said, "This stuff will kick you like a grown horse. Better take it easy."

But, James considered himself a man now, on his own, off to America to make his fortune. Anything John could do, he could do. So, he gulped down the liquid, which burned like a molten river all the way to his stomach, and prepared to go back into the cabin for a second helping.

John laid a restraining hand on his shoulder and cautioned, "That's enough for now. Let that settle in your belly."

The only casualty of this happy affair was Ben Smoot.

After several cups of the whiskey, he grew quarrelsome and ended up inviting Mrs. Anderson to share his bed and commenting on the curve of her thighs. There was no way he could determine the curve of her thighs because of her voluminous skirts, unless he had been looking when he should not have been.

When Mrs. Anderson told her husband of the insult, he confronted Smoot and the runty individual quickly drew his knife and would have plunged it into Anderson if John McCredie had not been observing the encounter. He grabbed Smoot by the back of his neck and marched him over to Captain Hurlbert and related what had happened.

"Put him in irons," Hurlbert commanded his first mate and the drunken passenger was led away cursing and screaming that he would "get even."

"We'd better watch him if they release him before this trip ends," James told his brother later. "I think he means to harm you."

"Let him try," John said.

The second week aboard the *Patrick Henry* was pleasant except for the cursing, alternated with loud singing, of Ben Smoot in the brig adjacent to the quarters of the steerage passengers, and the passengers spent all of their daylight hours on deck. Toward the end of the second week, about sundown, John and James were standing in the bow of the ship with John and Mary Anderson when James suddenly exclaimed, "I see birds." Off the port bow there were birds wheeling and gliding, outlined against the setting sun. Later some were observed resting on the water.

"What would birds be doing out here in the middle of the ocean?" James wanted to know.

"That means we are near land," John Anderson explained. "We should be in the vicinity of the Azores."

"I hope we can go ashore, if only for a moment," Mary Anderson said. "I'd like to stand on something that isn't moving." She had been violently seasick all of the first week of the voyage, but seemed to fare better when she could remain above deck.

Later, the passengers learned that they would anchor in the Azores to take on fresh water, but no one would be allowed to go ashore.

Two days southwest of the Azores, James and John returned to their steerage quarters one afternoon to find their rations had been stolen. Not one biscuit or bite of herring remained. Captain Hurlbert offered little comfort. "I warned you to watch your vittles," was his only comment. Later, he promised to look into the matter. The food could not have been stolen by any of the steerage passengers because there was no way they could hide extra provisions.

That evening the Andersons shared their diminishing food with the boys, but James and John knew they could not infringe upon the hospitality of the Andersons for very long. They realized their problem was a serious one because the voyage was less than half completed and without food they would starve. Captain Hurlbert said they could eat with his crew but they would have to pay for the food.

That night they discussed the situation.

John carried their money in a purse strapped inside his shirt. They had just enough to pay for passage from New York to Jacksonville and up the St. Johns River where their Uncle John Stewart McCredie had written he would meet them, at the place the Ocklawaha River entered the St. Johns. The agreement was that he would camp in the vicinity for a week beginning June 1st, 1854.

"If we use our money to buy food from the Captain," John said, "we won't be able to buy passage up the river."

There was a long silence, and then James remembered their last night in Whithorn, and the coin Janet had pressed into his hand. The next morning they took the coin to Captain Hurlbert and asked about food for the remainder of their trip to America. He examined the gold piece carefully and then announced, "For this coin you kin eat at my table."

Not knowing the value of the coin, James and John agreed, but they felt certain the tight–fisted captain had made a good deal for himself.

Later, upon discussing with the Andersons the theft and their deal with Captain Hurlbert, John Anderson told them that he had been warned by friends in London that some of the clipper commanders had a member of their crew regularly steal a passenger's food supply and thus force the passenger to buy food. The extra money went into the commander's pocket and not into the shipping line's funds. The passenger or passengers to be victimized in this manner were carefully chosen as they came aboard; those least likely to cause trouble with the company being singled out and warned to keep watch over their provisions.

"If I were you," John Anderson told the McCredie boys, "I'd report this theft to the owners of the line when we get to New York. In fact, I'll go with you."

This, they all agreed would be the wise thing to do.

Toward the end of the fourth week, as the *Patrick Henry* neared the Bermudas, the weather had warmed up to the extent that all hatches were left open day and night, otherwise the steerage compartment would have been uncomfortably warm. Steerage passengers were allowed to bring their mattresses topside and sleep under the stars, if they so desired. James and John did this one night and decided that they preferred the open deck and continued to sleep there on clear nights.

One day the wind died to a whisper, the sails hung limp and the ship barely stirred in the water. Crew members threw hooks and lines from the stern on the captain's orders to "catch some fish for a fresh seafood dinner."

These hand lines were effective and soon they had hauled aboard grouper and dolphin that were cut into fish steaks and then fried in oil in a large kettle hung over an iron "fire pit" on the afterdeck.

All passengers were invited by the captain to enjoy their first meal of fresh meat since they had left Liverpool and cups of warm ale were handed around during the meal. This lack of wind continued for two more days and the passengers began to fear that their arrival in New York would be delayed to such an extent that they would not make connections with the ships moving north or south along the American coast, but the wind returned and soon the *Patrick Henry* had rounded the Bermudas and was headed on its final leg to New York.

The nights were mild and the boys continued to sleep on deck. James liked to lie on his back and watch the twinkling stars, which seemed near enough to pluck out of the sky like picking grapes from the vine back home. The cobbler's shop in Whithorn and his old home in Glasgow seemed part of another world like one of the stars winking at him from the night sky.

One night he asked John if he thought they would ever see David and Janet and their brothers and sisters again.

"Yes," John answered.

"I don't see how you figure that," James said, sadly. "We won't have the money to go back to Scotland. Maybe it'll take years, maybe forever."

"We just have to work hard and save our money so we can bring them to America, too," John said. James couldn't see his brother's face, but he imagined the set of his jaw and knew he meant what he said.

These two brothers were, in many ways, like two peas in a pod. Both were big for their ages, fair of skin, dark haired and strong of limb. James was the smaller of the two, which came from the age difference, but he showed promise of being as big as John when he reached twenty–five. Both boys were stingy with words, smiled seldom and kept to themselves most of the voyage. The Andersons sensed their shyness and decided that it was due in part to "homesickness," John Anderson told his wife. Then he added, "You can't get much out of a Scotsman, tight with money, tight with words."

"I think they're just overwhelmed with being so far away from home," Mary Anderson had said. "They need some good friends."

And so, the Andersons became good friends. Mary arranged little picnics on deck, using food from their scant store, and used the occasion to try to pull the young McCredies out of their self–imposed shells. She taught them a few English songs and finally got James to sing some of the songs he had learned in school.

Mary Anderson agreed with her husband that while the two boys were a lot alike in physical appearance, in manner, in likes and dislikes they were basically different. Of the two, John was the doer, the one who would stride fearlessly into the face of danger. He had worked as a farm hand and was good with animals.

He liked to work with his hands and never seemed to worry about anything. On the other hand, James was more of a thinker type. He had read every book he could buy or borrow. His little room at home still held a small treasure trove of books, including his favorite, Lorna Doone. How that scholarly bent would affect him in pioneer America remained to be seen.

The days passed, the weather became cooler as they moved northward, and then late one afternoon as the sun was about to plunge below the horizon, leaving a trail of crimson, there was a cry of "Land Ho" from the crow's nest. The young British sailor told James, "It's probably Maryland. Wind holding, we'll be in New York in a few days."

COLD BEFORE MORNING

On the morning of May 30th, the passengers of the *Patrick Henry* went on deck to find land directly ahead of the ship. They were anchored at the entrance to New York harbor, awaiting an incoming tide, and among those on deck was Ben Smoot who had been released from the brig by Captain Hurlbert with orders to his crew to "watch the little beggar." About ten o' clock the anchor came aboard and the *Patrick Henry* moved under light sail toward the shipping lines's dock up the Hudson River.

The boys, as well as the other passengers, stood in the bow and along the starboard rail, completely mesmerized by the harbor commotion and the tall buildings along the waterfront. They were fascinated by the steam engines, ships that towered above the sailing vessels and the black smoke that poured from some of them that were getting up steam to depart made them look like sea monsters.

Suddenly, in the midst of all this wonder, there was a cry, "Grab the bloke, he's going overboard!"

Then there was a splash. It was Ben Smoot. His head bobbed up and down as he swam toward the wharf. Someone called the captain. "Forget it," said Hurlbert. "He's a bad one. He'll die on a rope someday."

The boys wondered if they had seen the last of Smoot.

After the ship docked, they gathered their meager belongings and joined the crowds seeking coastwise passage to the south. Their father had made arrangements through the *Patrick Henry* owners for them to go south on the clipper ship, *Savannah*, operated by Benton and How Line, serving the U.S. Eastern seaboard. Captain Hurlbert directed them to the line's main office.

At Benton and How they showed their papers and John was about to pay for their passage when he made a sickening discovery. His money belt was empty. He turned to James with a grim look. "Now I know why Smoot jumped ship," he said.

The boys were stunned. They were in a strange land. Help was more than three thousand miles away. The ticket agent returned their papers and said he was sorry.

"He's sorry," John thought. "That's not much good right now." Then, he saw the look of anguish on his brother's face, and knew he had to take charge. "Come on, James," he said, his voice as lighthearted as he could make it. "I've got an idea." He took James back to the *Patrick Henry* and told Captain Hurlbert their plight. All thought of reporting the captain to his superiors because of the missing food had vanished with the discovery of the empty money belt.

Hurlbert was silent for a long time, his piercing eyes on the two young men before him. Finally, he said, "I think I can help you. That is if you want to work fer yer passage. The line says I got to take the *Henry* south to Savannah to pickup cotton and lumber before goin' back ter Liverpool. The coin ye give me will pay part of yer passage and ye kin work for the rest. Eat with the crew. What yer say?"

John nodded his head. "When do we leave?"

"Two days," Hurlbert said. "But you two stay aboard. The ship needs cleanin.' Report to Mr. Marlow." Tom Marlow was first mate, a decent sort of fellow, but harsh on those who failed to work hard, and he had been seen using a whip on sailors who lingered over their chores.

As they put their gear back in the steerage compartment, John told James, "At least we'll get to Savannah, and then, we'll work something out to Jacksonville. One thing is sure now, we won't be able to meet Uncle John at his camp at the mouth of the Ocklawaha River. It could take ten days to two weeks for us to get down there and he will leave to go back to Orange Springs at the end of this month."

They reported to Mr. Marlow and were put to work swabbing the deck, and continued with that work until the *Patrick Henry* sailed on June 2nd. The journey down coast was uneventful, and slow. Only a light breeze blew most of the days so the ship was able to maintain just a few knots speed. Finally, on June 10th they turned into the harbor at Savannah and the boys' first reaction was that the town looked a lot like Liverpool.

As soon as the ship was tied up at the dock, Captain Hurlbert went ashore to see about his cargo. As he left, he said to John, "You boys remain aboard until I get back and maybe I'll have some news about a job that'll take you to Jacksonville."

He came back in half an hour, a scowl on his face and obviously out of sorts. His first order was to Mr. Marlow to weigh anchor and get the ship underway. John and James had been standing on the wharf but hurried aboard to see about getting their baggage off before the *Patrick Henry* sailed back to England. Hurlbert came up puffing and fumin.' "You boys get to work. My cargo's another day's run down to St. Marys. That's not far from Jacksonville and you could walk down there if you have to."

The next afternoon the *Patrick Henry* entered the St. Marys River between Georgia and Florida and sailed west to the harbor.

They found a bustling small town with a row of docks along the river and about sixty buildings, including warehouses, dwellings and official offices, including the director of the port. The harbor was so crowded Captain Hurlbert was forced to anchor offshore and wait his turn to dock so he could load up his cargo. This didn't help his feelings. "Another day or two wasted," he grumbled to Marlow.

James and John went ashore in a small boat to speak with the port director about work in the village and were told they might try the Ross Inn down the street facing the St. Marys River.

When the boys found the Ross Inn, they stared in disbelief. It was like many English inns they had seen back home. The innkeepers, Jean and Marion DuFour, were cordial and sympathetic after hearing the story of their trip across the Atlantic and the efforts being made to reach their uncle, John Stewart McCredie, at Orange Springs in Florida.

"Dat work'll be hard," DuFour said, frankly. "Everything from cookin,' waiting tables, cleanin' up and throwing out them as had too much whiskey. "He looked at John's size. "You kin handle dem drunks, oui?"

John nodded.

"We kin accommodate you two on the third floor. Might be a bit crowded. Some nights three or four to a bed." He grinned. "The food and drink's good, though."

They hurried back to the ship to get their baggage and found Captain Hurlbert stomping around like a man bewitched. Seems that he was about to empty all his ballast in the river so he could take on cargo when someone on the dock called to tell him there was a one thousand dollar fine for releasing ballast at any spot not designated for that purpose.

To keep from being fined, Hurlbert had to raise anchor and go a mile from town to a mud flat designated for ballast.

The boys learned that the foundations and the chimney at the Ross Inn had been made from stone ballast discharged in the river by ship captains who had released their ballast by night.

The young British sailor took them ashore with their baggage and on the way warned them about the Inn. “Got ghosts,” he said. “Haunted. A headless pirate.”

John laughed in disgust. It sounded like some of the stories he had heard along the waterfront at Whithorn.

“You kin laugh,” the sailor said heatedly, “but there’s more than ghosts, like a knife between your ribs in the middle of the night.”

Back at the Inn, James asked Mr. DuFour about the ghost. He roared with laughter. “You heard dat tale soon already. Thought you might. It’s fool talk up an’ down dat east coast. I ain’t never see ghost.”

John spoke up. “It’s not ghosts worryin’ me. It’s men with knives in the middle of the night, tryin’ to steal our money.”

“Dat you’ll have to keep dem eyes on. It kin be rough here. I said that befo.” DuFour turned and started up the stairs. “I’ll show you yer room.”

The third floor room they entered was large, with a ten–foot ceiling and four, oversized double beds, each one with a deep feather mattress and four pillows. "Take dat one," DuFour said, pointing to a bed near a front window. "Yew two only ones in it less some people come in durin' night. Put things under dat bed."

He turned to go. "Come down, we'll have us a leetle sip of ale and speak of work."

The boys noticed slop jars under the bed and wondered if their duties would include the emptying of such smelly things.

"That's woman's work," John said. "I'm not goin to touch them."

Later, over the ale, he learned that their chores did include emptying the slop jars each morning and was unable to hide his dislike for such work.

"Yew kin take it or leave it," DuFour said. "They's sure to be work here dat's not to yer likin,' but if yew want to sleep an' eat at Ross, yew'll do as I says, or as Mrs. DuFour says, oui?"

John nodded in assent.

For light there were lamps with whale oil for fuel, and they had to trim the wicks each day and keep the lamps filled. The floors had to be swept daily and scrubbed every week. Firewood had to be cut and stacked in the kitchen for the ten–foot–wide fireplace where the cooking was done in iron pots that hung over the flames. DuFour said there would be other jobs as they came up.

"How old' s this place?" James asked their new boss.

"Who dat knows. Some, they say 1760. Dat make it close to one hundred. Could be more, could be less," DuFour answered. "Somethin' yew ought to know. Tween them two top rooms is a hidden passage. Folks who knows kin move from room to room without usin' dem doors."

James had visions of a secret door opening behind his head and a hand coming through with a knife aimed at his throat "How will I ever sleep up there?" he wondered.

That question was answered at the end of the first day of work. Both boys were so tired when they were allowed to go to bed after midnight that they slept all night until they were awakened at daylight by DuFour shaking the bed and demanding they get down to the kitchen.

During the days that followed, on some of their chores around town, they met the Rev. George McRae at the First Presbyterian Church, who agreed to take their wages each week for safekeeping.

He agreed with them that their room at the Inn, even on their persons night and day, might not be a safe place for money. This turned out to be a wise decision.

Toward the end of June one night after they had retired, but had not fallen asleep, John felt a hand moving around over his waist. Through habit, he continued to wear his money belt to bed even though it was empty, and it was obvious that the owner of the hand was seeking the belt. John went into action, almost as fast as a striking snake. He grabbed the hand, and at the same time flung himself off the bed to the floor.

The quick movement was fortunate because John's assailant had a knife in his free hand and lunged downward at the spot where John would have been had he not moved.

John's fall to the floor, however, caused him to lose his grip on the hand, and as quietly as he came the assailant fled through the secret panel. James lit the whale oil lamp but the dim light showed no evidence of the intruder, except the place where the feather mattress had been slit.

The room was in an uproar, the seven occupants swearing and complaining about being disturbed. The commotion brought DuFour to the door with his lamp, but, when he heard what happened he simply shrugged his shoulders and went back to bed.

On July 2nd, John met a man with a small sailboat who had to take some cargo to Jacksonville and he agreed to take the two boys along free of charge if they would help with the boat.

They gave DuFour notice, collected their money from the Reverend Mr. McRae and left in the twenty–eight–foot boat with Mr. John Bessent and a load of bagged pecan nuts.

Bessent was a man in his fifties, faded blue eyes, a deeply lined and tanned face and grey hair. He was a fisherman by trade but sometimes used his boat to haul cargo if it paid better than fishing.

The boys sampled the pecans from a small sack Bessent took along for food. "Where'd these come from?" James wanted to know.

"Trees all over St. Marys. Didn't you see 'em?" Bessent asked.

The boys shook their heads.

"The story is that Captain Samuel Flood found a cask of nuts out in the ocean about fifteen years ago and brought it to his home in St. Marys, then he went back to sea. His wife, Becky, got tired of seeing the nuts and decided to plant them and they grew into big healthy trees that eventually bore lots of nuts."

Bessent paused, holding up one of the pecans. "Becky Flood made pecan candy and pies and cakes and the neighbors wanted some of the nuts to plant. She gave them some, and now they' re trees all over town."

"They drop in the fall here, too," Bessent replied. "But these have been kept cool and dry and did not mold. Now with the rainy season coming, they will mold if they don't get on the market. That's why we're taking em to Jacksonville."

On July 5th, the small boat entered the St. Johns River and soon was tied up at the wharf on Bay Street. John and James helped unload the pecans, collected their belongings and set off down Bay Street to see about transportation up the river.

Jacksonville in mid–summer of 1854 was an exciting town. Although Bay Street was no more than a sandy lane along the St. Johns River, after the end of the Second Seminole War in 1842 the street had blossomed with all kinds of business enterprises, including many that catered to the river and ocean traffic; such as, rooming houses, bars, dance halls and gambling houses.

Steamships and sailing vessels came across the famous St. Johns River Bar weekly to load longleaf yellow pine for markets all over the world. From the west, wagons rumbled in on the newly built plank road with cotton, hides, tobacco, cane syrup, and other products from the plantations that spread out from the city. The Plank Road went as far west as Lake City, known then simply as Alligator.

As James and John walked west on Bay Street, they were attracted by a rising sound of shouting, cursing and screaming at a corner more than two blocks away. Suddenly, out of the crowd at that point emerged three men on horseback, riding like demons, beating the flanks of their horses with their hats and urging the steeds to run faster.

It was one of the Bay Street horse races that seemed to erupt on the hour as men drank and bragged about the prowess of their mounts. Betting by the participants and the spectators added the extra adrenalin that set off these contests on a moment's notice.

It was a dangerous sport that had citizens and city officials in an uproar because the streets, as primitive as they were, were made even more unsafe for pedestrians by these rowdy races.

The masts of the clippers that crowded the riverfront, sticking into the blue sky like huge matchsticks, the street fights, the drunken brawling, and the painted ladies who flirted their way along the plank sidewalk, kept James bug–eyed with wonder. Glasgow and Whithorn had been solid havens of civilization in comparison with this raw, untamed country.

They had rented a room in a waterfront rooming house for the night, but James feared that if they went to sleep they might be murdered in their beds for the small amount of money they had saved for their trip to Orange Springs.

The rooming house food was good, however, and with youthful appetites they ate into a pile of hot biscuits, fried chicken, rice and gravy. Early in the evening they had made arrangements to leave Jacksonville on a small steam launch that was going up the river as far as Enterprise to unload some household goods for an English couple, recently arrived from Europe.

The captain told them there was a small settlement where the Ocklawaha River emptied into the St. Johns and at that point they could go by pole barge to Orange Springs, provided there was one going up that narrow, crooked river to load or unload goods for one or more of the plantations along the way.

"If you could wait until November, there would be hundreds of pole barges going to Orange Springs for the oranges," Captain Josh Willingham told the boys.

"Oranges?" John asked. "Is that a good business around here?"

"Fortunes are being made now," the captain replied, "but in 1835 the cold wiped out the groves. The temperature dropped to seven degrees and there was even ice on the river. First time I ever seen that."

Captain Willingham promised to point out the large groves of oranges and grapefruit that he said were lush and green along the St. Johns River up toward the Ocklawaha River.

Despite James' fears for their safety at the rooming house, the night passed peacefully enough, except for the constant laughter of the young blades and the giggles of their lady friends.

The departure at daylight the next morning for the journey up the St. Johns was beautiful beyond belief. The waterfront was cool and quiet as the exhausted city slept following a night of revelry. At the wharf where James and John went aboard the *Hattie Brock*, a few mockingbirds were serenading the coming of day, and a pair of ospreys wheeled and turned like ballet dancers as they sought their breakfast along the river's edge.

Just a few miles up the river, as the launch moved noisily forward, James saw what appeared to be a large, scaly monster scurrying to get out of the way of the oncoming boat.

He jumped back from the rail. "What was that thing?" he asked in fright.

He had visions of sea monsters that had invaded the river and were waiting to devour him if he got too near the edge of the boat. On the docks at Whithorn you could hear stories of sea monsters and strange creatures from the depths of the sea if you cared to listen to the sailors who gathered with stories more gory and horrible than the last one to tell his tale.

A fellow passenger near James laughed. "Don't be frightened, lad," he said. "That's just an alligator, but he was a big one."

The man continued, "You'd better get used to alligators. Florida has more of them than just about anything else. Before you reach Orange Springs, you'll see alligators of every shape and size."

"Suppose a fellow fell in the river, would those alligators attack him?" James asked.

"Don't really know," the man said. "Never fell in." With that he laughed and walked away.

The first stop that afternoon was at a plantation wharf at Mandarin to take on wood for the boat's firebox. The boys were able to step ashore for an hour during the loading of the wood. They saw their first orange grove at first hand, the rows of green trees, loaded with little round green oranges that were well on their way toward becoming the large, golden fruit that would go to market in the fall.

"This is one of the most beautiful spots I've ever seen," John said. "I think I could settle down here forever."

A Mr. Wilson, who had a farm farther up the river near Green Cove Springs, spoke up. "It's right purty all along this river, but just a few years ago it was a dangerous place to be."

"How's that?" John asked.

"Ever hear of the 'Mandarin Massacre' in 1841?"

"Must have been Indians," John said. "I know there was a lot of Indian fighting back then."

"You're right about the Indians. Mandarin had forty or fifty families and the Indians raided some of them every once in awhile. In '41 a raiding party of twenty–one braves, came into the area. They watched the Hartley farm until they saw all the men leave on a hunting trip. Then they attacked, killing Mrs. Hartley as she was rocking her baby to sleep in front of the fire. They also killed a neighbour who was visiting her, and later a farm hand was found dead in the swamp."

"What happened to the baby?" James wanted to know.

"Oh, they came back later and killed the baby too."

Mr. Wilson added, "They was Hartley farms all over the area. It was a big family. The others heard the gunfire and fled into the swamp along the river and escaped, but the homes were ransacked and burned. By the time the hunting party came back, the families had lost just about everything they had."

James McCredie sat with wide eyes and open ears as Mr. Wilson continued to talk about the Indians.

"There's a mystery about another Indian killing," Wilson related. "There was a George Mott who fell in love with an Indian maiden—daughter of a Seminole chief. They were married according to tribal custom, but old George, so the story goes, failed to tell his bride and his new kinsmen that he had a white wife in New York, his old home. Also there were children."

"The time came when Mott wanted to see his New York wife and children so he left Mandarin and was gone two years."

"The Seminoles didn't take kindly to this so they were waiting for him when he returned. As he stepped off the boat, they seized him, dragged him into the woods and proceeded to torture and then kill him."

"That's one story. The other is that on the morning after his return, while he was getting water from a spring, he was shot dead between the eyes with a Seminole arrow that pierced his brain." He paused, looking to see if the McCredies believed him."

"Who knows the real story," he continued. "At any rate, there's a tombstone in the old Mandarin Cemetery on Mandarin Road that says he was killed by Indians on May 18th, 1836. Was he really married to a Seminole chief's daughter and was he killed because he dishonoured the tribe, or was this just another killing of a settler during an Indian raid? Who knows?"

"Any Indians along this river now?" James asked a little fearfully.

"No, it's quiet now. The soldiers came and built forts and chased em into the swamps down south Florida way. They won't come back. Too civilized up here now."

The *Hattie Brock* had left Mandarin before sundown and was moving toward Green Cove Springs. James and John tried to sit on deck and enjoy the richness of the sun setting on the river, but the mosquitoes had come down in such vicious clouds that they were driven into the cabin.

"We never had anything like that in Scotland," James told Mr. Wilson. "I believe those little devils would pick your bones clean if you stayed out on that deck," he complained.

"Nother thing you'd better get used to in Florida," Wilson said. "They's just about every bitin' insect in the world right here in this tropical paradise. It's beautiful here and warm and comfortable in the winter most years, but them mosquitoes and deer flies is somethin' else."

"Deer flies?" John said ,"What do they do?"

"You'll find out soon enough, my boy," Wilson replied.' "They're bigger than mosquitoes and you can't drive em off. They'll keep buzzing around your head until they gits their belly full of your blood."

"How can you sleep with that going on?" James asked.

"You sleep under a net or you keep a fire going with plenty of smoke to keep the mosquitoes away. The deer flies won't bother you after dark."

Then, the talk inside the cabin got around to the strangeness of the St. Johns River.

"I never seen anything like it," said Mr. Wilson. "You know we been heading south all day and yet we've been going up the river."

"How can you head south and go up river?" James asked. "That's crazy."

"You betcha boots it's crazy," laughed Mr. Wilson, "but this old state of Florida is like a big alligator lying in the sun with its rump sort of hoisted in the air to the south and its big ole snout heading downhill to the north. That would make water run down his back from south to north. So, that's the way it is. It's just like Florida was tilted all in the wrong direction. The St. Johns River is the only river in the state like that, flowing from south to north. Seems like it ought to be the other way round."

He concluded, "You'll learn a lot of interesting things here in Florida, beginning tomorrow when we get to Green Cove Springs."

"What's interesting about Green Cove Springs?" James wanted to know.

Mr. Wilson got up, stretched and yawned. "I'm turning in," he said. "Tell you about Green Cove Springs in the mawning."

Turning in sounded like a good idea so the McCredie boys decided to go to their tiny cabin. Sleeping was another matter, however. To keep the mosquitoes from attacking they had to close their door and the tiny porthole. On a July night that meant heat near the one hundred mark. They rolled and tossed all night, but finally got some relief just before dawn and then the mosquitoes were back until well after sunrise.

On subsequent nights they learned it was better to roll up in a blanket on the deck and at least have the benefit of the cool night air and a breeze from the river. Also, the mosquitoes were not as plentiful during the middle of the night. They did most of their dirty work just after nightfall and before daylight.

Another glorious daybreak on the river uplifted the boy's spirits and then there was coffee, hoecake, a pan fried biscuit–like bread that was filling when eaten with cane syrup and strips of smoked bacon.

As they approached the main landing at Green Cove Springs, the sight was breathtaking. The high, sandy bank was like a huge picnic area beneath a grove of the most magnificent and stately live oaks, magnolia and hickory trees the boys had ever seen.

"You haven't seen anything yet," Mr. Wilson said, as he appeared at their side. "As soon as we are tied up at the dock, I'll take you on a special sightseeing tour."

A half hour later, they followed Wilson up the dock and along a sandy street that was the town's main access to the river. That followed a clear, sparkling stream that ended at a spring the likes of which James and John had never seen.

The Spring was perfectly round and the water so clear you appeared to be looking into an empty rock cavern, more than twenty feet deep.

"There's something you need to know about the water in this spring," said Wilson. "It has all kinds of hearing qualities. It will cure just about anything, and I mean anything."

"Smells like rotten eggs to me," James said. "I don't see how anyone can drink that rotten water. Something must have died in it."

Wilson roared with laughter.

"You'd better get used to that too, here in Florida. That's sulphur you smell and it don't have anything to do with the taste of the water."

He leaned over and scooped up a cupped handful of the water and sipped it. "Sweetest spring water you ever tasted," he said. "Try it."

Both boys took a taste of the water and admitted it tasted a lot better than it Smelled.

Wilson's face took on a seriousness they had not seen before. "As I stand here, and as God Almighty is my witness," he said, "before the end of this century, people from all over the world will be coming here to be cured of everything from lung fever to crippled joints."

He grew impassioned. "There will be big resort hotels all over this area, like in Europe, and the steamboats will be arriving almost on the hour to discharge their ailing passengers. If you boys have come here to make your fortune, buy some of this land around this spring. It's going to be like gold by 1900."

They told him they were on their way to Orange Springs to live with their Uncle John Stewart McCredie and learn a trade.

"Orange Springs is another place like this," Wilson said. "That spring has healing qualities and I predict there will be hotels there also. The only difference is that Orange Springs is harder to reach. This spring is just a few days up river from Jacksonville and Jacksonville is going to be the funnel through which the people will flow to this resort."

Wilson impressed the McCredies with his fervour. "There's no river in the world like this St Johns," he said. "It's sprouted these mineral springs all along its course and each one is better than a gold mine. You mark my words."

With that they returned to their boat just in time to go aboard before it set out for Pilatka.

About the middle of the afternoon, the boys bid farewell to Mr. Wilson at his plantation dock. He had told them he planted strawberries, big, red and juicy, that were shipped north out of Jacksonville. "And my melons are some of the best in the world," he said. "The only problem is spoilage. We need faster boats to Jacksonville and we need ice from the north to keep the produce cool. That will come."

As he waved to them when the boat departed, he called, "Remember what I told you about them mineral springs."

That night James and John rolled up in their blankets on the deck as protection against the mosquitoes and the chill of the river night air, whispered as they talked about this incredible land in which they had come to live. Mr. Wilson had written his stories and his predictions on their brain in letters of fire.

Even after sleep overtook them, they dreamed of great, clear pools of water that gleamed with gold and they had visions of acre after acre of golden orange trees, spreading as far as the eye could see, a fairyland of soft moonlight and the peaceful singing of the St. Johns as it wended its way to the sea in broad sweeps from the sandy ridges of central Florida.

Truly, they had the "orange fever," and they had not even arrived at their destination.

The next day, the Hattie Brock's arrival at Pilatka (name changed in 1875 to Palatka) brought new surprises. As the boat approached this town on a great "elbow" of the St. Johns, it passed miles of beautiful orange groves. All up and down the river, along what is now East Palatka, were large groves, with their individual wharves for loading their golden cargo each fall and winter. Many of the old homes were two and three story Victorian houses with their gables, red chimneys and lightning rods and hand–carved upper and lower porch railings.

Pilatka was a thriving town, having just received its charter by order of the governor on January 5th, 1853. Pilatka in the Indian language meant "crossing over."

Pilatka's two main streets ended at the river where there was a row of docks and warehouses for loading and unloading passengers and freight. A number of townspeople were on hand to see who was on the River Lady, and among them was a portly man, large of build, and quite imposing in his stovepipe hat, plaid vest and heavy gold chain that draped across his middle.

He introduced himself to the few passengers as Colonel Hart and informed them he owned the only stagecoach that ran between Pilatka and Tampa—just in case any of them needed his services.

He spotted James and John as foreigners and approached them with outstretched hand. "Colonel H. L. Hart, at your service, sirs. Where you from?"

When they told him Whithorn, Scotland, bound for Orange Springs to live with their Uncle John, he became talkative.

"Now that's a shame," he said. "If you had been here yesterday I could have put you on my stagecoach and had you in Orange Springs two days earlier than you will get there by boat."

He waved his hand in a sweeping gesture at the river. "Big things beginning here," he said. "In another year I'll have steamboats running from here overnight all the way to Silver Springs. It's the coming thing. That ride up the Ocklawaha River is a sight all the world will be waiting to see in a few years."

"It's the most wild and unspoiled scenic river trip in America. You'll be at Orange Springs. Watch for the Hart Line boats going by next year."

No one knew, of course, that clouds of war were already on the horizon and that Hart's dream would have to be postponed for more than a decade.

Toward the middle of the afternoon, the captain of the *Hattie Brock* told the McCredie boys to get their things together. "Around the next bend we'll be pulling over to the Ocklawaha Landing. That's where you lads will be getting off."

"I never saw anything like it," John told his brother as they gathered their belongings. "Everybody down here is a walking salesman for this country. That Colonel Hart, Mr. Wilson, the folks back there in Jacksonville. They see the streets paved in gold and the rain bringing diamonds."

James nodded his head. "I'm beginning to feel the same way," he said. "We've got to get our family here with us somehow."

At the Ocklawaha wharf came a big surprise. As they stepped off the boat, they heard a shout. "It's them, my two nephews, risen from the dead!"

And then, their Uncle John Stewart was hugging them both at once, the tears flowing freely from his eyes. "I'd given you both up for dead these many weeks," he said.

James had never seen a grown man cry and it brought tears to his own eyes.

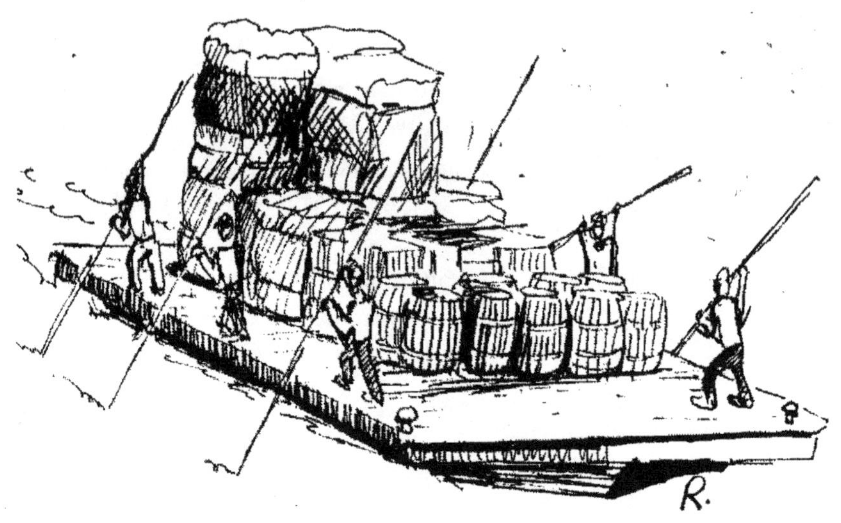

2

Orange Springs

After more hugging and crying and laughter at the same time, the boy's Uncle John became reproachful, chiding James and John for not writing. "Why didn't you write to tell me you would be delayed lads?" he asked. "We've been worried to death. Your mother has written three times to ask about you and I've not answered her, being too cowardly to tell her I believed you both were dead."

"You've heard from Mama?" James asked. "How could that be? How could a letter get here, three of them, you say, faster than we could?"

"The letters come on the mail steamships. We receive mail at Orange Springs once a week, now that the stagecoach runs from Pilatka to Tampa," their uncle explained. "There's also some mail for you boys from Scotland." He then added, seriously, "But, you haven't explained why you didn't write. It would have saved a lot of worry all around."

John, since he was the elder of the two, felt the responsibility of answering that question.

"We would have written, Uncle John," he said, "but we thought you lived in the wilderness and never received any mail. Also, we didn't have an address."

"You didn't need an address," their uncle replied. "Just, John Stewart McCredie, Orange Springs, Florida." He added, "You could have written your mother or father to explain what happened."

"As for that," John said, "we felt we would be here long before any mail would reach Scotland. It's a long story we'll be telling you."

"I want to hear all about it," the older man said, "but let us go to my camp. It's just up the river. Tomorrow we'll catch the weekly pole barge to Orange Springs."

As they carried the boy's belongings in two trips from the wharf a couple hundred yards to the camp, their uncle explained why he happened to be at the Ocklawaha Landing that particular day.

"I've been coming here every week or ten days to interview the captains of the boats that stopped, to find out what happened to the *Patrick Henry*. I wrote the clipper line in New York and heard that the ship had reached port, and that you boys were among the passengers. The main office had no word on the *Patrick Henry*, except that it had gone south to pick up cargo to take back to Liverpool. But there was no word about what happened to you two."

He continued, "The frightening thing was that I kept hearing from the captains that a ship had gone down off Cape Hatteras, with all hands and passengers lost but that no one knew the ship's name."

That night around the campfire, a yellow fortress against the mosquitoes and the pitch dark that surrounded them in the endless forest stretching along the Ocklawaha, James and John told their uncle all about their trip from Liverpool and how they had gradually worked their way down the coast to Florida.

"I'd like to get my hands on that Smoot," their uncle said. "But, there are lots of 'Smoots' in this world. You have to watch out for em."

Finally, emotionally and physically worn out, they wrapped themselves in blankets and went to sleep, except that James was the last to fall asleep. His mind was on the letters from home, his mother and father, his brothers and sisters, and he kept thinking what a strange turn his life had taken. In a few short months he had exchanged the security of a comfortable room and bed in a civilized town in Scotland, the love and comfort of a family, for a blanket and the hard ground of a wilderness camp site, which, for all he knew, was surrounded by alligators and other wild things, waiting for the fire to go out so they could attack and devour the three men. Certainly, the strange and often frightening howls and screams that kept coming out of the blackness of the hammocks and swamps offered no comfort. They only fed his imagination so that when a particularly terrifying crash sounded near–by, followed by the pitiful squeal of some creature caught in the jaws of a predator, his stomach tightened and he prepared to run, but run where?

His Uncle John had heard the noise and sensed his young nephew's fear. "Go to sleep, boy," he said. "That's probably a wild cat caught himself a rabbit. He won't bother us."

John Stewart had his two nephews up early. "Got to get everything down to the dock," he explained. "No tellin' when that pole barge will get here and we have to be ready. They won't wait here long."

James was curious to know what a pole barge was but he decided to wait and see. No use asking wasteful questions, he decided.

It was one of those rare days, a cool, clear morning with enough wind whipping up the Ocklawaha to keep the mosquitoes away. Daylight had arrived with a mighty chorus from the birds. "I never heard such a racket," John told his uncle. "Is it always like this?"

Uncle John smiled. "It's music to my ears. Those birds are telling me it's going to be a good day."

They had a quick breakfast of coffee and pan–cooked bread, then gathered all the gear and took it to the dock. It was a good thing they did because the pole barge came early.

James saw it approaching the mouth of the Ocklawaha about seven o'clock through a light mist. It was an eerie sight. At first the barge appeared to be a huge flat board with many men and mounds of bags loaded on top. He wondered if the craft was sinking. As it neared the dock, he could see that it did have a square bow and sides about two feet high. The barge appeared to be about ten feet wide and thirty feet long, and was poled by six of the biggest black men he had ever seen. Their shoulders and arms had become huge as their muscles in these areas developed far beyond the rest of their bodies from the long hours of poling the heavy barge against the current, half of each trip from Pilatka to Silver Springs and return.

James learned from his uncle later that the men were all slaves of the owner of the barge, Beeman White of Pilatka.

As soon as the barge was tied to the dock, one of the black men said, "Come bord, gen'man. We's hind schedule now."

The McCredies were quick to jump into the barge, piling their belongings in a corner of the stern, and the clumsy vessel moved into the crooked, swift Ocklawaha.

The two boys couldn't believe the power the blacks could apply to the movement of the barge through their long poles. The forward movement was provided by two men, one on each side of the boat. They simply put their poles in the water and "walked" down the side to the rear. By the time they reached the stern, two other men were at the bow with their poles, and repeated the process. A seventh black man called "Josh" steered the craft with a long sweep paddle.

"Well, Josh, you say you're late. How come?" the boys' uncle asked the helmsman.

The black man grinned broadly, displaying shining, white teeth. "Big Boss," he said "Made us wait foh train frum Jaxville." He pointed to a pile in the middle of the barge, covered with a piece of canvas. "Tools foh Massa Collins."

"Oh, you mean Neil Collins," the uncle said. He turned to the boys, "I'm doing some carpentry work for him now. His plantation is about four miles up the river from where we get off at Fort Brooke Landing."

There were times when the poles failed to touch bottom and the barge was steered nearer the shore until the men regained their power on the hard sand and shell–strewn bed of the Ocklawaha. The many twists and turns of the crooked, black river caused the pole men problems also.

"This must be the crookedest river in the world," James said to his uncle. "I never saw one in Scotland like it."

"They say here that the word 'Ocklawaha' is the Indian word for 'Crooked river.' Before we arrive at Orange Springs, you'll have to agree that the Indians gave it a good name; that is, if 'Ocklawaha' does mean 'crooked river,' " the uncle said.

Just before eight o'clock, as they moved silently around one of the many bends in the Ocklawaha, an unusual and beautiful sight stretched before them, all the way to the next bend.

The surface of the river was covered with many different kinds of ducks, so that it appeared an army could move across the stream on the backs of the birds. As the barge came into sight, the ducks moved into the air as though a signal had been given. They blackened the sky, shutting out the sun, as one would blow out a candle. These birds, by the thousands, flew around the bend and again settled on the water, because when the barge came in view again, there they were for an instant, then back in the air and around another bend.

They played this game with the birds until mid morning, when the birds seemed to vanish into the forest.

Young John McCredie, who had been an ardent hunter when the family lived in the Scottish highlands, drew in a sharp breath. "Whoo," he said, "what a place for duck shooting. Sure would like to have my gun."

"You'll get to do all the duck hunting you want to, lad," John's uncle told him. "The ducks up our way are just as thick in the morning and evenings as they are here."

At noon the barge stopped at a high, hard–packed sand bank, shaded by giant cypress trees. Beyond this small oasis was swamp water, dotted by cypress knees and an occasional alligator, lying in the water with only his head partly above the surface.

The elder John Stewart McCredie explained that the stop was necessary to rest the pole men and let them eat. He pulled some dried venison strips from a canvas sack, some cold biscuits and some cold, baked sweet potatoes.

"Better eat some yourselves," he said. "We got a lot of boatin' to do before we get to the Springs."

"Orange Springs is between thirty and thirty–five miles by river from where you got on the barge," their uncle explained.

"The pole barge will do about ten or twelve miles a day against the current, much faster going back."

"That means three days," James said.

"Bout that," his uncle agreed.

The afternoon on the river was like being in another world. Snowy white and large blue herons, egrets, an occasional eagle, were everywhere along with dour anhingas on tree limbs, where they stretched their snake–like heads and spread their wings in the sun to dry. Every log jutting into the river was filled with a family of turtles. As the barge got near, they went into the river with a "plunk," and then crawled back on their perch after the boat was a safe distance upstream.

And the alligators were everywhere.

"You heard about them things, I suppose," their Uncle John said, pointing to an especially large alligator resting on the bank. "That one will run twelve or fourteen feet. Probably several hundred years old."

As they approached Davenport Landing, there was a narrow portion of the river and the barge was swept beneath a mass of overhanging branches.

"Dem snakes!" screamed one of the pole men and about that time a stubby, evil–looking black creature about three feet long and as big around as James' forearm dropped into the barge right at the feet of one of the pole men as he was busy trying to get the barge back into the middle of the stream.

Without coiling or any warning the snake struck and sank its fangs into the black man's leg.

"Oh, Lordy, I'm bit to death," he moaned. "Lord, Lord, I'm comin' foh my judgment."

He dropped his pole and was on his knees, praying to the Lord to have mercy on his soul. Josh dashed to the stricken man, grabbed the snake behind its head, pulled it free and threw it into the river. Then he knelt beside the pole man and with his knife slashed the area where the fang marks showed as tiny red spots. As the blood began to flow he placed his mouth on the wound and began to suck blood, spitting it by the mouthful into the river. He shouted to the pole men to head the barge for the Davenport Landing.

In a few minutes they were at the dock and the boys' Uncle John ran to a blacksmith shed where two men were heating some horseshoes.

"We got a man's been bit by a cottonmouth," he shouted. "Need a red hot iron."

One of the men came running with a poker that glowed red on the end. He jumped in the boat and applied the end of the poker to the wound. The pole man screamed in agony and the flesh burned and curled and turned black as over–cooked bacon.

Then, Josh tied the leg tightly with a strip of rawhide and wrapped the wound with a piece of cloth obtained at the Landing. "Let's go," he said to the pole men. "We's hind schedule."

The barge swung out into the current and again headed up the Ocklawaha. The stricken slave lay in one corner on some empty meal and grits sacks, moaning in great pain. The boys' Uncle John took a bottle of whiskey from his pack and poured about a half cup of the fiery liquid down the man's throat. "You need this worse than I do," he said.

"Thank you, Massa Crady," Josh said. "That man hurt."

"That was a big snake," Uncle John said. "You think he'll make it?"

The black man hesitated. "Dunno, suh. If'n old Josh got duh pizen frum his blood, dat helps the Lord beat the Devil, an' he live." He shrugged his shoulders. "If'n not, he be cold foh mawning."

It was a somber afternoon as they labored toward Pinner's Landing, known locally as "Poor Man's Labor." The pole man appeared at times to be burning up with fever and at other times his large frame shook with chills. The elder John Stewart McCredie kept him drunk with large gulps from his bottle.

He shared some with the boys, knowing they had been shaken up by the experience with the cottonmouth.

"It's a good lessen to learn," he told his nephews. "This is wild country and if you fish this river, you'll see lots of snakes in the trees along the banks. Most of them are harmless water snakes, but some of them are cottonmouth moccasins. That's what you just saw. They are mighty poisonous. When you approach any river or creek bank, search the trees for snakes."

He added, "And that's not all. Those same overhanging limbs sometimes have wasp nests, specially this time of year. If you disturb a nest they'll swarm out at you and you'll feel like you been hit with red–hot flying needles. I saw a man standing in the front of his boat once. He touched a limb and the wasps came out and bit him in the face, nose, eyes, and forehead. He fell in the water and it was a week before we found his body. It's rough country all right."

"We met a man on the boat out of Jacksonville who had a plantation just south of Green Cove Springs who advised us to buy land around the mineral springs here," James told his uncle. "He said the visitors will be coming to the St. Johns River springs by the thousands to be cured by their waters. He said Orange Springs would be booming soon with visitors going there to drink your spring water. He said you'd have hotels and people coming and going by train and boats. You say it's rough country. Is it going to change soon?"

"That man hasn't been to Orange Springs for some time," the boys' uncle said. "We've already got a hotel that can accommodate up to sixty guests. The stage Line has a stop at the Springs where horses are changed and the people are already coming and going." He nodded his head, looking across the river at the dark forest. "But," he said, "I think your friend may be a hundred years early in his predictions."

The barge approached Pinner's Landing about an hour before Sundown.

The boys and their uncle quickly set up camp and John was told to start a fire for cooking and to discourage the mosquitoes. The pole men had a favourite campsite and busied themselves preparing for the night. James checked on the snake victim and found him in a kind of coma, but he was breathing quietly and the swelling in his leg appeared to have stopped.

John was having trouble getting a fire started. Already the sun was down behind the trees, leaving only a red gash along their tops and to the west. A fire was needed in a hurry. Josh came to his assistance. "Young Massa," he said, handing the boy a piece of pine wood, "try lighter'd knot; full of fire. You see."

John accepted the strange–looking piece of wood and placed it just above the pitiful little flame he had that threatened to go out any moment. As though by magic, the "lighter'd knot" grasped the tiny flame, curled it all around the piece of wood and soon there was black smoke lifting into the still air and orange flames dancing all over the wood, and soon on all the other logs on the fire. John couldn't believe his eyes. The knot was full of fire.

His uncle had watched the incident with an amused smile. "There's no magic here," he told his young nephew. "That is a pine knot from an old pine stump. It's full of the pitch they use to calk ships. Best thing you can use to start a fire."

Around their campfire that night, James wanted to talk about Orange Springs and the future of that part of Florida. It was obvious to his uncle that the boy had been sold on Florida. "You say the predictions of a boom for this part of Florida have come a hundred years too early," he said. "Why do you believe that?"

"We just lost the railroad," his uncle explained. "John Pearson came here in '45 and bought up the land around the springs and began to develop Orange Springs as a watering place." He paused. "You know what a watering place is?"

James shook his head.

"It's the same as a spa in Europe, a place where people with money go on a holiday to drink and bathe in the water for their health."

"Mr. Wilson talked about the spas," James said. "What about the railroad?"

"Pearson's partner in the development of Orange Springs was David Yulee, Florida's first senator. It was expected that Yulee's influence would get the Florida Southern Railroad routed through Orange Springs, but instead, the route selected went up near Rochelle. You'll meet John Pearson when we get home."

The uncle paused and looked at his nephew with sharp eyes. "Aren't you a bit young, lad, to be concerned about land developments and railroads? Why, when I was your age, all I wanted was a fine looking lass on my arm and a mug of ale."

"Uncle John," James said seriously, "we plan to save our money to bring the family from Scotland. Times are bad back there, and me and John don't want to spend the rest of our lives with an ocean between us."

"I'll help you," said the uncle, "but right now it's time to get a good night's sleep. The barge will be leaving early in the morning."

They built up the fire with some big live oak logs that would bum most of the night and then rolled up in their blankets with their feet toward the fire. They had learned that after midnight, even in the summer, the night air was damp and cool near the water.

As James drifted off to sleep, he could hear the snake victim still moaning on his bed of sacks on the barge.

Just before daylight a thunderstorm broke with all the fury of a hundred wild stallions stampeding through a cotton patch, as the boys' uncle described it later. "I knew we'd get rain," he said after the storm struck. "You can smell it coming in this country."

James was genuinely frightened. He had never heard so much thunder and seen so much lightning, coming so fast as to be almost continuous, and the wind came across the river in great waves that pounded the oaks and pines like an angry sea striking in fury against the coast. He was sure the forest would be torn apart and feared some of the trees or big limbs would come crashing down on their camp.

But like Florida summer storms, this one ceased as suddenly as it had begun; the clouds hurried away and the sun came up on time to reveal a wet world. There was good news in the barge, however. The pole man was up, hobbling on his swollen foot, but the crisis was over. Apparently, old Josh had saved the man's life by sucking the snake venom from his wound.

The cooking fires were all out and the wood was too wet to build a fire in time for a hot breakfast so they chewed on some dried venison and got back on the river.

When the sun was directly overhead they stopped at Riverside Landing to cook a hot meal. The pole men needed a big dinner to sustain them during the afternoon.

"What's that bright yellow spot in the middle of the river?" James asked his uncle.

"That's a big sandbar. Water's no more'n three feet deep out there," was the reply.

James eyed the cool river, tested the temperature with his bare foot and found it an inviting temptation, in view of the humidity and summer heat. But, he kept thinking of the big alligators they had seen at regular intervals during the trip from Jacksonville.

He turned to his uncle, "Think we could take a bath here?" he asked.

"Jump in," his uncle said. "Think I'll join you."

They all stripped and swam to the big sand bar, where they could stand up and enjoy the cool water as the current rippled around their bodies.

"Is the water really yellow?" James asked.

"You can drink it," his uncle said, raising a cupped hand filled with the clear liquid. "It's all spring–fed from many underground streams that come to the surface and feed into the Ocklawaha. The yellow colour comes from tannic acid in the cypress tree roots."

He pointed to some cone–shaped "stumps" that dotted the swamp around the towering cypress trees. "Those are cypress knees, really cypress roots, that come up out of the ground so they can breathe when the swamp is filled with water."

"I meant to ask you about those things," John said. "I thought maybe they were some kind of strange tree that hadn't budded out. Sure see some strange sights here in the tropics," he concluded.

Their Uncle John laughed. "Well, we're not in the tropics, but the country is different from Scotland."

The rest of the journey to Orange Springs was made without incident and late on the afternoon of the third day, the barge pushed to a large dock at Fort Brooke Landing. Fort Brooke had been an army post during the Indian wars. A small community had grown up around the fort to serve visitors who came by river on their way to Orange Springs, only two miles away.

As the barge was being tied to the dock, a number of local citizens gathered to greet any newcomers and hear the latest gossip from Pilatka. A big, redheaded, freckled–face man in his fifties pushed forward to greet the boy's uncle.

"Thought you'd be comin' in this evening," he said. "Got your wagon hitched and ready under that tree," he said, pointing to a large oak tree near a log cabin about a hundred yards away.

"That's right kindly of you, Clive," John Stewart McCredie said, grasping his friend's hand. "Want you to meet my nephews," he added. "Boys this is Clive Johnson. Clive meet my nephews. The big 'un is my namesake, John Stewart, and this one here is James."

"You mean them boys you said was lost at sea? Where in the world did they come from?"

"They come in on a river boat three days ago. I'll have to tell you all about it later," their uncle said. "We best be gittin' on home. Sun's gonna be down in less'n a hour."

"Shucks," said Johnson, "I thought you'd have supper with us. The missus is expecting you. She and Ellen got quite a spread ready." He grinned. "You can't disappoint Ellen, specially when she finds out you got these lads."

John Stewart knew all about Ellen. She was Clive's only daughter, as redheaded as her father and as spirited and pretty as any young women of eighteen in all the Ocklawaha River country.

"Well, I guess we could stay," the boy's uncle said. "That old hoss knows the wagon trail from here home better'n I do. She can find her way in the dark."

With Johnson's help, they gathered up their belongings and started toward the Johnson cabin where John Stewart's horse and wagon was tied beneath the oak tree. The boy's uncle waved to old Josh. "Don't work that man too hard," he advised. "Let that snake bite heal real good."

"Nassuh, Mister Crady," Josh said. "We's gwine let him he in de corner an' fatten up. Den we wuk the devil out'n him. You'll see."

At the cabin they created quite a commotion. Heads appeared briefly peeking from the open windows and you could hear the scurrying going on inside.

"Sounds like Ellen has seen you boys," Clive Johnson laughed. "She don't get to see many men her age round here."

Virginia, Clive's wife, greeted them at the door. "Come in," she said. "Supper's bout ready. John, we got some fresh trout from the river."

"Ginny, you know just what I like," John McCredie answered. "Where's Ellen? I want her to meet my nephews."

"Oh, you know young girls, John McCredie. She seen them nephews fore I did and now she's gone plumb crazy. Gittin' her shoes on and prob'ly her best dress. She'll be out in good time."

John laughed. "They ain't anything to git dressed up to meet," he said. "Look at em. Just like I'd plucked em from the swamp someplace."

He introduced his two nephews, who were too embarrassed to do more than nod their heads.

"Cat's got their tongues, I suspect," Ginny said. She sensed they might want to get more presentable before Ellen showed herself. "If you want to

freshen up, go out to the well house. There's a wash bowl an' some corn cobs you can use to comb your hair."

The men were all seated at the handmade, rustic table before Ellen Johnson appeared, carrying a plate of cornbread fresh from the oven. Contrary to what Ginny had said, Ellen did not appear the least bit ruffled by the young visitors. As her mother introduced the McCredie boys she looked them over calmly and said, simply, "Pleased to meetcha."

Under her straightforward gaze, the boys, lowered their eyes, but John had already noted that she had flaming red hair like her father and a few freckles across the bridge of her nose. Unlike the sallow complexions they'd seen among the women of the Florida backwoods, this girl's skin was clear and slightly flushed, "Like the sky when the morning sun's an hour high," John told his brother later.

After a meal of fried river trout, grits, roasted corn–on–the–cob, tomatoes fresh from the Johnson garden, cornbread and homemade butter, and chocolate cake for dessert, they sat around the table to hear the story of the boys' trip from Scotland.

The mosquitoes had arrived in swarms with the setting of the sun, but Ginny had numerous candles around the room beneath tin cups of camphor gum that kept most of the insects from their table.

By eight o'clock, John could hear his horse stomping the ground and neighing occasionally, a sign that he was restless and wanted to go to his own barn, so he bade his friends farewell and the three McCredies began the two–mile trip to John's cabin on the edge of Orange Springs.

John was a bachelor and lived on a small farm in a log house he had built. Behind the house was a barn and a carpenter shed where he kept his tools and fashioned furniture for his neighbours, some of whom drove their wagons over–night from as far away as Ocala, Micanopy and Gainesville to buy his cabinets or commission him to do special work for their homes.

James and John were assigned sleeping space in the loft that extended out over half of the house and was reached by a ladder that they climbed from the main room that served as living space, dining and cooking—the cooking being done in pots that hung in the huge limestone fireplace.

"Better get to bed," John told his nephews. "Tomorrow you start earning your room and board. We're working on the community church, and I'm behind schedule." He retired to his own tiny room that had been added to the main house.

John had trouble getting to sleep, but the fault was not the Corn shuck mattress that rustled every time he moved, but the steady blue eyes and long red hair that framed the most honest face he had ever seen. He kept thinking to himself, "What a self–reliant women she will be, just right for this wilderness."

James didn't have this trouble. He had already decided that Ellen Johnson was too old for him.

The next morning, in fair weather, the boys began work as apprentice carpenters, at the site of the community church.

They learned from their uncle that a man named John William Pearson had donated the land and built the church, the first one in Orange Springs, as an all–denominational house of worship. That was in 1853, the same year the town was platted, streets laid out and named. Pearson had fought in the Second Seminole Indian War and was mustered out in 1841. In 1845, in partnership with David L. Yulee, he had acquired considerable land in

Marion County, including all the land around the mineral springs that had been called "Orange Springs." He had previously lived in Alachua County and was a member of the County Commission of that County and lived at Newnansville, the County seat.

Pearsons' holdings in the area were extensive, more than a thousand acres of land in Marion and Alachua Counties, a general store, a cotton gin, a hotel and boarding house, a sawmill, and a machine shop. Working the land were more than a dozen slaves.

By mid–1854, when the McCredie boys arrived, he had dissolved partnership with Yulee who had failed to convince the railroad authorities to include Orange Springs as a stop on the new line. When the boys arrived he was in partnership with a John L. Livingston, and was doing business as Pearson and Livingston, but unfortunately for him, he had mortgaged most of his land and buildings to a man named Fones MacCarthy, who had invented a new kind of cotton gin for Sea Island Cotton.

Pearson was, however, a big name in the community which had prospered because his endeavours brought visitors from the north who came seeking health in the mineral springs and hunting and fishing in an area that was teeming with fish and game.

The first night James and John sat reading their letters from Scotland. Each letter from their mother showed that her fears and concerns were mounting. She could not understand why they hadn't written to her. First, she chided them for their neglect and then pleaded with them to ease her fears.

The family predicament in Whithorn had grown worse. Hides for leather were scarce and the price was high. They were barely able to keep from starving, Janet wrote.

John obtained a quill and some lampblack from his uncle and wrote a lengthy letter to Janet, explaining the reasons for their delay in answering her letters, and assured her that he and James were fine and would soon have money to bring them to America.

Toward the end of the week, the elder John Stewart noticed that his namesake nephew was unusually quiet and often wandered into the forest alone after supper. James was puzzled at his behaviour because he and John were close as brothers and it was not like John to keep to himself.

Finally on Saturday, the truth came out. On their way to the post office, John asked his uncle, "Are we going to church tomorrow?"

"Well, lad," his uncle replied, "that's up to you. I generally go, but I won't force you and James to go unless you wish to do so."

"We should go," John said. "Me and James need to meet the people here, besides you can see your old friends, like the Johnsons, that is if they are church–going people." He hurried along, "Of course if they aren't church goers you can still see your old friends."

The elder John Stewart believed he was beginning to see the light, but decided to have some fun at his nephew's expense.

"Well, now let's see," he said. "I believe most of the Johnsons attend church. Oh, yes, I am sure Clive and Ginny will be there."

There was a long silence, broken only by the creak of the wagon and the sound of the horse's hooves in the sand. Finally, John said, "Do the Johnson children usually attend church?"

"Why, yes," the uncle said solemnly. "I believe some of them do, yes, indeed, most of them do."

James could stand it no longer. "Uncle John," he cried, "what he's trying to find out is if Ellen Johnson will be there. He's been mooning around like a sick calf ever since he seen her last week."

The uncle turned to John and asked with a serious expression, "John, is this true? You mean that red–headed brat over at the Johnson place? Why, she's just a child."

John was indignant. "She's eighteen," he said, "and that's not a child."

The older John Stewart laughed and slapped his nephew on the back. They proceeded on to the post office.

At the little white community church the McCredies sat directly behind the Johnsons and John found himself sitting behind Ellen, her long red hair draped over the back of the pew and flowing like red gold toward the floor. He recalled with pleasure how he had sanded and re–sanded and oiled and re–oiled that very pew without knowing that soon it would serve as the place to show off such a treasure.

At one point during the service when he was stretching his long legs, one of them touched her foot and he was so startled he left it there for a moment, and then he noticed Ellen had not moved her foot. In fact, he felt her press slightly against him.

She began to rub her foot ever so lightly against his and the sensation almost blew off the top of his head. It was chemistry, it was lightning, it jumbled his mind, but he knew he liked it.

As the families gathered to talk after the service, Ellen walked directly up to John and said, "John McCredie, now that you're in Florida, you need to know all about it. Come with me. I want to show you something you've never seen before."

She led him to a large oak tree, draped with grey strands of a threadlike material that hung all over the tree. "That's Spanish moss," she said. "It makes a soft bed when you stuff it in a sack but it has bugs in it that will make you itch."

They talked and talked about the moss, hardly daring to look at one another, and then Ellen noticed that her father was glancing more and more in their direction to see when they would return so the family could go home to dinner.

"Pa's gettin' itchy," she said. "Suppose he's hungry. We'd better go back."

Before they rejoined their families, she looked up at John and said, "Pa said it'd be all right for you to call on me, if you care to, that is."

"I'll be coming," John said, and that was the way it began.

From then on, John went to church with the Johnsons and sat next to Ellen. John had Sunday dinner at the Johnsons. He and Ellen went fishing, horse–back riding, and visiting her friends on other farms near Orange Springs.

Then, one day in late August, on a Saturday, she asked him to go with her to gather fox grapes so Ginny could make wild grape jelly for the winter. They went on horseback, with two oak stave baskets hanging from their saddles. When they arrived in the area where the grape vines were great tangled masses of tentacles that seemed to choke out the small trees, they tied up their horses and prepared to pick the dark blue clusters that hung from the vines like small lanterns.

As John prepared to move away to pick in his own area that was lush with the tart grapes, Ellen warned, "Watch where you step. We've seen rattlesnakes in this area."

The words were hardly out of her mouth when she gasped, "Oh my," and sank to the ground.

John came running, just in time to see a rattlesnake as big as his arm glide swiftly into the underbrush. He knelt beside Ellen. She was calm as she pushed down on her black stocking to reveal two ugly wounds halfway between her ankle and her knee.

"John, do you have a knife?" she asked.

He took out his pocket knife. "You'll have to slash those wounds," she said, "and suck out the poison. I can't get to them with my mouth."

John remembered how old Josh had cut into the pole man's leg, so he cut the wounds with two X's and began to suck out the blood. During the ordeal, Ellen quivered slightly, but never made a sound. He wondered what he would have done if the situation had been reversed.

While he was doing this she tore a strip of cloth from her petticoat and tied it around her thigh. He could tell she was getting weaker. "We'd better get on one of the horses," she said. "You'll have to hold me. Got to find Doctor George."

On the way to town, John held her in front and felt the sweetness of the body against his for the first time, but all he could think of was what old Josh had said on the pole barge that day. The words were burned into his mind. "If'n old Josh got de pizen from his blood, dat help the Lord beat the devil, an' he live. If'n not, he be cold foh mawnin."

And that is the way it ended.

The funeral for Ellen Johnson was a simple grave–side ceremony in the Community Church cemetery on the southern edge of Orange Springs. The Johnson family arrived in their wagon with the coffin that held the remains of their sprightly daughter. Ginny Johnson, in her best black dress and hat, sat on the seat of the wagon, the tears long since drained from her sad eyes. The solemn–faced children were spread out around the coffin in the bed of the wagon, as though to protect their elder sister.

The coffin was cypress, built during the night by the McCredies. For young John Stewart the carpenter work was a heart–rending task.

At one point during the night, as they labored by the light of a few pine torches, John screamed out, "It's not fair," he sobbed. "Why did it have to be her?" he asked of no one in particular.

His uncle came over and placed his arm around the younger man's shoulder. "It can be a hard life in this country, lad," he said. And then he added, "No one ever promised you that life would be fair."

Every bit of knowledge that was known on the Florida frontier about snake bites had been used to save Ellen's life.

Dr. George had given her indigo root tea, boiled in milk. Raw turpentine had been cupped over the wound so that the fiery liquid was kept in constant contact with Ellen's leg where the snake had struck.

One Orange Springs citizen said later he was certain she would live because he had seen the green venom drawn out by the turpentine. "Turpentine'll do that every time," he said positively. "Brings the pizen right out."

Another man said he knew for certain Ellen would live. "It's a known fact," he said, "that when snake pizen reaches the heart, hit'll kill and that pizen had plenty of time to git to her heart, and she's alive. That boy sucked out all that pizen."

Several others concurred, nodding their heads.

They were all wrong. She died during the night, her leg swollen to the size of her waist, mainly because Doctor George had ordered that under no circumstances could the tourniquet that had been kept tightly tied above her knee be loosened. He emphasized that at all cost the poison–filled blood had to be kept away from her heart.

She was a fighter and it took most of the night for the indignities done to her body by man and reptile to take their toll. She died a horrible death and it was a year before young John Stewart McCredie could erase the tragedy from his mind. Much of the year his thoughts were of the redheaded beauty whose path had crossed his for such a brief time.

After the funeral he had told James, "I'll never get over this. I won't get married, ever."

"Don't make any rash vows," James replied. "Time has a way of healing everything. You'll find another Ellen Johnson."

Orange Springs was growing and the stage line was busy bringing in visitors and new settlers. The McCredies spent most of 1855 working on additions to the hotel and adding rooms to old residences, as families grew in size.

Orange Springs

The cool autumn days of 1855 were exciting times for Orange Springs. A large hunting party had come to the hotel in private carriages from the boat at Pilatka for ten days of shooting in the game–rich forests bordering the Ocklawaha River. The wives spent their days drinking the mineral waters of the spring or playing cards, and exchanging venison and wild duck recipes as they enjoyed the cool of the veranda and the absence of insects.

Most of the time the McCredies drove the wagon to take back supplies. The general store, which housed the post office and served also as the stage stop, occupied most of their morning.

Walter Combs, storekeeper, kept a barrel of whiskey in a side room for the "comfort and convenience" of his customers. Hanging around the outside of the barrel were a number of gourd dippers and it was the custom to sip a gourd full of the whiskey while the clerks filled your order and put it in your wagon.

The side room was out of view of the ladies who shopped for cloth, lace, thread and buttons, but they knew about the room and cast anxious glances in that direction if their menfolks tarried too long with the firewater.

Talk around the whiskey barrel varied from politics to farming to some of the "goings on" at the hotel.

On the national scene, politics in 1855 swirled around the weakening of the Whig Party. Florida had just returned David Yulee, a Democrat, to the U.S. Senate to replace its only Whig senator, Jackson Norton. To fill the gap left by the departing Whigs, a new group had emerged that called itself the American Party.

"American party me bloody bladder," exclaimed Tim Ferguson, Orange Springs' leading blacksmith. "They're Know–Nothings, an' that's a bloody good name for em. They don't know nothing an' they don't stand fer nothin' an' they aint gonna do nothin'."

The American Party members were known for many months as the "Know–Nothings" because they began as a secret society called "The Supreme Order of the Star Spangled Banner." Because of the Secretiveness of their meetings the members became the "Know–Nothings."

They stood for limitations on the admittance of foreigners to the United States. They championed the Protestant faith as opposed to the Catholic faith.

In Florida the new party took a milder course. At a convention in Tallahassee members formed a Leon County group and emphasized the name "American Party." Their platform stressed a belief in Americanism and the preservation of the Union.

Nothing was said about stopping or limiting the influx of foreigners or defaming the Catholics. Principal speaker at the Tallahassee meeting was Richard Keith Call, a prominent Whig leader.

Young John Stewart, as well as his uncle, was a staunch believer in the Democratic party line. His heritage of independence that came from the Scottish Highlands made him a strong states lighter.

"I don't believe that people should be beholden too much to their government," he told his friends at the general store. "Look around you," he'd say. "Land full of trees and wild game and lots of fresh, clear water, enough land for all the poor people in Europe, an' these Know–Nothings want to stop people from coming here."

He paused, his face flushed from the intensity of his feelings, and maybe from some of Walter Combs' whiskey.

"An' that foolishness about throwing out the Catholics. Do they want to set up some kind of state religion of Protestants? That's against the law," John concluded.

But one of his listeners was not content to conclude the discussion. Tate Parker was a big, red–faced fellow from Kentucky. He had just arrived in Orange Springs and had early established a reputation for being a trouble maker.

He came up to John and stuck his face up close and said, "Yer for them furriners cus yer one of em, all you Credies. I'm a member ov thuh Merican Party an'damn proud ov it. What yuh say tuh thet, boy."

John's right arm, seasoned by hammering and sawing all summer, moved so fast no one saw the clenched fist swing upward to catch Parker directly on his slobbering chin. All they saw was the big man go down like a wet sack of meal. He remained on the floor, out cold, while the McCredies and some of the others went outside.

John Stewart McCredie told his nephews to be ready for trouble, but none came. In fact, Tate Parker left Orange Springs the next day and was never heard of again.

One Saturday in late October, as the McCredies were reading their mail and sipping some of Combs' whiskey, John Stewart McCredie said rather casually to his nephews, "Think you could be ready to go to Micanopy on Monday?"

"Micanopy?" said young John. "Why Micanopy?"

"There's some carpentry work over there that needs to be done and I can't leave our job here," the uncle replied.

James was not sure of his ability as a carpenter at this stage and said as much. "You can do it," said his uncle. "John, here, is as good a carpenter as I am already and you're coming along. John'll be in charge."

And so it was arranged. They set off in a buggy with their tools at daylight on Monday and took the road to Cross Creek, where they could cross between Orange and Lochloosa lakes and then continue west until they reached the stagecoach road between Ocala and Micanopy to the north.

Two days later they were entering Micanopy from the south on Cholokka Boulevard, the town's main street that ran north and south for more than a quarter mile. John and James sought James L. Cooper, druggist at the Cooper and Mathers Apothecary. The boulevard was a broad sand and clay street, shaded by beautiful oaks and lined with a number of residences as well as several general stores. They found the apothecary's shop near the stop for the stage line that connected Gainesville and Pilatka. As they pulled up to the hitching post, the daily stage was just unloading its passengers from the north.

On their trip north from where they had met the Ocala–Gainesville trail, they had passed one grove after another and at one point, in the distance, they could see the sparkling waters of Orange Lake.

"I could easily learn to like this country," James told his brother. "Things are bustling here and the town looks prosperous. Might be a good place to settle the family when we get them here," he continued.

John nodded. "Looks good to me too," he said. "Since Ellen died I've been restless to get out of Orange Springs."

They found James Cooper to be a pleasant, fine–looking man in his early thirties. He left the drugstore with the two young carpenters to show them his log house on Ocala Street where he wanted two rooms added to take care of his growing family.

James was curious. "Don't you have any carpenters in Micanopy?" he asked.

James Cooper laughed. "We've got more carpenters and general labourers than most anything else, but the place is growing faster than we can get help to do the buildin.' You fellows would do well to move here. Micanopy is going places."

The McCredies said they'd already been giving that a lot of thought.

"George Riggs is making carriages as fast as he can and Henry Marchung's store's got about all the business he can handle," said Cooper. "I'll tell you. Micanopy is the right place to be. Everybody's planting orange groves on the side, and I'll bet this area is going to be the best citrus country in Florida. You mark what I'm telling you."

James and John spent the winter in Micanopy. There were a few days when the thermometer dropped below freezing for two or three hours before daybreak and therefore some of the citrus growers had fires going in the early hours of the morning, but everyone agreed that it was a mild winter.

Christmas with the Coopers was a new and exciting experience for the McCredies. It seemed Like a long time since they had been around small children at Christmas time. Christmas morning, long before daylight, the town erupted with gunfire and people shouting "Merry Christmas" to anyone who had ears keen enough to hear any words above the roar of the holiday warfare.

A small pine tree had been decorated in the main room of the log home with cut–out paper figures, popcorn strings and squares of paper on which the children had drawn their versions of angels and the Lord Jesus in the manger. Simple, handmade gifts were exchanged and then the day of visiting and eating began.

Spring arrived slowly in February with the budding of the wild plum trees and that's when James and John finished their work and packed up to return to Orange Springs, but they had promised the Coopers they would return to Micanopy.

Their Uncle John had good news for them when they arrived home. "There's enough money in the box to bring the family over. If we get to work on it we can have them in Florida before the end of July." The "box" was a beautifully finished and fitted strong box about eighteen inches long by six inches wide and four inches deep that their uncle had built of heart pine and kept in a secret compartment behind a removable brick in his large fieldstone chimney.

The young carpenters were overjoyed and the news set off a flurry of activity that included a trip by stage to Pilatka with the money to arrange through the bank the transmission of the funds to Scotland through a New York bank. There was sufficient money to bring the family and all the David and Janet McCredie household goods.

The next step was to make arrangements for the family in Florida. They agreed that Ocala offered the most promise for a shoemaker, and all three McCredies went by stage to that town to locate housing and a place for David McCredie to set up shop.

Then, a letter came from Janet saying the family would sail from Liverpool on May 10th aboard the *Justyn*. In addition to David and Janet there would be Margaret, age twenty–three: David, age seventeen: Thomas, age ten; and William, age six. Helen had elected to remain in Scotland with her new husband. Janet said they expected to arrive at Orange Springs early in July.

In a letter dated May 10th, 1856, Janet wrote her sons that the family would go aboard the clipper that day. She explained her letter was being dispatched through one of the fast steamship lines so it should arrive long before the family. The letter reached Orange Springs on a Monday, two weeks later, and from then on throughout the remainder of May and all of June, James found it difficult to sleep nights, filled with doubt about the safety of his mother and father and his brothers and sisters. He began to understand the agony his mother must have felt when he and John were on the high seas, and knowing of the storms and other problems he and John had encountered didn't help matters.

"I suppose I'm being paid back for not writing to Scotland when we reached New York," he told John. "I sure hope nothing has happened to them."

"That's nonsense," John replied. "I heard you tell Mama a hundred times not to worry about us, and here you are the biggest worrier of all."

The elder John Stewart McCredie understood his nephews' anguish and tried to lighten the load by making light of the worry. "I don't know what we're going to do with your brother," he'd say to John, within hearing distance of James. "He's about as lost around here as a string ball in high weeds. You'd better keep an eye on him. First thing you know he's going to nail himself to those studs instead of the boards."

"I've got my eye on him," John would reply.

Beginning in late June, the McCredies met every stage and every pole barge coming to Orange Springs, and then on July second it happened.

When James arose that morning he had a feeling there was something special about the day. "Maybe it's the weather," he thought. All the signs pointed to an exceptionally warm and muggy day with heavy thunder–showers in the afternoon. "It's stage day, too," he thought. "Maybe this is the day."

It was. The stage came rolling into town in a downpour about 2:30 p.m. Lightning rumbled in one constant barrage. About that time a man who had come in on horseback from Ocala decided he'd better get his horse to a safer place, since he had left the animal tied beneath a medium–sized hickory tree not far from the stage office. Just as he reached for the horse's bridle there was a blinding explosion of lightning and the man and his horse were knocked fifty feet from the tree.

They were both dead when examined. The man's shoes had been burned from his feet and the path of the lightning was etched from his head to his toes. "Oh my Gawd," one man screamed. "It's the punishment of the Lord."

"Punishment me bloody bladder," Tim Ferguson said later. "That man didn't know any more about lightning then a hog does about Sunday School." He shook his head in disbelief. "Tieing a horse under a tree in a storm."

That was the way the McCredie family was introduced to Florida, where they would spend the remainder of their lives.

3

Billy Bowlegs War

The McCredies were on the stage from Pilatka and scampered out of the coach in the driving rain.

"Mama, Papa," John and James screamed together, and from all the hugging and kissing going on in the wet street you might have believed it was a bright sunny day in May. One of the drivers restored reason to the meeting.

"You ladies ought to git in outen this rain," he said, and gently guided Janet into the stagecoach station, believing the rest would follow her like a mother hen, and they did.

In the dry, semi–darkness of the station some of Janet's calm was restored as well as most of her indignation, which apparently had been building during the long and tiresome journey from her homeland.

"John Stewart," she said, addressing her eldest son, "what manner of son be ye to drag your old mother half–way around the world to a savage land such as this? Oh, that poor, poor man, laying in the street." She slumped into a chair, a wet pile of black taffeta. She had put on her best sabbath dress for the meeting with her sons and now it was a sodden mess. "Oh, my beautiful Scotland," she wailed.

John and James knelt beside her. "Now Mama," James said, soothingly, "you'll love Florida. It's a clean, new land. Just give it a chance."

By the time they collected their belongings, the summer storm had passed, the sun was out and only a few puddles showed there had been any rain at all. The only evidence of the tragedy was the covered body of the stranger in the back of the station. His horse still lay in the street where it had been felled by the lightning bolt.

David and the other members of the newly–arrived family had said little during all the commotion. They appeared to be in a state of shock, but Maggie was the first to notice a change in her brothers. "Mama, look," she said, "they've got moustaches."

Both John Stewart and James had spent much time developing their moustaches so they would be fully–grown by the time their family arrived from Scotland and they had been disappointed that their mother had not noticed their "new faces" the minute she clapped eyes on them, but then, the electrical storm, the downpour and the death from lightning had disrupted the reunion of the family.

Now, they all gathered around the two young men, admiring the moustaches and the maturity they gave the young faces. Little William had to touch the hair that adorned each lip and summed up his findings, thus, "Feels like a brush," he said.

Eventually, they all piled into the elder John's wagon and headed for his cabin, which had been enlarged by two rooms to accommodate the rest of his brother's family.

Janet sat on the seat of the wagon between David and his brother. She was constantly fanning her face with her hat and sighing heavily. "Is it always this hot?" she asked.

James reached under the wagon seat and pulled out a fan made from a palmetto leaf. "Try this, Mama," he said. "That rain helped. It's much cooler now than before it rained."

"I know," Janet sighed. "Times were I thought I'd die in the stage from Pielatka. When we got out of the coach at the last stage stop, the heat of the sand burned my feet right through this good Scottish leather. I declare, this sand must be close to the fires of hell. James, are you sure we aren't below sea level?"

James corrected her. "It's not Pielatka, Mama. It's Pilatka. You spell it P–i–l–a–t–k–a but the "i" sounds like the "i" in "it." And, no, we are not below sea level."

He laughed. "As for the fires of hell, I spect they're around here some place, but I don't think they heated up our sand. The sun does that every day."

Janet perked up some when she reached John's cabin and saw the fresh vegetables, gathered from the garden that morning and cooked for their supper. They had been simmering with newly–dug potatoes in a big pot over hickory coals in the fireplace for several hours. "How'd you like some fresh–caught trout to go with those vegetables?" John asked his Sister–in–law. "I'd like that," she replied, "But where do you find a fishmonger in this wilderness?"

"You're looking at him," John answered. "I'll be back in bout an hour."

He turned to William and Thomas, "Want to come along?"

Janet intervened. "Leave William," she said. "He's kind of peaked and needs to rest. Take your brother."

Off they went and returned in a little over an hour with enough fish "to choke a bull gator," as John put it.

Supper was a happy meal. Just before sunset a breeze had risen to cool off the land and scatter the mosquitoes so they were able to eat in the hard packed yard that had been brushed clean by James and John while their Uncle was fishing. There was a large table and rough benches so they could all gather as a family.

Soon after dark, however, they were all ready for bed. It had been a long and exciting day and their weariness was evident in the drooping eyelids and lagging conversation. The younger boys were intrigued by the mosquito nets that hung over their beds and then dropped around them and tucked under the mattress after they were in bed. Janet said she felt like she was in some kind of sack and she didn't know that she was coming to Florida to spend the rest of her life in a fish net.

Her brother–in–law told her, "Janet you'll soon learn to appreciate them nets. Without them the mosquitoes would pick your bones clean during the night and you'd wake up in the morning no more'n a skeleton."

David had made arrangements in Pilatka for their household goods to be sent to Orange Springs by pole barge and the plan was to take them on to Ocala by ox cart. Brother John had hired a friend with two wagons and oxen to make the journey after the furniture arrived.

The next day, John asked his brother about William. "Is there something wrong with the boy?" he wanted to know. "He just sits by himself and never runs with the children, or is he still tired from the trip?"

"He has a touch of lung fever," David explained. "The poor lad has been like this for several months. We hope the change of climate will perk him up."

"You brought him to the right place," John said. "People are coming to Florida from all over the world to cure their lung fever. Make him drink some of the Orange Springs water every day. Do him good."

Two weeks later the furniture arrived and the very next day the David McCredie family was on its way to a new home in Ocala, by way of Micanopy. The wagon train, as James called it, was made up of two wagons of household goods, each one pulled by two oxen. Then, there was Brother John's horse and wagon, with members of the family riding with him, and James and John in their own wagon. They planned to settle in Micanopy and build a home for their father and mother.

The David McCredie family settled in Ocala and David soon had all the leather tanning and Shoemaking business he could handle. Good cowhide was scarce but deer hides were plentiful and there was a good market for the soft leather he produced from the wild creatures' skins. His deer skin moccasins were in great demand by the hunters who came from the north to track down the plentiful supply of deer in the vast forest that ran north of Ocala.

Despite this prosperity, however, and the fact the new home south of Micanopy was well underway, David and Janet were constantly worried about William. His health continued to deteriorate day by day and then in Mid–December he became ill with the dreaded diphtheria that caused the death of so many children, especially in rural areas. This illness struck just as all the McCredies were planning a Christmas reunion in Ocala. Because of William's lung condition, death came quickly. He died on Christmas Eve and was buried Christmas Day in Ocala.

The spirit of Christmas was all but forgotten as the members of the family walked in a drizzling rain to the little cemetery north of Ocala, trudging along a sandy road behind the wagon carrying the small box that contained the body of their son and brother, a small bundle, because William weighed less than fifty pounds by the time death took him out of his misery.

As he walked along David's thoughts returned to Scotland where he had lost his first William. "I won't believe the superstition," he muttered to himself, "won't believe it! The Lord just didn't intend for us to have a William."

Later in the afternoon, neighbours and friends came by to share a mug of hot toddy and extend their sympathies. Janet told David that night the warmth of Scotch kinsmen and friends in this new land was all that took her through this sad and dismal Christmas. "I'll never forget this day," she said.

The house for the McCredies was completed in mid–February, 1857, and the family was settled in the Micanopy area by the first of March. David's shoe business went well as he drew customers from parts of Marion, Putnam and Alachua Counties. In addition, the boys helped David put in more than fifty orange and grapefruit trees which they expected would augment the family's finances within a few years.

Toward the middle of June, a major topic of conversation in the mercantile store, at the Postoffice, drug store and stage stop was the growing Indian trouble in south Florida. Some referred to the new Indian uprisings as the "third Seminole War" and others called the activity the "Billy Bowleg's War." Word coming from the south was ominous —men, women and children killed, homes burned, crops stolen or burned.

"If Bowlegs is successful down there, he'll come this way," predicted John McCredie. "If the soldiers can't stop him, maybe it's time some of us did."

That appeared to be the sentiment all over Micanopy, and, indeed, north Florida as well. The pressure on Governor James E. Broome became so intense that an agreement was reached in June for the formation of ten companies of Florida militiamen to join with regular troops of the United States Army to deal with Bowlegs, Sam Jones and others. The number of Seminoles in south Florida was believed to be about one hundred fifty.

The ten companies began to form the first of July and John McCredie told his family at the supper table one night that he planned to join up. "There's a poster at the post office that says a Captain Stephens will enrol his company of Florida mounted Volunteers on July 20th at Ocala and I plan to be there."

"If you go, I'll go," said James.

Janet was stunned. She had not recovered from the loss of William—and now this. She left the table and went to her room.

The boys followed her. They found her sitting in her chair by the window, rocking slightly as she stared into the yard.

"Mama, now don't get upset," John said. "The enrolment period is only six months. We'll be back before you know it, and we can use the money."

"You know nothing of fighting," Janet said. "These savages can come up on you while you sleep and split your head. It's too dangerous." She looked the two young men directly in the eyes and said, "I want you to stay here."

"We're going, Mama," John said, and walked from the room.

James saw her wilt and felt sorry for her. He put his arm around her shoulders and said, "It'll be all right, Mama."

He followed his brother back to the supper table. David had continued eating after Janet left the room and he never mentioned the matter when the boys returned, but James noticed that his father was more somber than usual.

Even then the matter had not ended. The next morning, young David said he wanted to go with his brothers. No amount of pleading on Janet's part could change his mind and the elder David refused to take either his wife's or his son's side in the matter. Eventually, it was decided that David could also leave for six months to fight the Seminoles.

John, James and David were sworn in as privates in the Florida Mounted Militia at Ocala on July 20th. Each one had brought his own horse, saddle, gun and bedroll. A valuation of eighty–five dollars was recorded for James' horse and his equipment was listed at eighteen dollars. John's horse went on the record at one–hundred dollars, as was David's, but their equipment was only twelve dollars each.

Their unit was immediately ordered to report to Fort Brooke, near Tampa. There was no time to return to Micanopy for formal "good–byes", and the boys were glad to have it that way. They had feared a tearful parting with their mother. Each one wrote her a hurried letter and posted it from Ocala on that date. The forced march to Fort Brooke took six days, a pace that had a number of the company swearing and regretting their decision to go off to fight the Indians.

An Ocala attorney, Colonel S. St. George Rogers, was sworn in as commander of the Florida Militia in federal service on August 10th and hurriedly joined his outfit in Tampa.

He ordered five of his companies to Fort Denaud, where he set up his general headquarters, and sent the other five companies to Fort Myers to join up with federal troops there. The more than seven hundred Florida militiamen at the two forts spent August, September and the early part of October in restless anticipation of some kind of action when the rainy season was over. They drilled, cleaned their equipment over and over and fumed and fussed as the weary summer wore itself into fall. There were card games and fights. James wrote his mother, "Morn, if this keeps up, you can cease your worrying. We haven't seen an Indian since we've been here, and probably won't see any before the enrolment is up."

Then the rains stopped and the men were ordered into the field in small scouting parties to seek out the red men. Those in the mounted volunteers soon discovered their horses were useless in most of the marsh and saw grass areas covered by the patrol so the animals were left to graze at Depot Number One. "I hope we'll still have horses when we get back," John grumbled.

The patrols were torture. By day the McCredies waded in snake and alligator infested water, some of it waist deep, or through saw grass over their heads that cut their faces, arms and legs. By night they slept in trees and it was not uncommon for a soldier to fall from his perch in the middle of the night and land with a splash in the swamp water below and then thrash around, cursing the army, the Indians and the world in general.

One day, David McCredie was on patrol with a party of militiamen who were pushing and cutting their way along the Okaloacoochee River? After several days, during which men were dropping every day from exhaustion and returning to Depot Number One, they came upon a small Seminole village where the unsuspecting villagers were cooking a meal. They were ordered to go in firing and in the fighting that followed two Seminoles were killed and the rest of the villagers captured.

Among those captured was an Indian called Tigertail who said he was seventy–five years old. He and the other captives were told they would be sent to the reservation in Oklahoma.

David told his brothers what happened. "This old man said he wouldn't go. He said he would die right there by the 'black water.' The cap'n rounded em up and put guards all around. 'Watch old Tigertail,' he said. They tried to watch him but durin' the night he pounded up a glass bottle and ate the glass. They found him dead there in the sand, bleedin' at his mouth."

David paused. "I was sick at my stomach when I seen him. That poor old man killed hisself cause he didn't want to leave his home."

"I'm ready to go back to Micanopy," James said. "On my patrols we been destroyin' crops and burning down villages where there's nothing but old men and women. I haven't seen a gun yet."

John interrupted. "We joined up to do a job. Someone has to make this area safe for settlers. Nobody said it would be a church picnic. Anyhow, we have bout two more months to go."

As David's patrol was returning to Depot Number One, it was followed by Indian warriors who were sighted occasionally along the trail. Back at the Depot there was an attack on their grazing horses and many of them were killed, including the one John had brought from the McCredie farm.

Finding the main body of Indians was almost a hopeless task but the key turned out to be flat–bottomed boats that could be paddled and poled through the sloughs and the hidden creeks of Big Cypress Swamp. The boats were a new experience for the formerly mounted volunteers, but they were effective in finding hidden villages and supplies of grain and pumpkins.

The war continued as a kind of "seek and destroy" engagement. Using the boats, the militia kept the Indians on the move, unable to plant crops or build permanent villages. Ambushes were used on both sides. In one Indian ambush in late November, Captain John Parkhill of Leon County was killed.

Christmas, 1857, was one day to remember because it wasn't a special day at all but just another day in the sloughs and swamps and just keeping healthy and alive was an accomplishment. A bigger enemy than the Indians was the swamp water, which was poison to the soldiers' feet, exposed to its acid content day after day. John's feet got so bad at one time he had to return to Fort Myers and lie on a cot for a week with bandages up to his knees.

Another enemy was diarrhoea and chills and fever. On New Year's Day, Colonel Rogers moved into Big Cypress Swamp with all the healthy men he could muster out of five companies, a few less than two hundred men. All three McCredies were in this manuever, which proved to be their last before their enrolment was up. Sometimes walking and sometimes rowing or poling a flatboat, the patrols destroyed many bushels of stored foods, burned more than one–hundred houses in a number of villages and took all the horses, they found.

The Florida militiamen had been successful in seeking out and finding the Seminoles to such an extent that wheels were set in motion in Washington and at the Oklahoma Reservation to seek peace in south Florida, and the Florida patrols were ordered back to Fort Brooke on January 19th, 1858, the "war" was over except that some patrols were continued around the forts until the first week in February. John McCredie was paid one–hundred dollars for the horse he lost at Depot Number One and the brothers saddled up and headed for home.

The return of the Mounted Volunteers was a big occasion for Micanopy. On Saturday there was an all–day picnic with baseball and other games, followed by a box supper at the First Presbyterian Church. The Volunteers were happy to be home but some were bitter because they had not been paid. The lack of funds to pay the soldiers became a political issue and a topic of newspaper comment for many months.

The Florida News at Fernandina led the campaign to nag Congress into action with words such as these: "Unfortunately, the appropriations are exhausted, and they are turned adrift without a cent for the six months hard service in the Cypress. This is truly a hard case, and we hope Congressmen will not again subject the government to the humiliation of becoming a debtor to her soldiery. In conducting wars, it is bad policy to cripple vigorous measure by withholding means when it should be forth coming."

John, James and David were reluctant to talk about their experiences in the South Florida Indian war but as time went along they became more talkative, especially young David, the more impressionable of the three. One campaign, weighed heavily on his heart and he spoke of it one night after supper. They were all sitting around their new–fangled paraffin lamp in the living room of their new Micanopy home and the yellow–white light from the lamp made only a slight dent in the wall of darkness outside their windows and David thought of the blackness of the South Florida swamp. At one point in his narration he left the room, tears tumbling down his tan cheeks. It seems that a large scouting party with Captains Spark man, Carter, Lesly, and Bullock in command left Camp Rogers for an eight–day hunt in the Big Cypress. After travelling about ten miles they found the country too difficult for horsemen so fifty men under Captain Bullock were detailed as horse guard. They camped in the vicinity and were ordered to remain until the main force returned.

The next day they found a fresh Indian grave and decided to investigate it. The body was that of a very old man, with only two teeth, and because of his clothing, sash and shot–bag, the soldiers concluded he was an Indian of distinction.

On the third day, the party found and burned a corn house containing about twenty bushels of corn.

"The next day," David said, "two men got sick and we had to leave them in an old potato patch with two soldiers to guard them. I said to myself, 'They'll all be dead when we get back.' We had seen a lot of Indian signs and killed some hogs."

David said they walked for five miles in swamp water up to their waists before running into higher ground. "Then we saw this Indian with a gun. He begin to run but two of our men brought him down with their guns. He was young, like me, and scared," David said.

The Indian told Captain Sparkman through an interpreter that Sam Jones and Assinwah were on an island about ten miles to the south with thirty–five warriors and many women and children. The wounded Indian was left under guard and the detachment pushed on toward the island believed to be the hideout of Sam Jones.

"You wouldn't believe this," David said, "but that night we had to sleep in the swamp water with our heads propped up so we wouldn't drown. At nightfall there wasn't a piece of dry land anywhere."

The next day they reached the Indian camp but found it deserted. Sam Jones and his Indians had fled during the night.

At one point the Volunteers were fired upon from ambush. The soldiers rushed the Indians and wounded one, and although they followed him because of the blood in his tracks, they never caught him. What upset David was the little Indian girl. He said she was about eight years old. He found her sick and crying as she wandered in the tall saw grass.

That night the officers decided to return to camp. Many of the men were out of food and some were barefoot. On the return they stopped at the last Indian camp and found an old squaw, too sick to travel. She claimed to be the wife of Chief Assinwah and said the little girl was her child. She agreed to have the girl taken back to the main Volunteer camp and said when she was able she would come in with all her other children.

David told about their camp the next night. "I never seen anything like it," he said. "We was in bout twenty acres of the best hammock land I've ever seen in Florida. There was corn, rice, beans and potatoes every where. We destroyed at least a hundred bushels of corn and ten or fifteen of rice."

One day in a swamp they crossed on the way home, they found five cow–hide boats.

"What good are those things?" David asked his captain.

"That's the way the Indian squaws move their smaller children," the officer replied? "They put em in those things and pull em through the saw grass and swamp water."

They picked up the wounded Indian who appeared to be in good condition, and twenty volunteers offered to take him immediately to Camp Rogers for the reward money.

"That's about it," said David. "We was out ten days with eight days food. I hope I never see another swamp like that Big Cypress."

"What happened to the little sick Indian girl?" Janet asked her son.

"She died the third day after we found her," David replied, and that's when he left the room, tears streaming down his tanned cheeks.

"I didn't want the lad to go," said Janet "He's too young for such harsh things." She then left the room to console her son.

"I don't know what all the fuss is about," John declared. "They're all savages and we did what we had to do. The Volunteers did a good thing. The paper says so. I'll read it to you."

"We think we may now state definitely that the disturbances occasioned by the remnant of the Seminole Indians in our state, have been brought to a conclusion. The warriors left with Sam Jones to take care of him in his present advanced age, can do no more harm, and will no doubt leave for the West as soon as the old chief dies, which event must happen ere long as he has already reached a very advanced age."

"The question naturally presents itself, to whom does the credit belong for bringing about this happy and long looked for consummation? We unhesitatingly say to the Florida Volunteers and their enterprising commanders! Some credit is undoubtedly due to Major Rector and his Indian delegation, as successful and skilful negotiators of our persevering and brave Volunteers, into a willingness to emigrate. Their last place of refuge (the Big Cypress) had been penetrated, and their crops and habitations destroyed by the command of Col. Rogers. They had suffered several surprises and lost some men in these attacks, and they well knew the character of their foe, that what they had once done, would be repeated until there was no longer a safe spot left for them to rest upon."

"In this condition Major Rector found them, and his task was rendered comparatively easy. The Indians we believe confess to a much heavier loss in the different skirmishes with our cow boys than the whites ever claimed and the number of their fighting men therefore considerably reduced. They found themselves unable to continue the war for another season and wisely consented to emigrate. Our State is therefore happily rid of the greatest nuisance that has ever infested any country."

"This event, and now the certain completion of our Railroad, is destined to give our State an impetus forward, that will in a few years place her in the front rank of Southern States. Verily, there is a good time coming!"

David, usually a mild and quiet man, completely under the wing of his out–spoken and impetuous wife, snorted. "Those poor Indians didn't have much of a chance, a few hundred against more than seven hundred farmers and tradesmen who want their land."

"Papa, you cannot stop progress," John said. "Don't forget about all the killing and burnin' before we went down there."

"I know all about that," their father replied. "The Indians were only doing what we Scots would have done if anyone had come into our Highlands to take our land and drive us some other place."

John saw he had better turn the conversation in another direction.

"The citrus trees are coming along fine," he said. David's face brightened. "That they are," he replied. "We'll be getting a crop next year if we don't get a late freeze."

"What about the railroad?" John wanted to know. "With all the new groves coming in down here we need the railroad nearer than Starke."

In the spring of 1858, the Florida Railroad had only been able to extend it's rails to Starke, although the plans called for the line to run to Tampa, with a spur to Cedar Key. A stage line connected with the railroad at Starke and extended through Newnansville to Gainesville, Micanopy, Flemington and Ocala.

"The line's out of money," David said. "There's a meeting in Ocala next week of representatives from Alachua, Marion, Sumter, and Hillsborough Counties to make plans for financing the laying of the tracks to Tampa. George Leitner is representing Micanopy."

The Ocala meeting produced a plan whereby landowners interested in the railroad would pledge their property against bonds to be sold by the Florida Improvement Fund. Former Governor James E. Broome was present and stirred the landowners into action with a passionate speech favoring the extension of the railroad at any cost.

Spring was a nice time in Micanopy because the gentle weather was accentuated by the smell of orange blossoms as the groves began to bloom. The green trees by day were a sparkling mass of white and by night fountains of sweet smell that permeated the entire community.

The fascinating topic of conversation in the town, however, was not the orange groves, the blooms and their sweetness, but the agonies of a man named McNair.

James had met him at the post office one morning. McNair was begging for money to have a doctor cut "two snakes from his stomach." His story was that a Doctor Higgins (he never revealed where this doctor Higgins was located) had given him medicine that relieved him of a third snake but the good doctor had refused to cut into him to remove the other two snakes because he said McNair would not survive the opening of his belly.

According to McNair's story, the larger of the two snakes was "generally stupefied" and caused little distress to McNair except when it was hungry. The smaller snake, he said, was always moving about, biting him on the inside and generally making life miserable.

"Aren't you afraid to have your stomach opened up?" James asked.

McNair was quick to reply that he would rather die than continue to live with the reptiles torturing his insides.

McNair sat in the shade on Cholokka Boulevard, allowing the curious to feel his stomach, and many swore by the hide of the Devil that they felt the smaller snake moving around.

None of the town doctors had examined him, or given him money. Doctor Montgomery said the incident reminded him of the story about the Indian on the reservation who went to the government agent to get whiskey for a snake bite. The agent was so impressed by the honesty and sincerity of the man, he agreed to give him the whiskey.

"How much do you need?" he asked.

"Four quarts," the Indian replied.

"Four quarts," the agent exclaimed. "Why do you need so much?"

"Him big snake," the Indian said, calmly.

Dr. Montgomery said evidently McNair had a "big snake" inside him that demanded stringent measures.

As fall approached, incorporation of the Town of Micanopy caused much heated post Office conversation. John asked his father how he felt about the subject.

"I'll vote for it, lad," David said.

"Doc Mathers is against it," John commented. "In fact, all the doctors say they will vote against it. Payne, Montgomery, Stewart, Cooper."

"It'll mean more taxes for them, and us," David said. "That's why they're against incorporating the town. They own most of the property here. In the long run, it'll help all of us. Yes, I'll vote for it. I believe the folks here will approve incorporation."

David was right. The vote in September was three to one in favor of incorporation.

4
Civil War

The old family clock, brought from Scotland with great difficulty, was striking 9:30 as Janet and David McCredie lay in their bed on an April evening in 1859, discussing their sons.

"I fear we'll have nae grandchild from these two," Janet said.

"John's almost thirty and James is now a man." There was a note of anger in her voice as she continued. "What're we to do with them, David? They have no interest in girls. James follows John like a puppy dog. They're as thick as fleas on Old Black. They drink with lads down at the grogg, do their carpenterin' and no church socials, no visitin' around."

"Don't fret, lass," David soothed her. "Give em time. This is new country an' the men marry late."

"You had three children when you was John's age," said Janet. "I fear they're two bachelors."

"We'll see, we'll see," David said. "It's been a hard day in the shop. I'd like to sleep now."

Then he remembered. "James is in the town band with his fluterina. May be that will lead to something."

"Fluterina my foot," Janet complained. "That won't bring any grand–children." She sat up in bed. "David, you've got to do something about them boys. Talk to them or something."

"Go to sleep," David said. "I'll see what I can do."

The next night at supper, David had some news. He told the children, "Your mama an' me have been invited to ride the Florida Southern on an excursion from Gainesville to Fernandina to celebrate the arrival of the railroad in Gainesville. We'll be leavin' early in the morning on the 25th."

Young Thomas spoke up. "Pa, I heard about that from Jeff McNair. His sister, Betty, is goin' an' a lot of girls from the church. Why can't we go?"

"You weren't invited, that's why," David said to Thomas.

Janet turned to her youngest son. "You say all the girls are going?"

"That's right, Ma," Thomas said, "an' if all the girls in town are goin', I don't see why we can't."

Janet told Thomas, "This is a thing for older people, Thomas. You'll have to grow up and then maybe you can take such a trip."

She looked at David. "I'm not going" she said firmly. "It would be too hot and tiresome, David. We're too old for this kind of thing. I want John and James to go instead." The look on her face said to David, "Don't you dare say no."

David knew what she was trying to do. So did the boys.

"Mama, you're pushing me and James at the girls again," John said. "I'll go on that excursion, but not for the girls. I'm not ready to be hurt again."

"It's time you forgot about the Orange Springs girl. She's not comin' back, you know," Janet said.

This made John angry. He resented it when his mother kept referring to "that Orange Springs girl," instead of to Ellen Johnson. To him the redheaded, light–hearted girl of the Ocklawaha River had brought warmth and starlight into his often–times dour Scottish nature, and he feared he would not find another to brighten his days. To get back at his mother, he said, "I'll probably be a bachelor." He left the room to take some scraps of deer meat to the dogs.

John brought news from the post office a few days later that a mass meeting of Alachua County citizens had been called for April 23rd at Newnansville, the County seat, to discuss the railroad situation. Tempers were short and the slavery problems with the north were all but forgotten as local attention turned to the Florida Railroad and the need to extend it beyond Gainesville to planned terminals in Tampa and Cedar Key.

Target for most of the wrath was Governor M.S. Perry who had refused to sign the Internal Improvement bonds that would provide funds for the railroad to extend its line.

Talk was that Governor Perry was holding out to get the route of the railroad changed so that it passed by his plantation.

Purpose of the Newnansville meeting was to draft strong resolutions calling for validating other signatures to go over the head of the Governor. David and his older sons attended the meeting. As citrus growers they were vitally interested in seeing the railroad extended south and west near Micanopy.

The citizens who met in Newnansville were all of one mind. They quickly organized with Samuel R. Pyles as chairman and Dr. J. Crews Pelot as secretary. A committee of George W. Boston, Jesse T. Bernard, J. C. Pelot, Samuel B. McLin and Dr. P. W. Cato was appointed to bring in suitable resolutions.

While the committee members were absent about their business, the citizens stood around in small groups discussing the situation.

"This is no time for pussyfootin' around," John told his group. "We've got to let the Governor know we're out for blood, his if necessary. I doubt that Governor Perry ever went hungry in his life. This railroad is a matter of food for a lot of people."

Heads nodded in approval.

"I trust the language that goes from this place will be hard–hitting and straight to the point," David said. "What the Governor has done appears to be better suited to a monarchy than to the citizens of a free state."

The resolution was stern and full of rebukes for the Governor. One section of the document ended with a sentiment similar to the one expressed by David McCredie. It said:

"Resolved, That Governor M.S. Perry's whole course in relation to our Internal Improvement scheme, and particularly his autocratic acts as president of the Board of Trustees of our State, in refusing to sign the bonds of the Florida Railroad company, and in rescinding a wise resolution of the said Board of Trustees, should meet with a proper rebuke throughout the state. For such high handed dictation is better suited to the serfs of Russia then to the citizens of a free and sovereign state."

Two days later on April 25th, 1859, the McCredies gathered with other citizens of Alachua County at the depot in Gainesville for a 7 a.m. departure on the excursion to Fernandina.

A correspondent for the *Fernandina News* later wrote that "The morning was one of Spring's loveliest children, and its balmy influence communicated cheerfulness and elasticity (sic) to the hearts and countenances of the joyous company."

The departure of the train, which must have brought out a tremendous poetic impulse on the part of the correspondent, was described in these stirring words, "At seven o'clock the hoarse whistle of the locomotive warned all to be seated, and a few moments after, the iron horse, freed from his restraints, bounded rapidly forward to his destination."

James had brought his flute and as the train pulled out into the country side, he began a lively tune, "Grand Norma March," followed by "Rosalie."

Soon there was singing all up and down the three–car train and the morning passed rapidly. Despite the fact they were scheduled to have dinner on their arrival at Fernandina, passengers were sampling picnic lunch baskets throughout the morning. Around noon, they arrived at Callahan Station and saw telegraphic wires for the first time.

"That's a good thing," said John. "Soon we'll be in touch with all the centers of commerce throughout the country. It should help in the marketing of our oranges."

"I can see the day coming when trains will be running all over the state, maybe even through the Big Cypress," said James. "More and more people will discover this beautiful land of sand and pine and they'll come pouring in like the Huns who invaded Western Europe. I'm not sure I'd like that."

John laughed. "What happened to your dreams of great, green orange groves, whose fruit will fill your box with gold? The more people who discover Florida, the sooner that dream will come true."

"I'm about to change my mind, I suppose," James mused "I like things as they are."

"Well, you needn't worry," his brother answered. "These things take time. I doubt if all that progress will take place in our lifetime."

At 2:30 p.m. the train reached Fernandina, the "Island City." The visitors were greeted by the booming of the wharf cannon and the shouts of hundreds of citizens who had gathered to meet the inland guests.

They were whisked away to three hotels, the Pioneer, the Whitfield, and the Florida. The McCredies went to the Florida Hotel and were soon dining on a feast of fish and oysters. After dinner they were given the choice of carriage rides through the city or a pilot–boat tour of the waterfront. The ladies with the group at the Florida Hotel preferred the boat trip so off they went down the bay. John and James also preferred the boat trip because they wished to see the part of town called "The Old Town," where they had first stepped ashore in Florida in 1854.

"The Old Town" was not much changed from their first view five years earlier, but the rest of Fernandina was an eye opener. There were a number of handsome hotels like those in which they were staying. Centre Street that extended down to the wharf where their train had come in was lined with numerous businesses and the area beyond had stately residences.

"I can't believe all this has happened in five years," James exclaimed. "John, you could be wrong about the progress not coming in our lifetime."

A brilliant ball for the visitors was held at General Patton's new hotel. "I'm not going," said John. "I don't have any clothes for such foolishness."

"We must go," James said. "We have to go in what we have. Besides, you're a good dancer. I've seen you and Ellen out dance everybody in Orange Springs."

"That was different," John said, looking at the floor. "It was Ellen."

"We'll go," said the younger McCredie. They freshened up and went to the ball. Sarah Jackson, a seventeen–year–old Micanopy school teacher, saw them come in the door and rushed over to John.

"John McCredie," she exclaimed. "You can be my first partner." She took him by the hand and before he knew what had happened he was on the dance floor. James soon had a partner, one of the Fernandina young ladies, and the evening went quickly. Not the entire evening, however, because supper followed the ball at a late hour.

This meal the correspondent described, "The supper table was bountifully spread with a profusion of most tempting viands, and the gay scene was enlivened by the continual discharge of small–arms in the shape of bottles of champagne, which were fired off in platoons in all directions. At a late hour of the night the gay company separated to seek balmy sleep, tired Nature's sweet restorer."

The return trip to Gainesville was made the next day without incident and all those who went from Alachua County had a foretaste of what the coming of the railroad would mean for the future of Florida. They saw their world becoming smaller.

The railroad situation was not much improved by July 4th,1860. Micanopy prepared a day–long celebration but friends in Lake City who wanted to attend faced a long, hot, tedious journey. There was no way to get to Gainesville by train, where they could rent a buggy for the remainder of the trip to Micanopy, but if you were courageous you could board the cars at 4 a.m. and go to Jacksonville, arriving at 8 a.m.

There was an eight–hour layover in Jacksonville, so the traveler needed to plan a day of sightseeing in the City on the St. Johns. The train left Jacksonville at 4 p.m. and arrived in Gainesville at 8 p.m. You could stay overnight in a good hotel like the Suwannee House and drive to Micanopy in the morning in a one or two–horse buggy.

The good side of all this was that you could get from Lake City to Gainesville, a distance of forty miles, by train, all in the same day. If you traveled between the same two cities by buggy, wagon or stagecoach, the trip took several days.

Despite the slowness of the train, everyone was eager to see the iron laid farther westward, and that was the major subject of conversation around town. The principal address at the July Fourth celebration dwelt at great length on the merits of such an enterprise.

The big occasion began at 8 o'clock when the meat went on the fire for the barbecue. Later in the morning a giant flag, with the words, "S. A.

Douglas" in large letters across it, was raised and then at 10 a.m. came the parade, consisting of twenty men on horseback, masked and wearing pasteboard hats. The masked paraders charged their horses toward a group of black and white children, to the amusement of the crowd.

The children scattered like a covey of disturbed quail and the parade passed on.

The parade was led by I. P. Garrison, Micanopy tailor, carrying the flag with Douglas' name on it, followed by the Micanopy Town Band, which included James McCredie and his flute.

At 2 p.m. Micanopy residents and their guests gathered at the Methodist church for a patriotic oration and the reading of the Declaration of Independence. The Declaration was read nobly by Robert Hall and then Andrew J. Neal, a young lawyer, delivered an oration that called on Floridians to maintain their sovereignty as a state despite any attempts to take away their rights. Then followed many toasts before the crowd adjourned to the tables laden with barbecue, fresh vegetables, pies and cakes.

There was one other aspect of the Fourth of July celebration that deserves mention. Posters in Micanopy advertised a balloon ascension by the famous European balloonist, Professor Henri D'Armand. The "Professor" appeared with his balloon, a fourteen–year–old girl he said was his daughter, and a Mr. Peterson, an assistant. As the balloonist set up his equipment on Cholokka Boulevard, the girl and the assistant circulated through–out the town, soliciting funds to pay for the balloon ascension. Their story was that unless money was raised there would be no ascension.

When the morning stage arrived from Gainesville, it brought along a woman who claimed to be the girl's mother. She said the child had been kidnapped by D'Armand some months before in Mobile, Alabama. She had been on his trail ever since.

Persons at the stagecoach stop directed her to the professor and she made the mistake of confronting him without a lawman to help her. D'Armand promised to produce the girl, who was still seeking funds somewhere in the town, but instead packed his balloon and accessories, hired a buggy and left town with the girl. Mr. Peterson, the assistant, was left behind, penniless, since he had already turned over his donations. The Micanopy residents were left cheated out of their money and the balloon ascension, the highlight of their July Fourth celebration.

James said to John that evening, "There was something familiar about that man. I know I've seen him before."

"I know," said John. "Struck me the same way. If I didn't know better I'd say he was that scoundrel who stole my money and jumped overboard in New York Harbor. Same build, same sneaky look, but that heavy beard concealed too much of his face."

"If he's in the area, we may see him again," said James.

As 1860 advanced almost every subject of conversation was lost in the fever of secession that gripped most of Florida. Communities all over the state had formed volunteer military companies for the defense of their homes. Such activity had been encouraged by the new Florida Military Law. Both Micanopy and Ocala had such units as "home guard" establishments.

One morning at breakfast, Janet McCredie appeared hollow–eyed and disturbed. She explained that she had not slept well. David wanted to know if she were ill. No, she said, she had just had a bad dream. She called them "visions."

"Visions, is it," exclaimed David, in some disgust. "Visions of what?"

"Don't you fun me, David McCredie," Janet replied. "What I see is fearful. As a child I suffered through the clan wars in Scotland and now I see them coming here. In my dream I saw our boys in tatters and scraps of uniforms. James was dripping blood from his arm and he stared straight ahead like some kind of spirit."

She closed her eyes as if to blot from her mind the unhappy picture.

"Aye, lass," David said, "I also remember the clan wars. With all the talk of secession and fighting, 'tis nae wonder you dream of such things, but what is to be will be."

"Don't worry about it now, Mama," John said. "We'll lick the Black Republicans in November and that will be the end of it."

But such was not to be the case. The Republicans won the presidential election in November with Abraham Lincoln and Micanopy, along with the rest of Florida and the South, became restless and active.

Secession talk was everywhere. Florida newspapers, including one in Micanopy, the *Peninsula Gazette*, published by J. R. Bean, Micanopy dentist, and J. J. McDaniels, were urging the state government to provide the Volunteers with uniforms manufactured in the South. "Why should we give military business to those who would take away our freedom?" the editors argued.

On November 22nd, shortly after the presidential election, Alachua County citizens met at the courthouse in Gainesville and passed resolutions calling on the state government to vote for secession and immediately to arm the Volunteers. A similar meeting was held in Ocala at the Marion County courthouse. The day of the Ocala meetings the Secession Flag, with a single blue star and the words, "Let us Alone," was flying from a pole on the courthouse square.

The newspapers also carried a number of accounts of "tampering with slaves." For example, a meeting of the Santa Fe Vigilance Society found Henri D' Armand guilty of tampering with slaves in that area. The Society recommended that one side of his head be shaved and that he be delivered to the Conductor of the Florida Railroad at Waldo to be immediately shipped North.

"I'd like to be the one to shave his head," said John McCredie, after reading the account in the newspaper. "Perhaps he has found stirring up the slaves more profitable than riding a balloon."

The slavery question was not paramount in the McCredie household.

"If war comes, it will not be over slavery," said the elder David McCredie. "This will be a war for the principal of States Rights."

The McCredie family owned no slaves, nor did it hire any of the black freemen in the area, for two reasons. First they were small businessmen and tradesmen and believed in doing all their own work. It was a tradition they brought from Scotland. Second, they were not extensive landowners with a need for slave labor, or any kind of hired labor.

The family stand on the slavery issue was summed up by David when he told his boys, "I don't believe in slavery and would nae have any, but slaves are property and I don't believe the government has the right to take a man's property without payment in a free and sovereign state."

By the end of 1860, John, James and David were heavily involved in the drills of the Micanopy Volunteers, wearing their blue cockade hats that were signs of their belief in the right of Florida to secede.

"Don't tell Mama," John told his brothers, "but the seeds of war have been sown and there's no turning back."

There was no turning back. Everyone appeared to be convinced that secession would not bring on war, or if it did, it would be a half–hearted war.

"War would ruin the North," one man said. "Grass will grow in the streets of New York City if war comes. The North can't live without our cotton."

Another man around the whiskey barrel said, "It'll be nothing. Most of the North will refuse to raise arms against us."

George Mason, a cattleman, was more to the point. "Why I could drink all of the blood that will be spilled in such a conflict."

John's comment to James on this kind of talk was bitter. "They sound like a bunch of children," he said.

The McCredie household was in turmoil. Young David, going on twenty–two, was of age, and had announced that he was volunteering for service in the Fourth Florida Infantry Regiment. Big brother John Stewart had been right. War between the North and the South was imminent.

Janet cried and wrung her hands, but to no avail.

"We left Scotland," she Complained, "to get away from bloodshed, men bashing in one nother's heads like so many empty gourds, an' poverty an' hate. Now in this savage land, it's to do all over again."

She stared out the window at the masses of yellow Amanda, growing in a great cluster in a corner of the front yard, which was enclosed by an unpainted picket fence of rough cypress.

The yard was hard–packed sand, swept clean with a handmade brush broom and up against one end of the front porch was a wooden trellis, spotted with red and white rambling roses. Janet took pride in her yard and her flowers, but this war business had turned everything else from her mind so that even though she was looking at the beauty she had brought about in the new barren soil, she saw nothing. The horror in her mind's eye had taken over her senses.

She turned back to James and David, who had been shuffling uneasily behind her.

"David," she said bitterly, "I'd just as soon shoot you now and get it over with, as spend my days waiting for one of your friends to show up with a handful of your belongings."

"Then, you'd better shoot me, too," James said quietly, "because I'm going to volunteer with David."

"I'll not hear any more of this," she shrieked and dashed for her room.

The boys let her go and quietly left the house to go to the Micanopy post office.

The year was 1861, in June, and events had moved rapidly since the election of Abraham Lincoln as president of the United States in November of 1860. Seven states, South Carolina, Mississippi, Florida, Alabama, Georgia, Louisiana, and Texas had left the union. In February representatives of these states met in Montgomery, Alabama, and formed their new government, the Confederate States of America, with Jefferson Davis as their first president.

Also in February, twenty–one states met in Washington at the Peace Convention to try to come up with some kind of compromise that would restore the Union by bringing back the seceding states, but no compromise was reached.

On April 12th, 1861, Confederate batteries fired on Fort Sumpter in South Carolina when President Lincoln sent in supplies, men and ammunition to strengthen that federal garrison. The Confederates quickly reduced the fort to rubble.

After that, there was no turning back. Lincoln called for seventy–five thousand volunteers and four more Southern states, Virginia, Arkansas, Tennessee and North Carolina seceded from the Union.

James and David enlisted on June 22nd, 1861, in Micanopy. A table had been set up on Chulokka Boulevard, near the post office, and there the young men of the town and surrounding communities had gathered to volunteer their services to the Confederacy.

One man was heard to exclaim, "By me bloody bladder, I'm ready to fight. Any cowardly president that has to crawl into Washington through the back door with his tail hanging ain't gonna sick his dogs on me. I'll fight em."

James and David looked at one another. "Tim Ferguson," James said. "I'd know that voice anywhere."

It was Tim Ferguson. He had arrived in Micanopy that morning on horseback to sign up. They greeted their former Orange Springs acquaintance, who was in a belligerent mood. "Floridy won't go back to the Union til they gits rid of that Black Republican," he said. "Impeach him or ride him out of Washington on a rail, is what I say."

"You can't restore law and order with more disorder," James said. "If the President doesn't have the confidence of the people, then he should resign."

"He ain't gonna resign. James, you know that, unless somebody makes him," Tim said heatedly. "I'm fer sendin' a few hand–picked Southerners up there tuh take care of the scoundrel. I'll volunteer for that duty."

"Well," James replied, "We're here to volunteer for duty in the Confederate Army right now. We'll have to see where that takes us."

They all signed up and were told to wait for further orders, but to be ready to leave Micanopy at any time. Both had enlisted for twelve months duty. It was a sad day at the McCredie house.

Janet took to her bed, looking red–eyed and frail. John had agreed to remain on the farm to look after the citrus grove and perform general farm chores while his father ran the cobbler's shop, but he made it clear that if he was needed in the Confederate Army later he would go.

Orders arrived assigning the boys to Captain Fletcher's Company G of the Fourth Florida Infantry regiment. They were ordered to report at Cedar Keys on September 14th, David as a private and James as a member of the company band.

Janet came out of hiding and took charge again. Apparently, she had feigned a serious illness so that her sons would give up their foolhardy venture into the Southern army. Once the enlistment became final, however, and she realized her ruse had failed, she set about with great determination and energy getting the boys ready to leave Micanopy.

All of the Alachua and Marion County area was in a war frenzy. The Micanopy churches had farewell picnics on the church grounds for the departing volunteers, and piles of warm clothing of all kinds were knitted, crocheted and sewn by mothers, grandmothers and women without men–

folks for distribution to the soldiers who would be heading for camps in Georgia, Tennessee, Alabama and South Carolina.

Janet added her share of items from stockings to neckpieces to underwear. "Mama, we can't take all those Clothes," James protested. "Even if we get them to Cedar Keys, there will be no way we can take them to our first encampment."

On the surface, there was an air of festivity that hovered over all of the going–away events, as though these men and boys were going off on an alligator hunt to Orange Lake.

The day of departure came. A neighbor had agreed to drive the two young men in his wagon to Cedar Keys, a journey of four days. The wagon was loaded with food and clothing, and John shook his head as he saw the size of the load, but Janet had insisted that nothing be left behind. "We'll never get away with all that stuff in the Army," he said. "You know how light we traveled in the Indian campaign."

James whispered to his older brother, "We'll be sending a lot of it back in the wagon."

Parting with their father was almost formal, a brief handshake, a "Take care of yourselves, boys," and then David turned back indoors, but James saw him hastily wipe the back of his hand across his eyes.

John hugged his brothers and told them in a whisper, "I'll be with you ere long."

Janet followed them to the wagon, and, with trembling hand, gave each one a small Bible. "Keep them in the pocket over your hearts," she told her sons.

She watched until the wagon was out of sight. "When you left Scotland in the gray light of dawn," she told John, "I felt something in me had died. Now, this, this," she faltered. "Tis more than a mother can take."

John put his arm across her thin shoulders. "It'll be all right, Mama," he told her. "It's just a year's enlistment. This war won't last that long."

Days at the farm dragged by without word from the boys. July, August and then September, all oppressively hot and sticky months went by and each day Janet surveyed David as he came in to see if he had a letter. Then on October first a letter came from James. He had been mustered into the company band on September 21st but there were no instruments so the band members spent their days drilling with the infantry, breaking and setting up camp as practice, and cooking their own issued rations.

"You won't believe this," James wrote, "but we're sleeping in a cannery the Army took over. The smell at first made nearly everybody sick, but now we don't even smell the crabs. At least it's dry when it rains. I guess we smell to other people because when we go into town they turn up their noses when we pass by."

There was no word about how long they would be in Cedar Keys, but at least Janet knew James and David were well.

In November James wrote that things were unchanged at Cedar Keys except that his company had been ordered to help with the production of salt by the civilians in the area. The salt, they were told, was badly needed by Confederate troops encamped throughout the South. It was also used to preserve beef transported by train for Army use.

James complained about the Army's requirement that they pitch tents just for practice. "The ground here is solid rock," he wrote. "Try to drive a tent peg."

December began as a happy time. The McCredies and their Micanopy neighbors arranged to send ten barrels of oranges to Cedar Keys for their boys. They also expected to get several barrels of smoked mullet in return for barrels of oranges they sent along for the fishermen. John drove one of the wagons in this wagon train of citrus, which arrived in Cedar Keys on December 10th.

He found his brothers' company had been moved to Fernandina to join the rest of the Fourth Regiment.

Nevertheless, the oranges were distributed to other Florida volunteers on duty at Cedar Keys and the wagon train returned to Micanopy, loaded down with smoked mullet that had been salted down in wooden barrels.

John fussed and fumed all the way home because his brothers had not written about their removal to Fernandina. Truth of the matter was he dreaded to tell his mother that he had not been able to present her Christmas gifts to her soldier sons.

James and David found duty at Fernandina to their liking. They quartered at Fort Clinch, just completed that year, and named for Gen. Duncan L. Clinch, Seminole War leader. The Confederates had taken over the fort at the outset of the War to protect ships moving in and out of the port. Duty there consisted for the most part for James of playing stirring marches for the parading soldiers. As a private, David drilled, stood guard duty on the fort walls, cooked for his company when his turn came around, and spent his off–duty time fishing with a hand line just below the fort walls.

The parades were the best part of the Fernandina duty. The soldiers marched from Fort Clinch into town and down Centre Street to the wharf, where the band played for the citizens. All along the line of march women and children, pretty girls and old maids cheered and waved their handkerchiefs. It made a boy feel like a man, and to die for one's country was a way of being a real man.

In January of 1862, Janet heard some shocking news at a church meeting where the ladies were sewing and knitting for the soldiers. Lucy Williams said she heard that five men had died at Fort Clinch from dysentery. "The water's poisoning our men," Lucy reported. "They say two of the men are from Micanopy."

Janet went to bed that night with a tight band of fear squeezing her chest like an iron corset. She kept waking up, every hour or so as she heard James calling her name. Either it was an omen or she was hearing her son calling to her from some place outside of this life. She awoke in the morning, exhausted and limp, unable to leave her bed.

When she told David of her dreams and anxieties, he stroked her hair. "You'll make yourself ill," he said. "Drink a cup of hot tay and try not to worry about the boys. You'll get a letter soon."

Letters came, but not to the McCredie family. One Micanopy soldier and one from McIntosh had died at Fort Clinch and had been buried there. The war had come home to the area and the mourning began.

The Presbyterian Church bell began to toll its dismal message just after Janet and David retired for the night. She wondered how many more times it would toll before the dreadful war was over.

War arrived at Fort Clinch the middle of March 1862, with the arrival of Federal gunboats, loaded with soldiers and artillery. Being outnumbered, the Confederates withdrew their troops and ordered Fernandina evacuated. The Florida Fourth Infantry Regiment was sent to Camp Langford, near Jacksonville. As the last train was pulling out of town, loaded with refugees and some troops, cannon on the gunboats opened up. Two cars of the train were struck and several civilians were killed. The train stopped just out of gun range long enough for a detachment of soldiers to blow up the bridge.

Toward the last of March, the Fourth Regiment was ordered to move to Corinth, Mississippi.

On May 14th, John McCredie went to Orange Springs to join Captain Pearson's Independent Company, Florida Volunteers, which had been formed in the area to ambush and harass any Union Boats that might use the St. Johns and Ocklawaha Rivers in that area.

John later wrote James that the day he left was the most agonizing time of his life. "I felt like I had stabbed Mama with my deer knife," he wrote. "She just sat on the porch, pale, her eyes without expression, like two empty pools. It was as though I had abandoned a child, a poor, helpless child."

Janet was almost out of her mind. She feared the Yankees. What would they do if the Union soldiers came marching into Micanopy? She and David were old. Who would protect them? A fourteen–year–old son and an old maid daughter? John had left them to the mercy of the enemy in a savage land.

In June the Fourth Regiment began a series of moves that began in Chattahoochee, Florida then up the Apalachicola by boat to Columbus, Georgia. The troops left the boat there in the early morning and marched all over Columbus while the ladies along the line of march wept. At 11 a.m., after going more than twenty–four hours without food, they were allowed to camp, build fires and cook gingerbread and "bakers bread."

James wrote his father that he had never seen so many men in his life who had never seen a musket or a bayonet as those in the Confederate Army at Montgomery.

The next move, the last of June, was to Mobile, where the Third Florida Regiment and five other regiments had assembled to form the Army of Mobile under Brigadier Jones of Alabama, James wrote. The forces were gathering for a move into the battle areas around Chattanooga and Lookout Mountain.

James didn't like Mobile. It rained all the time and their rations had been cut. They had to stand eight–hour watches on the streets of the town as an addition to the meager town police force. The citizens seemed to resent their presence and prices were outlandishly high.

"I'd sure like a ripe watermelon," James told his brother one afternoon.

"You kin have all you want for ten dollars a melon," David replied.

They were just about to go off guard duty. "I know," James said. "I can't eat melon at that price."

Tim Ferguson heard the remark and when they had returned to camp he sauntered over to the McCredie boys. "How'd you like a watermelon, free," he grinned.

"You must be crazy," David said. "Ain't nobody in this town gonna give you anything fer free."

"Some of the other fellows been gittin em," Tim said. "You jes follow me."

They walked about a mile to the edge of town and just off the trail was about an acre of melons, ready to be picked. Each one got a melon and then they sneaked back into camp for a melon feast with some of the other men.

A few days later, James returned to camp from his turn at guard duty with a worried look on his face. "What's eatin' on your gut?" Tim Ferguson asked.

"Colonel Hunt's been arrested for letting his men steal watermelons," he said glumly. "We ought to go to headquarters and tell em the Colonel didn't have anything to do with watermelon stealin' cause we did it."

"You dern fool," Tim said. "This is the army, man. The head man always gits his foot put to the fire. We can't do the colonel no good. They'd just git us too."

James knew he was right, although the incident disturbed his sleep.

Then came the order to move again, this time to Chattanooga. So, the watermelon incident was forgotten.

Then came a night of horrors.

On the train somewhere between Pollard, Florida and Montgomery, Alabama, the car occupied mostly by Company G broke down in a deep clay cut. It broke loose from the engine and came apart, scattering men and equipment all up and down the track.

James found himself lying alongside a soldier whose leg was pinned Underpart of an axle. The man was screaming for help but without a light James could do nothing. The scene was one of utter confusion, men calling out for friends or relatives, and the night as dark as the inside of a cave.

Finally, they got some lanterns after the engine had backed up with the other cars. Two soldiers were dead, several with broken arms or legs, one with a concussion, and one had all his front teeth knocked out. In all, eight were either dead or injured.

James and David found one another and also their friend Tim Ferguson. By noon order had been restored and they left for Greenville, Alabama, where the wounded were left for treatment. Then followed another night on the train before they reached Montgomery.

By then, the soldiers were exhausted and hungry. They had not eaten for twenty–four hours, and despite the fact that Colonel Hunt had orders to transport his regiment to Chattanooga without stopping, he did let his men stop long enough to cook two day's rations. He didn't know when they would get to cook again. He knew there was a strong possibility the regiment would be ordered into battle on arrival.

At Marietta, Georgia, the troops were greeted by groups of young women singing patriotic songs like "Maryland," "Dixie," "Bonnie Blue Flag," and "Cheer, Boys, Cheer."

On July 26th they arrived at Chattanooga and set up camp near the base of Lookout Mountain. On August 1st, Colonel Hunt was placed under arrest for letting his men stop to cook during their journey following the wreck.

"I've never heard of discipline like this," James told David. "Already three men have been shot for being away from camp without orders. They called them 'deserters.' All they were doing was trying to find some food."

"I've been hungry enough to steal food from one of the farms," David complained. "You know what the rations are now—a little over a pound of flour, a pound of beef or a pound of bacon, an' the bacon's full of skippers, an' a little salt each day. How can a man live on that?"

"Don't forget the five ounces of sugar we get each week," James said. "But, at least the band's improving. Music is beginning to sound real sweet."

David grinned. "It ought to," he said, "you got instruments now!"

That night Tim Ferguson came to their campfire. The temperature was already in the low thirties and all the Florida boys were huddled around fires. He paced up and down in front of the fire.

"What's the matter with you, man?" James wanted to know. "You're acting like you're carrying a problem across your shoulders as big as a hog."

"That's it," said Tim. "I know where I can git us a hog. By me bloody bladder, I'm so empty, I could eat one all by myself."

"You'd better forget it," David said. "They'll shoot you in the army for stealin' a hog."

"Don't worry about me," Tim said, and disappeared into the darkness.

About two hours later, he was back with thirty pounds of hog meat in a sack. James felt his stomach fall into his shoes. "Now, he's done it," he thought.

They began roasting the hog meat over the coals and the smell drew men from all over the camp. By the time they shared their bounty, Tim, James and David got very little of the meat.

Then, disaster struck. An officer, unknown to any of the men, moved into the circle of firelight. He surveyed the scene for a moment, then said, “Who killed that hog?”

There was silence for a moment and then Tim spoke up. “I did, sir,” he said.

“Come with me.”

They moved off into the darkness. The next morning the regiment was called to fall in by companies. In front of the soldiers, as they stood at attention, was Tim Ferguson, tied to a pine tree.

There was a sharp command and a firing squad marched into position. James looked on in horror. The rifles cracked and poor Tim slumped against the tree, shot through the heart.

“My God,” James thought “Killed for a pig that he scarcely got to eat.” Then he was sick.

Janet sat on her front porch, rocking gently, with James' letter from his camp near Chattanooga in her hands. A little curl of blue smoke escaped from her tiny clay pipe.

Shock and disbelief shone on her face as she reviewed in her mind the death of Tim Ferguson, but she was even more concerned about the lack of food for the Confederate soldiers. She looked again at the letter.

"Me an' David are cookin for some of the noncommissioned officers," James wrote. "We get a dollar a month from each man, an' that money is used to buy food for us, when we can get it."

James wrote, "I've lived on nothin' but meal for a week. No meat, no lard to cook the meal with, just water to make a paste and then bake over some coals, not even any salt It's not too bad if that's all you've got to eat."

David came home about that time and Janet told him, "We've got to send some boxes of food to Chattanooga. If our boys are not shot to death, they'll surely starve."

"It's a hard, hard war, ass," David replied. "John McCormack was in the shop today. He had a letter from his son, Jeff. The Confederate Army is losing more men from disease and hospital care than in battle. All they kin do for a wound in an arm or leg is cut it off– and then most of them die from the amputation."

David was right about the hospital. James and his brother had learned that if you were sick it was better to remain in camp as long as possible and not go into a field hospital, unless it was a matter of life and death. Their company's clerk, Washington Ives from Lake City, had told James about one soldier who got his foot mashed in a railroad collision and his leg was cut off in three places before he could be saved.

"I would a great deal rather die than to undergo any such operation," Wash said. "I'm not afraid to die, but I am afraid to be butchered up."

Amputations had become so common in the hospitals that every soldier was afraid of any kind of limb fracture. In fact, soldiers in Company C of the Fourth Regiment were so afraid of being attended by army doctors that they paid one dollar per soldier per month for Doctor Shaffer of Madison, Florida, to come to their camp to attend them during the winter of 1862, Wash told James.

By late September, 1862, General Breckenridge's division arrived in the Chattanooga area from Baton Rouge, Louisiana. The Army of Mississippi, some one–hundred–thousand strong was gathering for a big push against the Yankees. James wrote his family that despite its one–hundred–thousand man strength, the Army of Mississippi had an effective fighting strength of only fifty–thousand men, because of illness and lack of conditioning of many of the men marching and fighting in mountain country. He said he had heard of more than three–hundred men of the Florida Third Regiment dropping out on one march, because of the rough terrain.

The first week in October, James became seriously ill with pneumonia. In a letter home, he called it "bilious fever," but he did not tell his family how ill he actually had been. During the illness, all of the able–bodied men of his regiment moved by train to Nashville. Left in Chattanooga were about two–hundred men who were too ill to move, including James and Washington Ives.

Both James and Wash remained in their tents, lying on their blankets for three or four days before the fever subsided. "I believe I would have died if I had gone to the doctors," Wash said.

By the 20th of the month they both moved on to Murfreesborough, Tennessee, with the other sick soldiers and all the regiment's baggage, where they caught up with their outfit.

Prior to the move to Murfreesborough, the build–up of Confederate troops in the Chattanooga area had been impressive. One afternoon, James and David watched from a hillside the movement of troops across the Tennessee River. Objective of the movement of eighty–thousand men across the river was to attack General Buell and then go on to capture Cincinnati. Approximately sixteen–hundred wagons, drawn by sixty–four–hundred mules took the troops and supplies across the Tennessee on a bridge of flats. It was estimated the wagon train was between five and six miles long.

As the boys watched the troop wagons crossing, James said to David, "This could be a crucial time for us. If the Confederacy loses this army, she's finished." Wash Ives had put it more directly. "All the youth and strength of the Confederate Army is here," he said. "We could finish up this war in six months or it could go on for twenty years."

As the big battle approached, the band played more often to keep spirits high. At guard mounting time, the band played such tunes as "Troubadour," "Rosalie," "Grand Norma March," "Mobile Quickstep," and "Cheer, Boys, Cheer." At the battle of Lavergne, less than twenty miles from Murfreesborough, the Thirty–Second Alabama Regiment lost all its band instruments so the band members used those of the Florida Fourth. Commenting on their performance, Wash Ives wrote his father, "They perform splendidly, and their 'Down in Alabama' makes everyone's blood rise to the point necessary for charge bayonets."

As rumors flew around the encampment, indicating the troops would be ordered into battle at any time, morale was high despite the gathering of groups of friends to discuss their chances of being alive after the fight.. Wash Ives summed up their fears in a letter home that read: "Day after tomorrow I think General Forrest will march us on to Nashville, and if he does, this may be the last letter you'll receive from me for Gen. Forrest is a brave and dashing officer and the Fourth of Florida and thirty–second of Alabama bear the brunt of the fray."

"You speak of seeing me at Christmas. I only wish it were so I could see you all once more, but the way things are working out it is very doubtful if I ever see Florida again. If I should happen to get killed some of the boys will write to Pa, as I've made a bargain with them, but I hope the Yankees are not as strong as it is said for four–thousand of us have got to whip about ten–thousand of them out of their entrenchments. I see Henry Wood is wounded and a great many others whom I know are either killed or wounded."

"I guess the people would sooner rely on the Fourth than any other regiment Florida has in the field. The citizens of this city (Murfreesborough) say they believe our regiment will fight to the very death and some of the boys are as anxious to get into battle as I would be to see you all. At any rate, just beat the 'long roll' and you'll see sick and well hurrying into the lines and the battalion is about twice as large then as at other times."

The Nashville attack failed to materialize, despite the fact the troops had been ordered to cook two days' rations in preparation for the order to move out. As the days passed James and David wondered where the war was. The area seemed too peaceful. The town clock in Murfreesborough could be heard all over the camp and the spires of two churches could be seen jutting above the treetops. One spire of bright metal glittered in the sunlight like a silver pyramid. Daily, Murfreesborough ladies visited the camp, bringing warm clothing and pastries. The clothing was welcome since on the 25th of October there was sleet during the night.

The Florida troops spent all day on the 26th in snowball fights and general merriment. Some, less able to stand the cold, huddled around their fires.

On Christmas Day, 1862, the Honda Fourth was encamped a mile north of Murfreesborough. All furloughs had been canceled by General Bragg "for the duration of the emergency." Pneumonia had spread like a blight through the encampment, aided by the cold and rain that penetrated some of the tattered and flimsy uniforms like icy fingers. Gunfire had begun at noon on Christmas Day and continued until night, only to begin again at first light.

James and David met briefly Christmas afternoon to exchange greetings, probably illegally because they were encamped on opposite sides of the sprawling camp, and there had been orders for each man to remain with his unit.

On the 26th, three men were shot for desertion; and one was hanged on order of a general Court–martial. The nature of his crime was not known, although rumors were always spreading silently throughout the camp like drifting leaves. This was especially true on this particular Christmas night, and the word was that he had sneaked out Christmas Eve to sleep with a village girl.

"A heavy price to pay for a night in the hay," David said.

The sentences were carried out during a cold, stinging drizzle that lasted all day and into the night.

On the morning of December 28th, the camp began to hum. Word had come for the Florida Fourth to move at once to the Lebanon Pike. "Some turnpike," James said. "It's nothing more than a wagon road with deep ditches."

"Those ditches might be good places to hide in heavy gunfire," one of his fellow band members replied.

As they approached the turnpike they could hear firing and soon bullets were sniping off branches from the trees over their heads.

"Into the ditches," came the order.

No one had to be told. They lay there most of the day firing in the direction of the gunfire that was coming their way. They were cold and miserable in the drizzle that had been falling almost constantly for several days.

Just before dark Florida's First, Third and Fourth regiments were brigaded with the Twentieth of Tennessee and the Sixtieth of North Carolina under General William Preston and marched into a wooded area to camp for the night. They were allowed to build split rail fires from wood taken from the farm fences, but even with the fires, they slept, if sleep came, with the cold as their only companion.

At daylight they drew rations of flour and bacon. "How are we gonna cook this stuff," a band member wanted to know. In this emergency the band had left its instruments at Murfreesborough and had been issued rifles and ammunition to fight with the infantry.

They ended up using enough water to make balls of dough, flattened out like biscuits. Stones were heated red hot in the rail fires and then the bacon and dough were cooked on the stones, despite a steady drizzle that made the stones sputter and sing as the raindrops touched them.

The next day the Yankees could be heard cheering as they charged a unit of Confederates hidden behind a stone wall along the Franklin pike. This engagement took place only a mile and a quarter from where the Florida Fourth was entrenched. A courier brought news that the Yanks had been turned back after each charge, leaving hundreds of dead and dying.

Everyone agreed that they would really be in it the next day, the last day of 1862. The prediction came to pass. No one slept much that night. The rain had soaked their blankets, the campfires of the Yankees were in plain sight and no one knew when they might attack. Occasionally cannon balls would whistle just over their heads, followed by a few minutes of rifle fire.

"They're gittin' on my nerves," said another of the band members.

"That's just what they aim to do," James said. "Try to get some sleep."

What happened on December 31st is best described by Wash Ives who wrote it all down for his family.

"The firing is sublime, if such it may be termed, for the roar of musketry is as regular and quick as touching the two lowest keys on the piano, and the cannon are firing as fast as you can think. We marched about one–hundred yards nearer the fight at quick time when another aid halted us.

We double quick back through the field and waded Stone River, wetting us up to our knees, and formed in line of battle just on the west side of the creek or river."

"We had thrown off our blankets and coats before crossing."

At the creek ambulances were crossing with the wounded, and one man walking with his arm shot off inquired what regiment as our beautiful flag passed him. Being told 'Fourth Florida,' he said, 'You'll do it up right Pay them for my arm.' A little soldier about the size of Albert was in one of the ambulances and appeared to be hit in four or five places. His back, I think, was broken, but he bore it like a man, except as the wagon would jolt he'd groan.

"As we formed in line of battle there was a Confederate, the first dead man I had yet seen, lying on his back with a cannon ball hole through his breast I could stick my head in. I thought then how soon I may be Uncared for like him but I uttered a short prayer, leaving my safety with Him who can save."

As the regiment moved into and out of clumps of woods, James kept looking for his brother, David. The regiment passed through a picket fence and in doing so broke ranks during the hottest kind of fire from sharp shooters in a cedar thicket. In the midst of this, some companies of the North Carolina Sixtieth passed by under orders to retreat.

Then, James saw David, a sergeant, at the head of his unit. All were running and firing at the sharpshooters. Suddenly, he saw David spin and fall to the frozen ground.

He started to run toward his brother. "Get back here, McCredie," his bandmaster called out.

"But that's my brother who just fell," James said in anguish.

"If he's dead, you can't help him," came the reply. "If he's alive we'll get him out after dark."

James knew that if he disobeyed he could be shot on the spot so he got back in line but kept his eye on the crumpled figure of his brother. Then, he saw David turn over on his back, clutching at his right shoulder.

"At least, he's still alive." he thought.

That night the wounded were brought in and transported in an ambulance wagon to the field hospital near Murfreesborough, David among them.

James was unable to get word about David's condition until after the retreat to Tullahoma, Tennessee.

As for the retreat, everyone felt badly about that. Wash Ives said it this way in a letter to his folks. "I want to tell you a great many things, but I am unable to do so at present. The Yankees never hurt me or the Army half as bad as the retreat."

But the Yankees had hurt the Army. The Florida Fourth Regiment in that final assault on the center of the Union line lost fifty–five killed and wounded.

David had taken a rifle ball in his right shoulder that left his arm useless, but without complications his life would not be in danger and he would regain the use of the arm, the army doctor told him. At his request he was given a medical furlough home for recuperation.

"I hate to leave you here," he told James as he departed on a wagon with other wounded for Chattanooga, where he would go by train to Florida. "I'm afraid the worst is yet to come."

"Don't worry," James said. Then he grinned, "Maybe they'll let the band play and we can kill the Yankee's music."

David had been right. The worst was yet to come. Prior to the retreat that took the remnants of the regiment to Tullahoma, the regiment pulled deep into a large clump of cedars for the night, but few of the men got any sleep. They were without blankets and the ground was frozen solid. Also the main Yankee line was only a thousand yards to the north.

On the afternoon of January 2nd, the regiment lay in the cedars until mid–afternoon, when the men were ordered to march to a point east of the Yankees and form a line of battle.

Enroute they marched through piles of unburied dead. Confederates and Yankees, scattered around like rag dolls left by children at play. The sight was unnerving, since many of the dead lay on their backs with arms uplifted to the sky as though seeking God's help to stop the slaughter.

When the Fourth was in position, the Confederate batteries opened up and the infantrymen charged. This was probably their finest hour because they were outnumbered about five to one. When the retreat was finally sounded, the toll for the days of fighting at Murfreesborough came to one–

hundred and sixty–three killed and wounded and thirty–one missing out of a strength of four–hundred and fifty–eight.

By the time the regiment arrived at Tullahoma on January 9th, Wash Ives' second bout with pneumonia had turned to yellow jaundice, no doubt agitated by the fact the unit had lost all its tents and the men had to sleep in the open during a cold winter rain.

Wash felt he bore a charmed life. On the final charge he had one rifle ball that cut a hole in his pants, and another cut some hair from his right temple. A man fell, mortally wounded, on either side of him.

On January 20th, he wrote his father, editor and publisher of the *Columbian* in Lake City, "I want you to write a piece urging the people of Florida to plant gardens and raise poultry. I would give five dollars for a head of cabbage. Eggs sell at a dollar and a half a dozen but generals get them all. Tennessee is completely eaten out and twenty years from now she won't be in as good condition as before the war, and I have no idea the war will end under twenty years, for I've seen a thing or two myself."

It was May, 1863. The brigade of which the Florida Fourth Regiment was a part had been transferred to Mississippi to relieve other Confederates at Vicksburg. James McCredie sat in deep thought beside the Mississippi River. He tried to put the war out of his mind as he watched the river, moving almost invisibly and silently before him.

"The war's like that," he thought. "It'll go on just like this ole river, forever and forever."

The battle of Murfreesborough had put to rest a lot of myths about the Yankees. In the early days of the war, the Confederates bragged a lot about how one Southerner was equal to a hundred Yankees. Wash Ives messed with the band and they all talked about the Yankees as fighting men.

"There's no more use of talking about the Yankees being inferior troops," Wash said. "Those we fought shoot as well as any man can, and they've got the best artillerymen the world ever produced."

Wash also believed an army traveled on its stomach.

"They have everything to eat that a soldier can wish, even preserved vegetables," he said. "It's the camp fare that's killing off so many of our good men," he complained bitterly. They all agreed he was right.

He had written his father, "I long for fish, birds and oysters. I could almost shed tears I wanted some so bad, also some eggs."

James often marveled at this young man from Lake City, who at nineteen was such a boy in many ways, yet mature in thought, well educated, and a man in every respect on the battlefield.

There was the time when it seems half the regiment gathered around to watch Bob Bigelow pull two of Wash's teeth. The teeth were infected and were causing Wash great pain. The answer was that they had to come out. Some of the bigger fellows held Wash down, his mouth propped open with a wooden peg, and Bob, his triceps bulging, practically pried and yanked the teeth from Wash's mouth, leaving the mouth bloody and bruised. Wash never uttered a sound, but at times his eyes bulged out like they would pop.

David McCredie went around muttering, "I never seen anythin' like that before."

On July the 1st, the Florida First, the Third and Fourth Regiments engaged the Yankees near Jackson, striking the enemy flank and coming away with two–hundred prisoners and the colors of the Twenty–Eighth, Forty–Fifth and Fifty–Third Illinois regiments. The loss was one man wounded, who later died. James wrote his father, saying that the Florida Fourth "captured two colors by itself."

Following this minor victory, however, the fortunes of the Confederate Army in Mississippi were ebbing away because of conditions in general; scarce food, worn–out clothing, careless officers who were not considerate of their men.

In August, a rumor spread throughout the encampment that General Robert E. Lee had resigned. Wash wrote his father: "I never heard as much talk of desertion and deserters in my life before as I have in the last few weeks. From rumors in camp I suppose at least one–thousand men have deserted from our ranks and gone home. Probably they will return, as I think they will. The most loyal troops are Floridians, Georgians, Kentuckians, South Carolinians and North Carolinians."

"The problem is, Uncle Jeff ain't feedin' us proper," said Jimmie Rawls, a member of the band. Sickness, battle losses, and furloughs had diminished the band to the following members: I. C. Canova, William G. Brock, M. C. Pemberton, Socrates Prosperos, I. Bowen, Jimmie Rawls, J. H. Young,

Charles Young, T. A. Pollard, William Pennington and Sherman Daniels, in addition to James."

Each band member took his turn at preparing food. Jimmie Rawls had just drawn rations for three days, consisting of one pound of beef, three ounces of bacon, three–tenths ounces of salt, and three pints of cornmeal, mixed with shorts.

"They call that food for three days!" Jimmie snorted. "I kin eat that much in one sittin."

James wrote his mother that the men, for the most part, had not changed their clothes in seven weeks. "Men stand guard with nothing on but a hat, a pair of worn–out shoes, a shirt and a pair of drawers. Their pants have so many holes in them they can't be patched."

Apparently, the men could buy extra things to eat but their complaint was the high prices and the fact the officers bought up all the available food since they had more money to spend.

The boys in the band had a way of making campfire light bread when they could get a pound of flour. First, they boiled a handful of clean fodder in a quart of water; then, they took out the fodder and strained the water. The yeast was made from the "strainings" by letting it set overnight. Then they put in the dough, which was allowed to rise about two hours and then baked in an iron kettle over hot coals.

In late August the regiment was moved to a camp near Chattanooga on the Tennessee River. At night James and David could see the fires of the Union soldiers, across the river. One morning David was sent with a picket patrol down the river, and as they took their positions behind the trees that lined the river bank they could see their enemies doing the same thing across the river.

"Hey, Yank, what yuh have for breakfast?" David called out.

"Same as you, Reb," came the reply. "Smoked sausage, grits, hot biscuits, cane syrup and fresh milk. They cook our breakfast in Chattanooga at one of your fine hotels."

David laughed, and all his men laughed uproariously. They knew the Yanks had not captured Chattanooga, and they suspected the Union soldiers had the same kind of breakfast they had, cold cornbread and beef jerky.

Back in camp, James thought to himself how like Sunday the day had begun. There was bright sunshine except for the dark haze over the mountains where the mist and fog of the morning still hung. The smell of the hardwood fires was pleasant and the men were relaxed, talking, shaving and cooking. Some were singing or whistling bits of hymns despite camp gossip that the Confederates were assembling a heavy force for an early engagement with the Union forces.

The band members gathered in mid morning and began playing popular tunes like "Kissing Through the Bars," or "Switzer's Farewell."

Wash Ives was writing another letter to his family. "I tell you we are a dirty, tired, and I may say naked set," he wrote. "Three fourths of the men have not a single pair of shoes, and no drawers, and only a shirt, hat and pair of pants apiece, and some of them are threadbare. If this army is not clothed soon, it will be naked. The whole army is in good spirits but it is hard to see barefoot men marching on such roads as there are here."

By the middle of September, the Confederates in the Chickamauga area numbered more than fifty thousand. All night on September 20th Wash Ives and twelve other men cooked two days' rations for the Fourth Regiment, numbering two hundred twenty–four men, and on Sunday morning loaded the food into wagons for transport to the men who had been fighting all day Saturday.

The journey was a nightmare. Cannon boomed on all sides, punctuated by the rattle of rifle fire. They received incorrect directions and went twenty–seven miles instead of seventeen to reach the battlefield. More than five hundred wounded Confederates passed them during the day, headed for the camp hospital. At another time they counted seventeen–hundred Yankee prisoners being sent to the rear. Dark had descended on the ghastly sight of bloated men and horses before they reached the battlefield hospital. Wash wrote later that he "saw a surgeon cut off a leg" and "twenty wounded from my regiment."

The bridge over the Tennessee River was so choked with dead horses it was 10 p.m. before the wagons were able to get across. They pushed on, threading their way among the dead, seeking their regiment, which by then was without food or water. At one point they recognized a Florida man from the First Regiment when one of the drivers took a light to look. Beside him lay a wounded Yank, an Irishman with his back broken, who begged them not to touch him.

The night was freezing cold and despite the man's pleas to be left alone they covered him and built a small fire. As they drove on they could hear him praying.

"Oh Holy Mother," he was saying, "take care of my saintly mother, take care of my saintly mother..."

They found their regiment as day was breaking on a cold and gray Monday morning. The men joked and poked fun at Wash. "Whar yuh been, Wash?" one bearded soldier asked. "Yuh cook them rations in Floridy and pull them wagons up here with gophers?"

"That's about it," Wash replied. "We knew you fellows weren't hungry. Figured you'd whipped the Yankees and took all their fine rations."

Fact was the men hadn't eaten for a day and a half and had been in battle without water for more than twelve hours. The only water they had came from a small stream where they had filled their canteens and the water Smelled from the dead flesh of men and horses lying farther upstream.

The Fourth Regiment's loss was about fifty men killed, wounded or taken prisoner. The entire Confederate loss was reckoned at twenty–five hundred killed, wounded and taken prisoner. The Union loss was estimated at three–thousand killed and wounded and fourteen–thousand were taken prisoner. Morale was high in the Fourth because among the pieces of artillery taken from the enemy was the Michigan battery that had played havoc with the unit at Murpheesborough.

October 1st rain and sleet fell on the troops for seven hours in trenches eight miles south of Chattanooga.

Within a week many of the men of the Fourth were down with various forms of lung and throat illnesses, among them Wash Ives.

James McCredie was somber when he spoke with David about Wash's illness. "I don't think he's going to get well this time. He's burnin' up with fever and choking to death. Someone should write his folks."

"Lt. Kilpatrick did," David said, "but who knows when they will get the letter."

That's when Ben Dart took over.

Ben, a free black man, had been hired by Captain McKay to do his cooking. After the captain left the regiment, Ben did some cooking for Wash Ives. Hearing of Wash's illness, he went to Wash's tent with a cup of hot green tea and forced it down his throat, which was swollen almost to the point of complete closure. He was at Wash's side daily, making up his pallet, dressing his blister, and feeding him pap made with flour, whiskey and sugar.

Wash never knew how Ben obtained the flour, whiskey and sugar. Usually doctors drew these supplies for the sick and then kept them for their own consumption. Usually arrowroot was used in making pap but this too was in the hands of the doctors.

The "fly blister" was a poultice of hot mustard that stretched from ear to ear and down onto Wash's chest. The army doctor had ordered that it be worn for six days to cure the swelling inside his throat. Wash wrote home about the pain of the "blister."

"My throat does not hurt me inwardly, but my blister is now pretty painful. Dr. Hearn's instructions were when he sent it to put it on for six days but we only left it on three. If it had been six I do not know what kind of a place it would have left. The black man Ben has been very attentive to me, dressing my blister regularly and attending to everything I desired, but he had nothing suitable to dress it with."

"First, he had no sweet oil so he used castor oil which cured it too rapidly and now he uses neatsfoot oil. He also used a salve made of suet and neatsfoot oil."

Wash continued in his letter to describe his "diptheritis." He wrote, "It is no light disease and painful enough nearly to make a man shed tears. It is a disease of the throat similar to 'Choking Quincy.' The first in arriving was a high fever, and a continual longing or inclination to be swallowing wind, and as I would compress my throat to swallow, I would experience about the same feeling as if I had swallowed a pin cushion and someone was trying to pull it back the wrong way foremost."

Wash described his sickness later by saying, "It would have taken just a little more exposure to put my weary bones beneath the cold sod of Tennessee."

"I'll tell you what," James told his brother, "that Wash Ives has a flare for the dramatic."

Occasionally, James and David were able to get together in the morning to exchange information contained in letters from Janet. One day early in

November they were sitting with other members of James' band group by their campfire when they spotted great "V's" of wild ducks headed south.

"What a sight," David said. "I wonder when they'll begin to gather on Tuscawilla Lake back home? Remember how many hunts we went on in November of 1860?"

"Yeah," James responded. "A couple of wild ducks roasted in these hickory coals would go a long way to make this war more bearable."

"They're flying too high to reach with a rifle even," David said.

"I suppose so," James said with a sigh.

The war at that moment seemed far away, although cannon could be heard on both sides, firing every few minutes. It had been that way for a month. The Confederates were on Lookout Mountain and the Union troops occupied both sides of the Tennessee, including Missionary Ridge below Chattanooga. From the camp of the Fourth Florida Regiment the Confederate troops could see the pickets of their enemy and watch the soldiers at morning drill.

Periodically, the pace of the firing would pick up and the cannon were so loud the ground around the Confederate camp trembled. "It's like a hundred hogs were dropped from on high," was the way Wash Ives described the pounding.

Before there could be any more discussion of duck hunting or furloughs home for Christmas, the band boys and David were ordered on picket duty to relieve some of their fellow soldiers in the regiment.

About the middle of the morning, Lt. Frank M. Mitchell of Company K showed up with a work detail to dig rifle pits for those on picket duty, since it had become standard procedure for the Union soldiers, also on picket duty, to shoot every now and then at any moving target on the Confederate side.

Lt. Mitchell sat on a log to supervise the work detail. "It's such a beautiful morning," David thought as he used a pick on the partially frozen ground. There had been rain during the night, now frozen on the limbs of the trees like millions of twinkling stars as the sun filtered through the thick forest.

Suddenly, a Yankee battery opened up on the Confederate work detail and a twelve–pound shot, called a "Lampost," struck the lieutenant just below his knee and came out halfway up his thigh joint.

The following morning before breakfast a number of his fellow officers and friends gathered around Mitchell to wish him well. He was in good spirits and asked one of the men, "Hey, Joe, did they leave enough stump on that side for me to ride a horse?"

Lt. Joe Williams told a lie. "Sure, Frank, you got enough left."

Frank laughed and said, "Oh well, I can still ride and get around then." By 7 a.m. he was dead.

The quartermaster was ordered to build a coffin so the body could be sent back to Florida.

Wash Ives reported to the band members later that "soldier–like, they built the coffin a little too small for him and had to crowd him in with his amputated leg." The body was buried near the camp, but it was assumed that Mitchell's brother would take the remains home later.

Lt. Mitchell had just returned from a furlough in Florida.

Life in Micanopy in 1864 differed little from the years prior to the Civil War. The town had no military importance, unless one counted David McCredie's shoe shop, the cotton gin, the cotton growing in the fields and the oranges on the trees in the fall, as important to the Southern cause, since David's shoes went to the army, the cotton after being ginned went through the blockade to England to provide funds for the Confederate government and the oranges were shipped in barrels north to soldiers in the field.

But all of those things happened prior to 1864. In 1864, the rails had been destroyed so the trains could not run north. The stage ran only occasionally and thus mail from their sons and husbands reached Micanopy ladies late, and sometimes never.

David drilled on Cholokka Boulevard with the local militia of old men and lads scarcely twelve years old. But the enemy never came, and it was just as well. The "locals" might have damaged one another more than the enemy, and besides, there was hardly any ammunition. Families that had powder and shot saved what they had for hunting in the hammocks for squirrel, turkey and deer to provide meat for their tables.

Janet, however, lived in a state of panic, despite the serenity of life in Micanopy.

She had horrible dreams in which she saw her sons dying on some faraway battlefield or she stood by while her youngest son, Thomas, now seventeen, was dragged off to war, or told her he was going to help his brothers.

Then in early June, when the oranges and grapefruit trees had shed their white veils of aromatic blossoms, when the cardinals were back building nests in a crabapple tree just outside her kitchen window, Janet received one confirmation of her fears.

A letter from James, dated May 25th, 1864, told her that David had been taken prisoner at the Battle of Atlanta on May 16th and was a prisoner of war in Illinois at Camp Alton.

David had brought the letter to her and handed it over without comment

Janet read a few words and then fled to her room to her favorite rocker where she rocked silently, fearing to read the rest of James' letter.

David followed her. "Read the letter through," he told his wife. "It's not that terrible. He is off the battlefield now."

"Those Yankee prison camps," Janet said fearfully, "are the Devil's own house. He'll die there. We won't be seeing our David again. I know it. I feel it in my bones."

David tried to soothe her. "Don't fret so lass," he said. "He'll be coming back. If you must borrow trouble, don't borrow that kind."

"What about William Coffee?" Janet asked. "That was Elsie Green's cousin. He was only seventeen when he was wounded, captured and thrown in prison with a broken thigh. They say his mother in Madison stands in the road day after day, looking and waiting for her youngest to return. Poor soul! She'll never see him again."

"He'll be out when the war ends," David said.

"War ends," Janet wailed. "This infernal war's never going to end."

The town's gossips fed her fears. There were tales of deserters who raped and murdered. Two such deserters were caught near Lake Tuscawilla south of town and hanged on the spot.

The deserter situation was real. It became so bad in Taylor and Lafayette Counties that a Major Bowden with three hundred cavalry and two–hundred and twenty–five infantrymen made a raid out that way in an attempt to rid the area of deserters. This was wild country, full of swampland and thick hammocks and thinly settled by a few cattlemen and hunters so that it was a natural area to hide deserters from Georgia, Alabama and Florida.

The tales about the major in the newspapers were enough to frighten the most courageous of the North Florida women. He was so determined to carry out his orders that he went through the deserter–infested Counties leaving everything in waste as he passed through, putting houses, furniture and crops to the torch.

Most frightening of all, however, was the fact he made prisoners of women and children who could not prove that their fathers or husbands were fighting in the Confederate service.

The women and children of the suspected deserters were sent to Tallahassee and kept under guard for months, and then released.

One day, Janet met her friend, Elsie Green, at the post office. She had just received a letter from Tom Andrews, a young man from Lafayette County who told a harrowing tale of Major Bowden's exploits as he dealt with deserters and innocent men he thought were deserters.

"Major Bowden and his command," he wrote, "reached my father's home on Cooke Hammock in Lafayette County in early spring of '63, the cavalry coming in first and the infantry following up that night or next day. As for myself, I was frightened out of my wits. I never had seen so many men and horses at one time in my life. I thought there must be ten–thousand of them; they were very orderly and did not molest a thing on our farm. My mother stopped three negro women from farm work to cook bread and potatoes and a great many other things the soldiers wanted cooked, and had nothing in which to cook them."

"My mother kept every oven pot, skillet and frying pan red hot until they left, which was about four or five days. My father, E. E. Andrews, had an old rock mill for grinding corn. It was run by hand–power and some of my father's negro men run it night and day, grinding meal, which my mother had cooked and served to the soldiers that would come to eat at our table. Many of them wanted to pay for their meals, but she would not take a cent from them."

"My father saw Major Bowden and had quite a talk with him. I think he was instrumental in saving the lives of several men and a lot of property that would have been destroyed was spared, but later on the deserters made short raids into Lafayette and Taylor Counties, burning some valuable properties belonging to Confederate soldiers and others that were loyal to the Confederate States. Some of the most important were the McQueens and Cottrells at Old Town on the Suwannee River. They all owned many slaves and had large plantations of hammock land, fine houses and stock which was all destroyed."

"While encamped on Cook's Hammock in Hankins settlement the cavalry made raids in different parts of Lafayette County, occasionally capturing a deserter and burning all vacant farm houses. I remember one morning seeing a squad of cavalry coming up with three or four men marching ahead of them. It did not take me long to find out that they were prisoners. Next morning, two of them were released and I suppose two of them were condemned to be shot."

"One of them was named Adams and the other said his name was Hill. It seems a lieutenant and ten men were ambushed and shot into at night. Several were wounded and one or two were killed. The Lieutenant was badly wounded. Adams was accused of knowing all about it. Major Bowden had strong circumstantial evidence connecting him with the shooting and he also had a bullet hole in his hat when he was captured, although he had a leave of absence from his company in Tennessee, but all the same he was condemned to be shot."

The story went on in this manner. It seemed that Adams knew Andrews and sent a man to get him but Andrews failed to get the message until the two condemned men were already being m arched into the hammock to be shot. When he did receive the message he put his horse into a full gallop and finally overtook the Major and the detail that had been ordered to carry out the death sentences.

Andrews asked to speak with Adams.

"All right, Andrews, but I never allow anyone to talk with the brutes when I'm going to have them shot in a few minutes."

"Before God," Adams told his friend Andrews, "I am innocent and can prove an alibi if I can be spared twenty–four hours. I was home with a sick wife and there were several women and a doctor there at my house that night. I didn't leave the house a minute for I thought my wife would die. For God's sake, beg for my life until tomorrow morning."

The poor man was on his knees, pleading with Mr. Andrews.

"I think my wife's father will be here with a sworn affidavit to that effect from five or six different people that was at my house that night."

Andrews went to Major Bowden to plead the case.

"You're a fool, Andrews," the major swore. "The brute is telling lies, nothing but lies. I'm gonna do my duty."

He started to walk off toward his squad with the rifles.

"Now, see here, Major," Andrews said firmly. "I've known Pat Adams for more'n ten years an' I've never known him to lie. He's tellin' the truth, all right. If you shoot him now, it'll be no more than murder."

The Major stopped, and then turned around, his face black with rage.

"He's got until morning, but I swear to you I'll have him shot at sunup if I don't git some evidence he's innocent. I know a dirty, thieving liar when I see one."

Andrews got on his horse and left at a trot. He told his wife later, "I guess I'm a coward. I didn't want to hear the shots I knew would mean the end of Adams and Hill."

Andrews' two sons, Tom and Dock, followed Bowden and his men into a dense hammock and saw the squad stop. Hiding behind a clump of trees they watched some of the men try to tie Hill to a small tree. He was a sallow–faced little man with hair as black as a moonless night but he fought like a mad man and in the struggle hit Bowden a blow in the face that brought a gush of blood from the Major's nose.

"Shoot the brute," the Major screamed. There was a rattle of musket fire and when the smoke cleared the little man lay dead on the damp ground

The two boys ran for home like a pair of frightened deer.

The Major, apparently satisfied for the time being, took Adams back to camp and placed him under guard.

Just before sunup the next day, Pat Adams' father–in–law arrived with papers that convinced Major Bowden of the younger man's innocence.

Bowden left the area with most of his troop the same day but left about one hundred men to continue searches for deserters. Two days later Tom Andrews wrote he saw Bowden returning with his men. Ahead of the troop was an old man, stumbling along as though each step would be his last.

"Ma," he called, "they're back an' there's an old man walkin' out front."

"Yes," she said. "I know that old man. He's old man Hickerson."

They asked for water for the men and horses, and while they were drinking Mrs. Andrews spoke to old man Hickerson. "You a prisoner?" she asked.

"Mrs. Andrews, I guess this is my last day on earth. They are going to shoot me."

"I hope not, Mr. Hickerson," she replied.

"Yes, he will, Mam," a nearby soldier said. "He'll be hung or shot inside of two hours."

The old man hung his head. "I can't help what my sons did, but if I am to die, I am not afraid. I am a good Baptist and I am fifty–seven years old and they can't cheat me out of much."

Even though the old man had been forced to walk ahead of the cavalry troop for twelve miles, they set off at a trot with Hickerson ahead and the horses on his heels as he ran for his life. Four miles into the woods they stopped and hung him from a pine tree and shot into his dying body.

Hickerson pleaded for his life, saying he was not responsible for the acts of his sons.

"Your sons are deserters and lead a gang of scoundrels that burn homes and steal stock. The beef is carried to Cedar Keys to feed more deserters who hide behind the protection of Federal guns," Major Bowden said angrily. "Their sin is your sin. Someone has to pay. String him up, boys."

The word was passed that the old man's bones hung for months before his sons got a chance to slip out and bury them. Tom Andrews wrote that he passed by the tree one day and it, too, had died.

There were rumors that a detachment of black troops was moving in great strength from the St. Johns River to Alachua County to take slaves, destroy crops and burn towns. In the dark of night, Janet, David and Thomas buried the family silver and other valuables in the floor of the henhouse. Janet was certain the enemy troops would strike at any moment

The war did come to Alachua County, first in a fifty–six–hour occupation of Gainesville in January of 1864 and then a full–fledged engagement in the same town in August.

Newspapers in 1864 often carried reports of the exploits of Captain J. J. Dickison and his men, a band of a few hundred cavalrymen who moved swiftly by night and harassed Federal troops, many times their number, all up and down the St. Johns River and westward toward Alachua County, if the occasion warranted such action.

Dickison was known as the "Grey Fox," and was not unlike Francis Marion, the "Swamp Fox," who performed with such valor during the Revolutionary War. They were alike in many respects. They were both daring, were always where they were not supposed to be, seemed to appear and disappear at will like ghosts in the night wind. They fought furiously and successfully against forces that greatly outnumbered them.

Dickison had been a plantation owner south of Micanopy on Orange Lake in Marion County before the war, but by 1864 the plantation, called "Sunnyside" had been ruined by neglect as Captain Dickison pursued his army life. Men like Dickison and William Owens, who owned another plantation, "Rutland," on Orange Lake were the landed gentry of the area and were highly regarded by the McCredie's and other Micanopy residents, especially the tradesmen who benefited from their patronage.

Dickison sacrificed more than his plantation to the war effort, however. The *Columbian* at Lake City reported the tragedy on August 10th:

"We have been politely furnished with the telegram, received at headquarters, announcing the highly gratifying intelligence of the repulse and shameful flight of a large force of enemy, near Pilatka, on the second instant, by Captain Dickison and his invincible band of heroes."

"Whenever Captain Dickison's name is mentioned, a thrill runs through every vein and gladdens every heart; and while we rejoice that the noble victor has added another wreath to his brow, we are called on to mourn with him at the heavy sacrifice it has cost him a beloved son, who fell, gallantly fighting his country's battles, and gave his life in her holy cause, and added another name to the long list of martyrs of liberty."

Captain Dickison had little time to mourn the loss of his son. On August 16th, a Federal force that included some four to five–thousand black troops, several artillery pieces and about four–hundred cavalrymen moved out of the Jacksonville and Green Cove Springs areas inland toward Lake City. These troops destroyed as they went, cutting telegraph wires and tearing up railroad tracks.

Late afternoon the Federal force arrived in the vicinity of Waldo and destroyed the Boulware and McRae plantations. Some of the Artillery units and all of the black infantrymen were left camped in the vicinity of the Boulware plantation and the cavalrymen raced on into the night toward Gainesville.

Just after sundown, a rider arrived at the Edward Lewis plantation, some twelve miles northeast of Gainesville, with news of the Federal approach and what had occurred at the other plantations.

Mrs. Lewis was alone. Her husband and eldest son were with the Dickison force. The news set the house into a frenzy. "Lordy, we's gwine be defiled an' kilt," cried a young serving girl.

"You jes shut yo mouth, girl," said Aunt Ginny, Mrs. Lewis' chef and cook and general overseer of the house servants. "Ain't no sojer goin' tech you."

Mrs. Lewis intervened at that point. "Callie you go get Uncle Rufe. Bring him here," she told the girl. Uncle Rufe had charge of the horses and mules, the wagons, buggies and blacksmith shop.

Uncle Rufe was instructed to bring four wagons, each pulled by four mules, and all the slaves he could round up.

The wagons were driven into the front yard and loaded with as much furniture, paintings and other household treasures as they would hold and then Uncle Rufe was instructed to hide them in a heavily–wooded area deep in one corner of the plantation.

The Federal cavalry arrived about midnight. Colonel Andrew T. Harris, commanding the Seventy–fifth Infantry of Ohio, ordered a detachment to search the house and when he discovered most of the valuables missing, began questioning the slaves. One young boy, Jenkins, who helped with the mules, was rolling his eyes and trembling all over when Colonel Harris approached.

"You, boy," he said. "What's been going on here?"

"Dey's back in dem woods," the frightened boy said, pointing to the southwest.

"What do you mean, boy? What's in the woods?" the Colonel demanded.

"The wagons, suh. The wagons."

"The wagons, you say? Whose wagons? What's in em?"

Jenkins knew he was in deep trouble. Mrs. Lewis' face was hard as Georgia marble. With his eyes on the floor and his chin on his chest, the boy mumbled, "Jes things."

"All right, men," the Colonel said to his detachment. "Take this boy and make him show you those wagons."

Later the Federals left the plantation with all of the wagons loaded with household goods, all the horses, mules and cows and one hundred twenty–five slaves.

Captain Dickison arrived at the plantation about daylight and when informed of the night visit there set out in pursuit. When he arrived in the Gainesville area he found the Federals had strong positions at the depot and all railroad crossings. Their one piece of artillery was positioned in front of the Beville Hotel.

What followed during that hot August day was Alachua County's great moment in Civil War history.

Janet McCredie said later she heard the pounding of the cannon all the way south in Micanopy, but that is doubtful.

The Federals found little resistance at Gainesville. The militia, numbering thirty to forty old men and boys and commanded by Judge Thomas F. King, had assembled to face the emergency but after one attack quickly realized they were greatly outnumbered and retreated to await reinforcements from Dickison.

Dickison, a master, military strategist, ordered two detachments, one on the left flank and one on the right flank, to surround the enemy so he could get the Federals in a crossfire. He opened up with his artillery pieces. The rifle fire from his left and right soon put the single Federal gun out of the battle. With his main force he charged into the center of the town and so furious was the fighting, the Federals believing he had arrived with at least fifteen hundred troops, retreated in two columns toward Newnansville.

One of the unusual features of this battle was the activity of the Gainesville wives and mothers. Even in the midst of heavy rifle fire, they went into the streets with water for the exhausted Confederate troops. They stood in their front yards screaming, "Charge, charge!" to encourage their men.

"Ladies, ladies," yelled Captain Dickison. "Go back into your homes. Please, get off the streets. You'll be killed."

He was everywhere on his horse, urging his men forward and entreating the women to leave the battlefield, but they remained until the last Yankee had disappeared from the town toward Newnansville.

Later the *Peninsula*, a Federal newspaper in Fernandina, reported that Dickison had attacked with a force of twelve to fifteen hundred and that, "Even the ladies of Gainesville fought like spirits from the land of fire and brimstone."

Fifty–two Federal troops died on the streets of Gainesville. The Confederate loss was three killed and five wounded. Two of the wounded later died. Prisoners captured, including some officers, numbered about three hundred and the Confederates also took two–hundred and sixty horses and a twelve–pound howitzer, along with the Lewis plantation wagons, still loaded with the family's belongings.

The day after the battle at Gainesville, David drove his horse and buggy there to deliver shoes that had been ordered by the Confederate Army. Janet went with him, more out of curiosity to see the hundred Yankee prisoners of war she had heard were being detained awaiting transfer to Andersonville Prison in Georgia, than by any desire to shop or visit friends. Shopping was a hopeless endeavor, anyhow, because Gainesville, like most other Southern towns, had little to offer the shoppers. Products that were available had to be sold at below market value to the Confederate Government for use by its Army, and this was a source of dissension and discussion by all who produced beef, cotton, hides and farm products for sale.

David complained about this Government Impressment Act as they drove around Payne's Prairie to Gainesville.

"We'll all be on the poor farm if this practice keeps up," he said. "I can't get enough for my shoes to more than pay for the hides."

"We've given the Cause our three sons. What more can the government ask?" Janet replied.

"All I ask is for those boys to come home," David said. "The rest we can endure, like all the other folks."

They viewed the prisoners, encamped near the depot and surrounded by guards. It was rumored that a detachment of Confederate soldiers would soon take them on a march to Georgia. The prisoners seemed re–axed and happy. They chatted with their guards and tried to make friends with the young ladies who strolled by occasionally to, "See the enemy."

Upon the departure of the prisoners Gainesville ceased to be an active participant in the war and by December it was evident to most people that the Southern pause was a lost venture and the war would soon grind to an end.

Christmas 1864 was a hard time for Janet. She had sent packages to David to the prisoner of war camp at Alton, Illinois, to James encamped in Tennessee and to John still in Fernandina, but she had not received any word from the boys for several months.

Then, in mid–January she received a letter from James from Camp Chase, Ohio. He was a prisoner of war, having been captured on December seventeenth near Nashville.

Janet prayed for the war to end quickly, fearing that if it dragged out her boys would die in prison. She had heard horrible tales of conditions in the Confederate Prisoner–of–War Camp at Andersonville in Georgia, and she believed the Yankee prisons could be no better.

The surrender of General Robert E. Lee on April 9th, 1865 brought other worries to Micanopy and its citizens.

At first, the surrender was greeted as a rumor and then by panic when the story was proved true. Alachua County had about thirty–eight hundred white and almost forty–five hundred black residents when the war ended and the rumors spread like whispers in the night that the blacks were arming to take over the town.

"Do something," Janet wailed at David. "Put bars on the windows like in Scotland, or else we'll all be murdered in our beds."

"Janet, you know that's nonsense," said David. "The colored people here are not criminals. We've known most of them for years. They're peaceful and family folks. But they will need help to get by this change in their lives."

Late April, John walked into the yard one day as Janet was hanging out clothes. This bearded, gaunt man with his uniform almost in threads, almost frightened her to death.

"Don't come near me," she told him. "My husband is here and he is always armed." This was not true. David was in town and he never carried a weapon of any kind, except a small knife.

"Mama," John said. "I'm John, your son. Don't you know me?"

She did recognize the voice and flew into his arms.

They just stood there holding one another, the big man and the frail woman, locked as if their blood would flow together and sustain each other.

Then, Janet backed off and looked carefully at her son whom she had not seen for nearly three years. "John," she said, "you're skin and bones. Come into the house. You need fattening up, starting now."

David arrived home in March and James came in May, and for days all they did was eat.

They said little about the war until one evening as they sat on the porch enjoying the last rays of the setting sun and the lightning like speed of the bullbats as they searched the skies for mosquitoes, James said something that placed a period at the end of all that had happened.

"We should all believe in miracles," he said. "When David and I were with the Florida Fourth Regiment in Georgia and Tennessee in 1862 we had nine–hundred and twenty–six men and forty–seven officers. When the surrender came on April 26th this year there were twenty–three left."

"It wasn't your time," Janet said simply.

5

Micanopy

1866

It was spring again, the orange and grapefruit trees were in full bloom and the warm evenings were so laden with the sweet breath of the groves all over Micanopy that it was almost impossible to sleep. On such nights, Janet McCredie would slip quietly from the warm spot in her bed alongside David and with her shawl wrapped tightly around her thin shoulders go out into the front yard and sit in the swing near the rose garden.

The mosquitoes of summer had not yet returned so she could enjoy the perfume of the night without being tormented out of her thoughts.

As she sat there, her thoughts were on the months that had passed since her boys had returned from the dreadful war. She never thought of it in any other terms, except "that dreadful war." She had just about resigned herself to the reality that she would never be a grandmother to children from her sons.

She sighed. "How could they remain unmarried in such a romantic place. The flowers in the garden, the perfume from the groves, the softness of the moon, the mystery of the shadows cast by the pine trees—it's like a poem," she thought. Even at sixty–six, the thoughts sent little ripples of ecstasy through her body. Then she noticed a red glow to the west, just above the trees.

"That's odd," she thought. "The moon is still up and the sun has been down too long to leave any sign of light."

Then, she heard the clanging of the first bell. Soon all the church bells were ringing in clarion tones, warning of something wrong. David, James, Thomas and young David came from the house. Seeing Janet in the swing, they ran to her. "Mama, what's wrong, what are you doing here?" James asked.

"Just enjoying a perfect night," she said, "but look there," and she pointed to the western sky.

"That's a fire," said her husband. "Looks like it could be the old Smith farm where that new family from South Carolina moved to last month. Let's go, boys."

John came out and they all went to the barn for their horses. As they passed by on their way to the lane, David shouted to his wife, "Janet, go inside. It's too cool out here. This dampness will make you sick."

"Fi on you, David McCredie," she said to herself. "Where's the romantic fire you had in the Scottish Highlands?" Her lips curled in a half smile as she thought how he never let night dampness curb his wooing of her on colder nights than this. "He never feared I would catch me death of cold then," she thought.

By the time the Micanopy menfolks arrived at the old Smith farm, they found the Domino family, the newcomers from South Carolina, in the yard, vainly trying to stop the fire in their barn. They had been awakened by a neighbor who had heard his dogs barking. The men formed a bucket line from the well but the fire was a roaring monster, eating the fat pine boards like some kind of red–eyed dragon. The buckets of water seemed only to annoy the beast.

Fortunately, the night wind was away from the farm house so there was no danger to their home, but the frantic scratching, neighing and bellowing of the animals inside the barn was more than the women folk could stand. One young girl sat on the ground her head in her hands, weeping as though she had lost everything she had.

Young David McCredie saw her and sat down beside her. "Don't cry, Miss Domino," he said. "Your house is safe and so's your family. You should be joyful."

The girl raised her head and looked at the ruggedly handsome man beside her. The moonlight softened his face and she sensed his strength and gentleness.

"Name's Susan," she said, "and who be you?"

"David McCredie."

That was how it began. David McCredie and Susan Domino, each twenty–seven years of age, eloped to Gainesville and were married in the Presbyterian parsonage one month after the fire.

Janet McCredie was elated. One of her dreams had come to pass. "Now," she told her husband, "it's time to take up the work of the cross. As Preacher Melton says, we've just been throwing pennies in its shadow."

David was visibly puzzled. "Speak up, Lass," he said. "You're talkin' in riddles."

"David drove his sheep to a good market," she said. "Now, we must see to it that the other boys do the Lord's bidding and marry quickly."

David threw up his hands. "Back to that again. Leave the boys be. If they want to marry, they'll marry and if they don't they won't."

Janet's lip formed a straight line. "The Lord needs some help in this," she told David, "and I intend to be his helper."

She had a plan. Another new family of South Carolina planters had bought a large farm south of Micanopy, and she heard they had at least three lovely daughters, all unmarried, and all of marriageable age.

On Friday in the early part of November she asked David, "When will we be grinding cane and making syrup?"

"There's frost due any time now," David replied. "Cane's already stripped and piled up. We'd better grind and start boiling soon, maybe a week from tomorrow."

"Tomorrow morning hitch up the buggy," Janet said. "We're going calling on the Winecoffs!"

"The Winecoffs!" David exclaimed. "We don't even know those people. I hear in town they think they're too good for folks like us."

"We're going to invite them to the cane grinding," Janet said. "They're just lonely folks in a strange place. Time somebody acted neighborly."

Cynthia Winecoff was a younger woman than Janet—maybe in the late fifties, Janet thought—with a cold face, black eyes and hair pulled straight back from her face and made into a knot at the back of her head.

She was dressed in fine black taffeta and Janet thought this odd of a Saturday since the other farm women in the Micanopy area usually dressed in gingham on Saturdays, even if they were going into town to help buy supplies.

Janet smiled. "We're the McCredies," she said. "This here's my husband, David. I'm Janet. We're going to be grinding cane and making syrup next Saturday. It sure would be nice if you folk would come over. Chance to meet some of your neighbors."

Cynthia turned to the door and called, "Jacob, some folks here."

Jacob Winecoff came onto the front porch. He appeared to be about David's age, with flowing white hair, piercing black eyes and a face that could have been chiseled from Georgia granite. "Looks as rugged as Abe Lincoln," David thought. He wore black pants and an alpaca vest with a heavy gold chain stretched across his trim waist.

The McCredies explained again about the cane grinding party.

"We're a big family," said Jacob. "Eight of us."

"That's fine, all the better," David said, wondering if he should step forward and try to shake this taciturn man's hand.

"We'll think on it," Jacob said tersely. "Come, now, Mother," he said, turning to his wife. "We must go into town."

He turned back toward the door, Cynthia following. At the door, he called back, "You folks come again."

On the way home, Janet exploded. "Well, I never," she said. "What strange people. They can just stay on their old farm and rot."

David laughed. "Don't be angry, Lass. Remember, you're throwing silver dollars at the cross now, instead of pennies."

The Winecoffs came to the cane grinding in a fine carriage, six on the two seats with their feet dangling just above the sandy road. There was Alice, nineteen: Mary Elizabeth seventeen: Kate, fifteen: Ella, twelve: Coleman, nine, and Jacob and Cynthia. The eighth person in the group turned out to be Nathan, the black house servant. He helped the ladies from the carriage and took the vehicle away to a shady spot under a large live oak tree.

David went to meet his guests, who were dressed more for church than a Saturday afternoon farmyard party. He called his boys. "John, James, Tom. You boys come an' introduce the ladies around."

The boys were fully aware of the Winecoff arrival. John had muttered under his breath to his brothers as the carriage approached, "Ma's playing Cupid again."

"Mmmm, I like that one on the front seat on the right side," said James. "She's sure beautiful."

By the time the boys reached the carriage the ladies had been handed down from the carriage by Nathan and were standing in a circle. James headed for the one he had described to his brothers.

At this time he was twenty–nine, full of self–confidence, the most serious of all the boys, brown–eyed, hair combed to his shoulders. He was muscular and trim from his daily work in the open. He was known for his politeness and some said he had a way with the ladies.

James approached the Winecoff young lady with confidence, sure of himself. Then something happened to him. He looked into her eyes, so soft and brown, like a doe deer's, and yet, full of laughter. He had his speech all ready but for the first time in his life the words wouldn't come. "I must be blushing," he thought. "I'm acting like an idiot."

The girl put him at ease in a moment. "I'm Mary Elizabeth," she said with a friendly smile. "I bet you are James McCredie. The girls all talk about you."

James found his tongue. "Talk about me! What do they say?"

"Oh, I bet you'd like to know," she teased. Then she took him by the arm. "Let's find some cool cane juice. I'm so thirsty I could drink pond water."

James laughed. "They drink pond water in South Carolina?" he wanted to know.

"You'd be surprised what they drink in South Carolina," Mary Elizabeth said, while her eyes made him feel like a young man of twenty.

They went to the well where several gallon jugs of cane juice were cooling deep in the dark water. James pulled up one and they drank the cool, sweet juice in gourd dippers.

"Come on, I'll show you around," James said.

They went to where Old Blackie, the mule was walking in a circle around the cane mill. He was tied to a long pine pole that was attached to the grinder. As he walked in his circle, in tracks already worn deep in the clay and sand, the mill turned. Stalks of red sugar cane were fed between the rollers and the muddy–looking cane juice dripped into a bucket.

"We came here too late to plant cane this year," said Mary Elizabeth.

"I'm glad you invited us over. I've been to a cane grinding every year of my life, I do believe. I'm glad you have them in Florida."

It was James' turn to tease. "What'd you expect to find in Florida, jes snakes an' alligators and savages," he said.

"Something like that," she admitted, coming close and looking him straight in the eyes. Then she laughed. "I do believe you're blushing again."

"We'd better continue our tour," James said briskly. He saw his mother watching them and took Mary Elizabeth over to her.

"This is Mary Elizabeth Winecoff," James told his mother. "Isn't she the most beautiful girl you ever saw?"

Now Mary Elizabeth was blushing. "Nice to meet you, ma'm. My sisters and brother call me 'Betty.' As for this James of yours, I'm not sure what I'll let him call me. He's right forward for an old man."

"Old man!" James shouted. But, she was dancing off toward a table where cookies and syrup candy were piled on plates, along with the cakes and pies and citrus fruit, tree–ripened from their own trees. James ran after her. "I'll teach you about old men," he called to her.

They spent the day and on into the night laughing and talking as the cane juice boiled in huge kettles, getting thicker and turning the color of dark honey. But before it all ended James had agreed to take her home from church the next day.

John had been attracted to Alice, the Winecoff's elder daughter. He later told James he learned that Mary Elizabeth was seventeen. "You're sort of robbing the cradle, ain'tcha boy," he said.

"She's really a lot more mature than that Alice, and a lot more fun," James replied. "She makes me feel young."

John scratched his head. "Well, I have to admit I'm not much taken with Alice. She is kind of dull."

A couple of weeks later, there was a box supper at the Presbyterian Church on a Friday night. James took the family's best buggy and drove to Micanopy with the intention of buying Betty's boxed "meal for two." She had asked him about his favorite foods, so he looked forward to a pleasant evening. The suppers were held to raise money for the church but the boxes normally sold for twenty–five cents. James had a dollar with him in case the bidding went to an unprecedented fifty cents.

At the supper James never let Betty out of his sight. He marveled at her grace as she moved along the tables, arranging place settings and decorations She had marked her box with a red rose and when it came up for a bid he quickly called out, "Twenty–five cents." There was a moment of silence and then a male voice from the back of the room said, "I raise that, Fifty cents."

James bid sixty cents and then turned to see Sam Watson grinning at him The Watsons were newcomers from Georgia, and apparently were "well fixed," as they said in Micanopy circles. Sam drove a fine, new buggy, pulled by a couple of the finest dapple grays in the area.

Watson went to seventy–five cents, James to one dollar and Watson called out, "One dollar and a quarter." It was all over. Sam claimed the box and his companion for the meal. James was somewhat consoled by the fact that Betty looked disappointed at the outcome. The one thing that hurt the most was that the buyer of the box supper had the right to escort the young lady home from the supper. That ruined his evening. He had supper with an old–maid school teacher, and went home, in a sour mood.

On Sunday at church there was Sam Watson on hand to sit with Betty. He had been invited by Jacob Winecoff.

Jacob Winecoff was a shrewd man. Although his wife shrugged off the idea as nothing to worry about, he had closely observed his daughter and this shoemaker's son as they looked at one another and concluded they were getting too serious.

"This James is too old for her," he told his wife. "He's only a poor carpenter, and judging by what he has achieved thus far in life, he'll never amount to anything."

On Monday just as the sawmill whistle announced the noon hour, James McCredie looked up from the piece of lumber he was sawing to see ahorse and buggy coming up the lane toward the unfinished house he and John were building on Lake Tuscawilla.

Actually he never even saw the horse and buggy. It was the radiant girl driving, her long brown hair tucked under her straw hat, her yellow cotton dress glowing in the noontime sun and her smile that left his legs weak and trembling. It was Betty Winecoff, the last person he expected to see after the incident at the Presbyterian Church the day before.

Without waiting for James to come to her, she scrambled from the buggy, tied the horse to a tree and ran to him with a picnic basket in one hand. "Time for dinner," she said. "Didn't you hear the whistle?"

James couldn't speak. He was almost shocked out of his mind.

"Well, say something, James McCredie," she said. "Cat got your tongue?"

"I can't believe you're here," he stammered. "Why did you come?"

"Oh, just because I was hungry," she teased. "I really didn't come to see you. I was just hungry for a picnic dinner beside a lake and this seemed a likely spot."

"Oh you, you kitten," James said. "Come on."

He took her arm and steered her to a grassy knoll under a tall pine beside the lake shore. He waved at John who had been observing the scene with amusement.

Betty unpacked the basket to reveal food he had not seen in many years. There was a tin of Scottish shortbread, imported from Edinborough, a little wooden box of smoked herring, also from Scotland, a bottle of French wine, some fried chicken and biscuits, filled with homemade butter.

"This chicken and biscuits are still warm," James exclaimed. "How did you work that magic?"

"They were still in the oven, silly, not more than fifteen minutes ago," Betty said lightly.

"You couldn't get here that fast unless you came riding on a big bird," James said.

"Well, maybe I did fly over," was her reply.

James became more serious. "I can see your horse has been running. You could overheat him—and you could get hurt, driving too fast. I would be really upset about that."

"Why James McCredie," she retorted. "You, upset, about a little old horse getting too hot?"

"Not the horse," he said. "You know what I mean."

"What do you mean. You have to say it."

"It's you," he blurted out, like some school boy. He felt kind of foolish and knew he was blushing all the way down his neck. "I couldn't stand it if you got hurt."

Betty leaned closer to him, with her shoulder touching his. "I know," she whispered. "I feel the same way, and I hate that stupid Sam Watson!"

James whispered back. "Then why did you invite him to sit with you at church yesterday?"

"I didn't invite him," she explained "It was Papa. He wants to keep you from seeing me so much. He told Sam about the rosebud on my box at the church supper so he could outbid you. He suspected you might not have a lot of money with you."

"What are we going to do, then?" James asked. "I don't want your Ma and Pa against me."

"Papa's not a bad man," she said. "He doesn't lock me in. I'm not like a pet dog to be tied to a tree and admired. I'll find a way of seeing you." She paused. "I want you to come to the house to see me just like there was nothing going on."

"Suppose your Pa sends me away. What about that?" James wanted to know.

"He won't do that He'll just be cold and unfriendly and hope you'll give up," Betty said.

That's the way the courting went for many months. They had picnic dinners together until the Lake Tuscawilla house was finished.

David said to Janet one night at supper, "I wonder what's the matter with James. We never see him any more and when we do he seems in another world."

Janet laughed. "Of all people, David, you should know the symptoms, as romantic as you have been all your life. Don't you know? He's in love."

John overheard the remark. "That's right, Papa. He's so in love I've been afraid he will cut off a finger or a hand with his saw one of these days. Sometimes he just goes through the motions of working."

"The Winecoff girl?" David asked.

"Who else?" John answered.

One day after work on the Micanopy house, James stopped in town to get some tobacco and didn't start home until after dark. He was brought to a sudden halt by two men who stepped out of the shadows and grasped the reins of the horse. "You be James McCredie?" one of them asked.

"Yes, I am," James said, "and what is your business with me?"

About that time James felt cold steel against his throat and then the unseen ruffian whispered in a gruff voice. "This be a warning. Stop seeing Betty Winecoff, or the next time we meet you'll get hurt, hurt real bad, mister."

While the man was talking, James had slipped his heavily–booted foot from the stirrup and suddenly jerked his head away from the knife and lashed out with his foot with all his strength and caught the man in the middle of his stomach. At the same time he touched his horse lightly with the other foot and yelled, "Go, Blackie." The horse leaped forward, jerking the reins from the hands of the other man.

He had felt the man with the knife double up and heard his gasp of pain and surprise. As he rode away he heard both men cursing and screaming that he would pay for his attack.

At a full gallop he continued on into the night, trusting his horse's sure–footedness and his instinctive feeling for the way home to avoid catastrophe.

Even though he had broken free from the ruffians, he was disturbed by the incident, fearing that Betty's father had hired the men to waylay him and warn him to keep away from his daughter. "Whew, what a bad relationship to have with a future father–in–law," he thought.

On arriving home he discussed the incident with his father and brothers. John was of the opinion that Jacob Winecoff was innocent of the affair.

James' father agreed. "He's a proud man, cold and Unfriendly, but I'm sure he wouldn't do a thing like that. That could cost him his daughter's love," David said.

"Well, who then?" James asked.

The brothers looked at one another and almost in unison said, "Sam Watson."

"I'll tell you what," John said, "we can find out without saying anything to Betty or any member of her family about tonight." He lowered his voice. "Here's what we'll do."

It was generally known among the young men of Micanopy that Sam Watson was a heavy drinker and that he visited the girls at Sadie Green's place a few miles south of Micanopy on the Ocala road every Friday night.

John owned a horse pistol that he had saved from the Indian campaign. He wasn't sure that it would even fire, but he knew that if it did it would sound like a cannon.

With James and Thomas he hid along the Ocala road the next Friday night and waited for Sam to start home. About midnight he came from the house, staggered to his horse and laboriously climbed into the saddle. He let the reins loose and the horse slowly started toward Micanopy. Apparently, the horse had been well trained to take his master home.

As the horse passed, the McCredie boys stepped into the road and grabbed the reins. "Don't go for your gun, Sam," James said. "If you do it will be your last move."

Sam sat up abruptly in the saddle. "What's the meaning of this. You can't do this. Who are you?" Then, he thought he was going to be robbed. "Don't hurt me," he pleaded. "I'll give you my money."

"I'm John McCredie and these are my brothers. We want to know why you hired two men to stop James and threaten to harm him if he continued to see Betty Winecoff," John said.

"I wouldn't do that," Sam blustered "It was not like that at all."

The road was wide and in the clear starry night the white sand and clay reflected enough light for Sam to see the long barrel of John's big pistol, a few inches from his head. "What you gonna do with that? I'll have my daddy report you to the town marshal," he said.

"You might not live long enough for that, if you don't tell the truth," John said in a cold, almost chilling tone. "Now why did you hire those men?"

"It was all just a joke," Sam said. "Can't you take a joke?" he pleaded.

"Joke or no joke," John threatened, "if anything like that happens again, we'll know where to come. Now I'm going to see how fast you can get away from here. I'm going to count to ten and then fire. You'd better be out of range."

Sam wasted no time. He started off at a full gallop before John could begin his count. Without even counting, John pointed his pistol in the air and fired. The sound was like a dynamite blast. After that, all they heard was hooves pounding the road into Micanopy.

It was not until Betty Winecoff and James McCredie were married that he learned she knew all about the Sam Watson affair.

One night in bed she said to James, "I'm glad you didn't shoot the little coward."

James was startled. "Shoot who?" he asked. "What are you talking about?" He thought maybe she had been dreaming.

"That Sam Watson," she said. "I know all about that night on the road to Ocala, out there near that dreadful woman's whore house."

James didn't know she knew such words. "How did you hear about that?" he wanted to know.

"I know a thing or two," she said, and that was all he could get out of her.

The marriage of James McCredie and Betty Winecoff had been a quiet affair on March 22nd, 1871, at the First Presbyterian Parsonage in Ocala, attended by a few friends. James was thirty–two and his bride just turned twenty. After the elopement and the marriage ceremony the couple returned by train to Micanopy and then left in the McCredie's only buggy for Gainesville where they registered at the Beville House.

The journey to Gainesville had been a tempestuous affair with friends at a gallop up and down the line of travel, occasionally shooting into the air with their pistols. Fortunately, the McCredie horse was old and not inclined to be disturbed by the commotion.

At the Beville House, the wedding party grew larger as it was joined by acquaintances from Gainesville. They created such a fuss with their fiddles and singing and shouting for the bride and groom to appear that James and Betty finally did come out on the porch to keep the hotel owner from calling the town marshal. Other guests in the Beville House were amused at first, some joining in the fun, but as the hour grew late they returned to their rooms, grumbling about the lack of respect that the younger generation had for its elders.

The newlyweds moved in with the McCredies, moving into a room formerly occupied by James and John. John had moved in with Thomas. As the weeks passed, Janet learned that her new daughter–in–law knew almost nothing about homemaking. As the daughter of a wealthy man, she never turned her hand at anything.

"I declare," Janet told her husband, "I wonder what that child has been doing all her life. You suppose she knows what to do in bed?"

David laughed. "If she don't," he said, "James'll be teachin' her a few tricks."

"James?" Janet exploded. "What's he know about handling a woman. He' s hardly touched one since he came back from the war."

"Well," David said. "Sam Watson is not the only man in Micanopy who goes to Sadie Green's place. James is not as innocent as you think."

Janet looked at him sharply. "David McCredie, what do you know about that whore's place? Should have been burned down long ago."

"Not a thing, my love." David laughed. "I do have eyes and ears, you know."

"Just keep it that way," Janet said, as she left the room to prepare breakfast.

Janet decided that her daughter–in–law must have learned something because Betty told her in mid–afternoon that she was pregnant. She searched the girl's body up and down and saw no signs of a pregnancy, but she knew it was probably too early to tell. "Have you seen Dr. Montgomery?" she asked Betty.

"He's coming to examine me tomorrow," Betty replied.

Dr. Lucius Montgomery, Micanopy's twenty–seven–year–old Missouri–born doctor, took Betty into her bedroom and made his examination. The pregnancy was confirmed.

One of the big events of the year for members of the Micanopy First Presbyterian Church was the outing at Orange Lake. The date for this picnic and excursion on the lake was set for Friday, June 16th, 1871. Despite her "condition," Betty begged James to let her go to the picnic. "All my brothers and sisters will be there," she said. James agreed but insisted on taking the day off and accompanying his wife.

The party of forty men, women and children of the church arrived at the lake just before noon and spread their food on rough tables that had been built for such functions by the men of several churches in the area. Judge George W. Means had sent his thirty–foot sailboat, the *Flying Cloud*, to the picnic area for the use of the Presbyterians. In command was John Worthington, a black man who was the boat's caretaker. Worthington had also towed to the landing several small, wooden row–boats for the use of those who wanted to fish for trout during the afternoon.

When the ladies had the tables loaded with fried chicken, potato salad, a dozen or more kinds of vegetables, pies and cakes and coffee, the Rev. Jack Melton thanked the Lord for such a fine day for their outing and they began eating.

The children were almost too excited to eat. They kept wandering from the tables to the large sailboat and would have climbed all over it if Worthington hadn't been standing at the bow, stern–faced and with folded arms that seemed to say, "You chilluns go eat yo dinner and stay way frum my boat til I say you kin gitin."

About 2 o'clock, Dorah Montgomery, announced it was time for a sail on the lake. She and Dr. Lucius Montgomery headed the committee that was in charge of the outing, and were overseeing the picnic.

Some of the men began to prepare for their fishing trips but thirty–six of the party began to go aboard the boat. Dr. Montgomery saw Betty McCredie among those boarding. "Not you, young lady," he said. "I don't think it would be wise for you to go sailing just now."

"But, Dr. Montgomery," Betty protested. "I feel fine."

He smiled and shook his head. "You stay on shore and take care of that baby," he advised. Dorah had heard the conversation. She smiled at Betty. "He won't change his mind, Betty. You might just as well give up."

John Worthington fretted about the number of people on his boat. "We's got too many folks on this boat," he muttered half to himself. "What's that you say?" Dr. Montgomery asked.

"I say dis boat too loaded," Worthington told the doctor.

Dr. Montgomery looked at the sun filled lake, the gentle waters and felt the light breeze that caused the sails to flap slightly.

"With no more wind than this, your boat will move slowly, and we won't be out long," he said.

Betty and James watched the over–loaded boat move slowly out into the lake. Children were screaming and the mothers could be heard ordering them to take a seat and stay there. James went to his buggy to get his pipe and tobacco and noticed the dark cloud that had suddenly begun to steal in from the west. At the same time he heard a rising rustling in the live oaks overhead.

He called to Betty. "Rain coming. We'd better make a shelter."

She joined him at the buggy and they were ready to get under the vehicle if the rains came. In five minutes the sky overhead was black and swollen, split periodically by lightning and the wind had the trees in a frenzy. James worried about the horses, all tied in a bunch under a large live oak tree about a hundred yards from the picnic area.

And then he looked on the lake for the Flying Cloud just in time to see it topple over. John Worthington had felt the freshening wind at his back and had begun to turn the boat around to bring his passengers back to shore when the squall struck him amidship and sent the boat over on its side. The time was 4 o'clock.

The men on shore were in turmoil. Some had wives and children aboard the sailboat. "Gawd Almighty," one shouted. "They'll all drown."

Despite the rain and wind they ran to the rowboats, including James, and started paddling into the lake. Betty was crying. "Ella's out there," she called. "She can't swim." Ella Winecoff was her youngest sister. Her other two sisters, Alice and Kate, were also on the boat.

Dr. Montgomery saw the boat going over and grabbed for his young wife but he was too late. She went over the side, struck by a boom of the mainmast, and was pinned to the bottom of the lake.

The storm passed as quickly as it had struck the excursionists, but the hours following the capsizing of the boat were like a horrible nightmare. The small boats moved back and forth bringing in those able to keep afloat and those who were able to cling to the overturned boat.

Before nightfall seven bodies had been recovered, including Dorah Montgomery, Ella Winecoff, Adda Shufford, Maggie Simonton, Florence McIlvaine, James A. Simonton's youngest son, Johnnie, and Isaac Bowen, a Negro who drove a load of young people to the picnic for the Powell family.

James and John worked by lamplight all night, building coffins. Betty had gone to her old home to be with her parents in their time of grief. As he worked shaping the wood, James thought of how joyful the day had begun and how quickly the joy had turned to tragedy and sorrow. It had been like that every day during the war.

The Orange Lake tragedy hung like an evil shadow over Micanopy all during 1871. One reason for this was that Janet McCredie would not let it go away. She told anyone who would listen about her "Omen."

Indeed, she had had an omen about a tragedy on the water since the day her sons had sailed across the Atlantic Ocean in 1854. "The dream has been coming to me for years," she said. "I kept seeing a boat going down in a storm. I knew something like this would happen."

"But seventeen years!" her friend Lucy Morrow, told her. "That's a long time for an omen to be around without coming to pass."

Finally, her daughter–in–law couldn't listen to any more omen talk. "Mama McCredie," she pleaded, "please don't say anything more about what happened at Orange Lake. My sister is gone now and I wish to remember her as she was and not what happened." She smiled, "Let's talk about my 'Manger' baby."

Betty always called her unborn child her "Manger" baby because she was certain it would be born on Christmas Eve.

Then, John Stewart McCredie gave the McCredies something else to talk about.

One day he had to go to Leesburg to get orange boxes and wrappers for the packing and shipping of the crop they expected from their groves in a few weeks. He came home in such a jovial mood, Janet asked, "John McCredie, have you been drinking?"

"Not the kind of drinking you are talkin' about," John said, his eyes sparkling with a kind of light she had never seen before.

"You're up to something, John McCredie," Janet said. "I can see it in your eyes. I want to know this minute what you've been doing."

"Nothing, really," John said, "but I am getting married in November."

"Married!" Janet exclaimed. Then she was all over the house, rounding up the family to share the news. They gathered in the kitchen where supper was being prepared.

"John's got some news," she said. "He's out of his mind, forty–one years old and talking about getting married!"

"You joking, John?" James asked.

"Course not," John said. "A man can get married anytime he wants to. Who said forty–one is too old?"

"Your mama just did," James said.

Janet broke in. "Course he's too old. Can't have any children. I want a houseful of grandchildren before I go to my reward."

"You'll get em Mama," John said, "Julia is just turned twenty an' she kin give you lots of grand babies."

"Lord in Heaven," Janet cried. "He's marrying a child. Bringing another child into this house for us to raise. You hear that David?"

"I hear it," David said "Sounds fine to me. I'll get the jug."

He went to a cupboard and returned with a gallon jug of Scotch whiskey. The men all took a deep swig from the jug. Janet wouldn't be quiet. "John, you're twenty–one years older than that child," she complained. "Old enough to be her father!"

"Mama McCredie," Betty asked, "did you take on this way when you heard James was marrying me. He's fourteen years older than me, you know."

"That's different," Janet replied. Then, she probably realized how inconsistent she was and turned to John and asked about his bride–to–be.

"Her name is Julia Virginia Hay of Leesburg," John told his family. "She was born in Tallahassee and now lives in Leesburg, where her father is in the citrus business. She's another Ellen Johnson, Mama, full of sunshine and laughter, but with long dark hair." Then John laughed, "You'll like her. She's like you. She runs things."

"Nobody pays any attention to me," Janet replied. "How can I run things?"

"You have your way, Mama," John said. "You have your way."

All the McCredies went to Leesburg on the early train on November 16th for the wedding. Betty and Julia liked one another from the moment they met. "Why, you're as young as me!" exclaimed Julia.

"What did you expect, an old woman with wooden teeth?" Betty laughed, pretending to be an old lady hobbling with a cane.

"We'll liven the place up, when I get there," Julia said. "Those McCredies won't know what happened."

After the wedding ceremony, John and Julia left Leesburg for Ocala to spend the night and then went on to Silver Springs for an overnight trip to Pilatka on the *Marion*, a seventy–eight–foot packet that was known for its fine food and cabin accommodations, especially for honeymooning couples. John had convinced Julia that he would like to retrace his journey, made in 1854, on the St. Johns and Ocklawaha rivers, when he and James had first arrived in the area. Julia said it would be fun and she wanted to know all about his trip from Scotland.

As they boarded the boat on November 17th, they were greeted by Henry A. Gray, the captain of the *Marion* and part owner of the vessel along with the firm of E.W. Agnew & Company of Ocala.

Captain Gray had owned and commanded the first steamboat on the Ocklawaha and had the reputation of being one of the most experienced steamship men in Florida. He showed Julia and John to their cabin and told them to feel free to inspect his boat. "It's the best of the river boats," he said, as he left them.

Julia bounced up and down on the narrow bed. "Its nice and soft," was her assessment, "but not wide enough for two people."

"It's wide enough." John said. "I'm going to hold you so tight there'll be lots of room." He took her in his arms and kissed her. Julia struggled free. "You can't do that now." she said.

"And who's goin' to stop me?" John asked.

"Captain's orders. He commanded us to inspect his boat." She took him by the ear and began leading him toward the door.

"So, this slip of a woman is going to lead me around by the ear the rest of my life, is she?" John thought to himself, "and I'm going to love it." He wondered if it went deeper than that. She was another Janet and as sure as the sun came up every morning, Janet set the pace of his life when he was at home.

They toured the *Marion* and marveled at the luxury of the dining lounge, and the spotless condition of the galley where their meals were prepared. The stern wheel that pushed the boat along was housed in a compartment with doors that automatically opened from the force of the turning wheel as the boat moved forward.

Power was provided by a steam engine that fed on fat pine wood that caused clouds of soot–blackened smoke to flow from the smokestack near the forward part of the boat.

"I've seen pictures in *Harper's Weekly* of steamers like this," Julia said, "but the paddle wheels were not shut up inside the boat like this one. Why is that?" she asked her husband.

"River's too narrow and crooked for side wheels," John explained. "And the rear wheel has to be protected from overhanging trees."

They spent most of the day sitting on the upper deck enjoying the seventy–degree temperature and blue skies of this perfect November day. John pointed out where the current was deepest, where treacherous logs lay hidden just under the surface, where alligators lay along the bank, almost invisible to untrained eyes, where the beautiful ospreys nested, and they watched great blue herons playing tag with the boat. At Orange Springs they tied up for a couple of hours while more pine wood was loaded aboard for the remainder of the trip to Pilatka.

Along with other passengers, Julia and John went ashore to stretch their legs and enjoy the singing of the black men who were loading the wood. Julia was skipping around and clapping her hands to the rhythm of the songs. An older couple from Ocala was enchanted by her youthful–ness and obvious enjoyment of life, and the woman said to John, "Your daughter is such a sweet child. It's a joy to watch her."

"She's my wife," John said bruskly and turned away to join Julia, who had overheard the remark and was trying to hold her laughter.

"Papa," she asked sweetly, "will you buy me a peppermint stick when we get to Pilatka?"

"I'll take a strap to your backsides," he replied. "That old woman is a busybody."

"Better get used to that, honey," Julia said seriously. "I'll always look like your daughter, but not in our bedroom," she added, cutting her brown eyes at him in a way that made his heart quicken.

John didn't know why he had been angered at the remark of his fellow passenger. He had known from the day Janet had called his bride–to–be a child that this kind of thing would happen, but it was none of their business. Most men of his time married younger women, but maybe not twenty–one years younger.

That night as they again sat on the upper deck of the *Marion*, where the view was best, bathed by a full moon and lulled by the flickering of the pine torches on the river, Julia whispered to John, as she held his hand, "It's like something in a poem or a beautiful dream. I've never seen anything so beautiful."

"I'll tell you what," John whispered back, "it's better than the nights James and I spent on this river in that pole barge with no sounds except the gruntin' of the slaves and the moaning of that fellow who had the snake bite. I like it this way much better." He squeezed her hand.

When they returned to Micanopy after the honeymoon, Thomas had moved in with a friend so the newly weds could have his room. It had been agreed that the time had come when some more houses had to be built for the growing family. James and Betty already had plans to buy fifty–one acres southwest of town from the Simontons, but they decided to wait until the baby arrived. John was looking at land northeast of Micanopy toward Paynes Prairie for his farm.

"I don't want to live in town," he told his father and mother.

By this time Micanopy had begun to look like a town in the middle of a huge orange grove. More than a hundred acres of trees were in and around the town and groves spread outside of town all the way beyond Orange Lake, around Lake Tuscawilla and north to Paynes Prairie.

Margaret McCredie had married George Shufford in 1866 and they already had a large grove. Her young brother, Thomas, had the citrus fever, and all James did was talk and dream about the acres of oranges and grapefruit he was going to plant.

The McCredies had discussed many times with their neighbors the economics of citrus culture. This was James' favorite topic. "You can put a hundred trees to the acre," he explained. "Each tree will produce about twenty–five hundred oranges, and in the Montgomery grove they've got some trees that will produce from five to eight–thousand oranges in a five–month growing season, from October to May. Can you believe how much money even ten acres of orange trees will produce after the trees are bearing well?"

"I can tell you," John said. "It's simple arithmetic, fifty–thousand dollars."

"That's right," James said. "The market now is two cents for each orange. One hundred acres will produce two and a half million oranges, and at two cents each, that's fifty–thousand dollars."

"I'll tell you something else," James said. "Even if the price fell to one cent an orange and you only had ten acres you could make fifteen–thousand dollars, and do all the work yourself, so most of it would be net profit."

Betty danced around the room. "When do we start planting more trees?" she asked. "With fifteen–thousand dollars a year I could get some new dresses and we could buy a new buggy and..."

James interrupted. "It will come," he said. "Believe me it will come. The price of oranges has been steadily rising since the war, even while the production has doubled in this area. The market is increasing and the Florida oranges from this area are so much better than those shipped from overseas, we can't lose."

James was right. All the northern newspapers were full of accounts about Florida's "lake region," meaning the Orange Lake area and an area in eastern, Alachua County that included Gainesville, Waldo, Hawthorne, Fairbanks, Micanopy, Saludia, Melrose, Banana, Gruelle, and Lochloosa. This area was described as being far enough in land to be "free of the malarian fogs of the large rivers and prairies."

The Orange Lake area was singled out for special attention.

One writer said:

"But what today makes this region more interesting than any or all things else is the great extent of wild orange groves. The largest in Florida, and probably in the world, are found growing here, generally upon points or headlands out into the lake."

"There are here about seven hundred acres of land covered with orange trees; many of these acres have several thousand trees growing upon each acre, the trees standing so thick that their tops form a perfect canopy overhead through which the sun's rays cannot penetrate."

"Within the past few years nearly all of these orange grove lands have been purchased by men who arranged to convert them into sweet orange groves."

Micanopians laughed at some of these stories. David told John, "That fellow who saw all them wild orange trees must have got hold of some of your whiskey. Lord Almighty, imagine thousands of orange trees on each acre, so tall they shut out the sun." He put his newspaper down and walked outdoors, shaking his head.

There were wild orange trees, lots of them in the Orange Lake area, but nothing like the newspaper reported.

On December 5th, about three o'clock in the morning, all the McCredies were in their orange grove, keeping the fires going against the likelihood of a severe freeze. They had been there all night, including Betty, who was already nearing her ninth month.

Suddenly, she supped to the ground, clutching her swollen abdomen and gasping with pain.

She called out to James and all the folks came running, "Get Doctor Montgomery," she said. "It's time."

James saddled a horse and headed into town only to learn that Doctor Montgomery was in his grove on Orange Lake, fighting the cold. By the time he and the doctor had reached the McCredie home, James learned he was a father. Mary Ella McCredie had arrived, three weeks early.

Betty had planned to go home to her mother to have the baby on Christmas Eve since she firmly believed she would have the baby that night, but it was not to be. Possibly the work in the cold orange grove had brought on labor, although Doctor Montgomery had said he didn't believe so. Anyhow, Betty smiled at her husband and said she had her Christmas present early.

"Mine, too," James said. He kissed her and went back to the orange grove to spread the news that he had a beautiful, dark–eyed daughter. "She looks just like her mother," he told them.

Christmas Day, John and Julia told everyone that she was pregnant and they could expect another grandchild in the house. That called for another round of Janet's powerful eggnog. "Somebody better get to building another house real soon," Janet said, eyeing her second daughter–in–law.

"Already under way," John told his mother. "I signed papers on the land yesterday. We'll be in our new farm house before my son arrives."

"What do you mean, son?" Julia wanted to know. "Suppose I want a girl–child?"

"I know it's going to be a boy," John said simply, "but if it's a girl I'll be just as happy."

As it turned out, neither one got his wish. A baby boy was stillborn on August 10th. Julia had gone home to Leesburg to be with her mother for the birth. The sad news came through a passenger on the train who had been asked to deliver the message to Janet McCredie. A.H. Mathers, Micanopy mayor and postmaster, had been at Micanopy Junction when the train arrived and agreed to deliver the message himself.

"I'm sorry to bring such tidings, Miz McCredie," Mayor Mathers said, "but the fact is the poor lad hung himself on his cord comin' into this world. Nuthin' a doctor can do about that."

That afternoon James rode out to John's farm on the edge of the prairie to be with his brother. The large, comfortable clapboard house stood in a live oak grove on the edge of the prairie that spread out to the horizon like a sea of grass with great masses of fluffy clouds drifting overhead.

"What a beautiful spot for a home," he thought to himself. "There's no place in Florida quite like it–almost like a western prairie." The fieldstone chimney was almost as wide as one side of the house and tapered to a small spout high above the house. The wide front porch was shaded by one of the oaks and John had built several rockers and straight–backed chairs with deer hide seats for pleasant evening relaxation before the mosquitoes came.

He found his brother in his workshop, making a small coffin of cypress in which to bury his son.

"I'm terrible sorry, John," he said. "Did they name the boy?"

"No name. When we made coffins for those folks who drowned at Orange Lake last year, I prayed it would be the last for a long spell—and now this."

And then, for a moment, he lost his composure. "Dammit, James, what is there about this land that eats up children. The cemeteries hereabouts are full of tiny graves. Papa lost his. You remember, Little William died in Ocala not long after Mama and Papa arrived here."

James put his arm around his brother's shoulder. "That's not fair, John," he said. "It's not the land. Mostly it's ignorance. The day will come when we know how to keep these things from happening."

John raised his head and smiled slightly. "You're right. I sound like Mama. You know how she hated Florida when she first arrived."

John took the coffin to Leesburg on the night train and carried the little body to Lone Oak Cemetery the next morning for burial. As he left the cemetery after the brief ceremony, he thought, "There lies my son, but who knows, who cares. I suppose in a hundred years it won't matter anyway."

He returned to the Hay home to be with Julia and when she saw him she was dry–eyed and said simply, "John I want to go home."

New Year's Day, 1874, in Micanopy began sparkling clear, and cold. James stood on the McCredie back porch and looked at the orange grove, five acres of trees stretching to the east. Thick pine smoke was still rising from the fires that had been burning since before midnight. He was not worried, however, about the orange crop, even though much of the fruit was still on the trees. He knew that the freezing temperatures had not been on the grove long and now the sun was coming up and soon would cast its warm glow over the town.

James loved these brisk, Florida winter mornings. As he walked to the outhouse, the sand crunching beneath his feet, he almost felt the stabs of red light from the rising sun that was painting a backdrop for the still dark oaks and pines, and the acres of orange trees. The cold boards of the outhouse seat brought him back from his thoughts of the pleasant morning. "At least I don't have to worry about centipedes biting my rear this time of year," he thought.

He noticed the box of lime used as a disinfectant in the outhouse was about empty and made a mental note to get a new supply from Center's store that day.

James had been up most of the night and went back to the house to fix his breakfast and go to bed. On the back porch he broke a thin coating of ice on the water bucket and took it into the kitchen where he found Betty making a fire in the woodstove.

"You know what happened last time you were in and out of the groves, fighting the cold," James said to her. She smiled. "I kin feel it in my bones. This one will come on time. That's a few more days."

"It's not in your bones you're feeling that youngun," James said. "From where I stand it's poking way out front, an' that means a boy."

"Oh, you and yore boys," Betty said. "This one's been comin' on real gentle like. It's another girl, I kin tell," she added with conviction.

She was right. On January 8th they had a baby girl and named her Addie.

James looked long and silently into the little pine cradle he had made for his first daughter. "How very beautiful this one is," he thought, "another just like her mother." It was time to do something about a new house, and more orange groves to support his growing family. Besides, David and Janet were beginning to show their age and needed more peace and quiet than a house full of babies would create. Betty was a natural–born mother, and he knew she would produce the babies he wanted.

Betty looked up from her bed. "Mister," she asked, "have you seen my husband? He's about yore size, with sad, dark eyes and a long, long face."

The high, old–fashioned four–poster bed came to James' waist so he did not have to bend down very low to kiss her. "If I see the lazy scoundrel bout town makin' eyes at the pretty widow Hawkins, I'll tell him I been kissin' his wife," James grinned at her.

"You kin also tell the Widow Hawkins if she asked you to share her supper box at the church this Wednesday night while I'm havin' babies, I'll poison her well," Betty answered.

"And you would too," James said as he kissed her again and then left the bedroom, after taking another look at little Addie.

In July, John and Julia presented Mama and Papa McCredie with another granddaughter they named Annie Julia. That same month James and Betty bought their fifty–one acres from James and Sarah Simonton on the southwestern edge of Micanopy, down an oak covered lane on the west side of Lake Tuscawilla.

"It's not far from a certain spot under a big, old oak tree on the lake where I lured James for a picnic dinner while he was working in a house nearby," Betty explained. "I do believe it's the puniest place in Micanopy for a house—and room for hundreds of orange trees."

After the first of the year, James began clearing his land for the new McCredie house and his orange grove that would stretch to the west behind the home. By spring he had set out more than a thousand new trees and had the foundation ready for the house. Betty was pregnant again and he wanted to have the house ready when the baby came in June, but there were delays because John had to help with the carpenter work and John was busy with his farm planting through the spring months.

The baby, James' first boy, came on June 20th and was named Frederick William. They decided to call the boy Fred and James was slightly uneasy about that. He was afraid that he and Betty were swayed from calling him William because of James' two brothers, both named William, who had died as small children.

He finally dismissed the fears with a shrug of the shoulders and proceeded to spoil the baby boy.

The house was finished in August and the family moved in on the 19th. It was beautiful, Queen Anne in design with three dormer windows, a wide porch across the front on the first floor and another smaller porch beneath one of the dormer windows on the second floor. The house was built of heart, yellow pine, made from trees cut from the property where the orange trees were planted. It sat on brick foundations high off the ground so that the front porch was reached by five pine board steps and the crawl space beneath the structure was hidden by lattice work.

A four–pane bay window was placed on the front of the parlor, which was located on the right as you entered the front door.

An unpainted picket fence surrounded the house. Most Micanopians called the pickets on the fence "palins."

After the move to the new house Betty and James took their first walk from their home to the west shore of Lake Tuscawilla. It was said the lake was named for the daughter of old Chief Micanopy, a beautiful Creek princess.

As they stood beside the lake in the late afternoon on the last day in August, Betty turned to her husband. "Well, you have your son and a new home," she said smiling. "Are you satisfied?"

"Nope," James said "I want a lot more. Got to have many sons to take care of us when we are old."

"Oh, James McCredie," Betty said, "you'll never be old. I won't let it happen."

James looked at her rich, black hair, her soft eyes, the curve of her body, and thought, "She doesn't look like she ever had a child. Please, God, when the time comes, take me first. I never had any kind of life until she came into it, and I won't have any if she goes first."

"A copper for your thoughts," Betty said. "You look too sad!"

"It's nothing," James said, laughing. "See, I'm happy."

"Is it Mama and Papa McCredie?" Betty asked. "I know you've seen what I have. They're both breakin' and I'm worried about them. There are times when Mama McCredie looks at me like she's trying to figure out who I am."

"Yes, I know," James said. "When Thomas marries they'll have to come and live with us."

After that it appeared to other Micanopy families that Julia and Betty were racing each other to have the biggest families. Julia had a daughter,

Janet McCredie, named for her grandmother, November 24th, 1876. Thomas married Sally Blake that same year but remained at home with his new wife to care for his parents.

Betty gave James his second son on May 1st, 1877. They named him Thomas for James' brother, and called him "Tip," to avoid confusion in the family. Tip was destined to live longer than any of his brothers and sisters, but no one knew that when he was born.

All the McCredies went to an all–day church meeting with dinner on the grounds the last Sunday in August in 1878 and it was obvious that Julia was pregnant again. No one said anything, waiting for Julia to break the news. As they were spreading the food on boards placed on a line of carpenters' saw horses, Georgia Carruthers, a neighbor who lived on the next farm to John and Julia, came up.

"Oh, Julia," she exclaimed, "you're caught again."

Julia's face turned fiery red. Without a word, she flung a basket of biscuits into her neighbor's face and stomped off to where Betty was working.

"Old busybody," she stormed. "Why doesn't she keep her meddlin' in her own family. I wasn't 'caught.' I wanted this baby."

"No use to fret," Betty said. "We know you and John want lots of babies, same as me and James. Don't let her worry you."

The baby was born January 22nd, 1879, another girl, who was named Margaret Elizabeth, after John's sister, Margaret.

James and Betty went to see the new baby, "John is disappointed," Julia said first thing. "Looks like the only boy we'll ever have is the one that died. It's some kind of curse."

"Don't be silly," Betty said. "You'll have boys. You'll see."

The race was still on, however. Betty had another son on March 6th, 1879. This one was named Jacob and called Jake, for short. He was destined to be a bachelor all his life and follow the carpenter's trade, like his father.

When he saw the new son, John said to James, "You'll have to give me the formula. I can't seem to sire a son."

James had a twinkle in his eye. "Brother," he said, "when you get a little older, I'll tell you how it's done."

"Don't you get smart with me," John said angrily, and went out on the porch.

"Whew!" James told Betty, who had heard the remarks. "I didn't know he was so itchy about that. I'll be more careful."

"I guess you'd better," Betty said dryly. "Because, he's bigger'n you."

By the middle of August Janet had become difficult to manage. Days went by when she didn't recognize anyone. She often was re–living another part of her life, back in Scotland. She turned against everyone she loved, scolding David and her son and daughter–in–law for imagined injuries. As a result, David shuffled around like some kind of lost soul. He ate little, never smiled and took to his jug.

The last week in August she brightened up, got out of her bed and announced that she had to go to Leesburg to see her eldest daughter, Helen McCredie Marshall, the wife of Robert Marshall. Helen had remained in Scotland with her husband for a few years after the McCredie family had sailed to America in 1856, and then she and Robert joined them in Florida, settling in Leesburg.

"But Mama McCredie," Sally said, "you know Helen's been dead ten years."

"Rubbish," Janet screamed. "You're all against me. You trying to keep me from my daughter." It was a difficult day. James and Betty came over and it took all of them to keep her in bed. Finally, to humor her, James and Betty bundled her up and took her in their buggy to their home. They got her to go by telling her that Helen was waiting there for her and would take her to Leesburg. They left David behind, a forlorn figure, bleary–eyed and in a world of his own. He seemed childlike, hardly aware of what was happening.

Janet turned to look at her husband of fifty–two years as the buggy moved out of the yard. There was a slight smile on her pale face, as though she were seeing him for the last time. Sally watched the scene with tears running down her cheeks. She was not sure she could hold up to what was happening. "Dying is such a lonely journey," she thought. "It must be traveled alone."

At the James McCredie home they put Janet in a bright, sunny room on the first floor, but it was so strange. The moment she was back in bed she ceased to be part of their world, and on September 4th, in the evening while Betty was trying to feed her, she turned her face to the wall and died, quietly.

As she helped bathe her mother–in–law and dress her for burial, in the same black dress she had worn when she arrived from Scotland twenty–three years before, Betty wondered how many more times she would have to perform these last rites for someone during her life time. Family and friends gathered in the parlor to sit with the body, candles flickering, and voices low, as though the dead could hear. The next day Janet was buried in the Shuford plot in the cemetery. Her daughter, Margaret, had married a Shuford.

The hardest part was to come. David was moved in May of 1880 to the house in which his wife died. He had become more of a burden than Thomas and Sally could bear. They had to dress him and feed him and hide their whiskey from him.

When he escaped James' and Betty's watchful eyes, David roamed the streets of Micanopy, searching for Janet. Each day, when he arose, it was the same routine. He begged to be taken to Thomas' home to see his wife.

"Thomas and Sally are keeping her from me," he would say. "My own son and daughter–in–law. Why are they doing this?" He would shake his head sadly, and go back to his room, where he sat in a rocking chair all day, staring out the window.

When he was told that Janet was dead, he looked at the speaker and said, "I'll see Janet today. Thomas will let me see her today."

Then, on June 14th, 1880, right after breakfast, he appeared clear–eyed and alert as he announced to James and Betty, "Janet has gone to the grove to pick some oranges for Margaret. I'll go to help her."

There were no ripe oranges on the trees during the summer, but he went into the grove as his family watched to see how far he would go. About a hundred yards from the kitchen, he sat beneath one of their oldest trees and did not move. When James went to check on him, he was dead, his eyes open, as if staring into eternity.

He had lived nine months and ten days after his wife died, his mind never accepting the fact of her death.

"Now, his search for her is over," James told Betty.

After the death of his father, James was sad and depressed. Almost every day he told Betty, "I don't know where the years went. They passed like the wind and now I wish I had done more for Mama and Papa. Maybe they would have been happier and lived longer."

"There is enough guilt for all of us." Betty said, "and you needn't try to bear it all. That's too much for one man."

"Papa always talked about going back to the Old Country for a visit. It was his dream, and I meant to see that he got there. Now, it's too late."

"It's time to stop all this," Betty told her husband, almost angrily, "Mama and Papa McCredie were not unhappy. All they ever wanted was for us all to be here together. They enjoyed their grandchildren. Doctor Montgomery said they did not die from unhappiness or misery or discontent. He said they just plumb wore out."

Although David and Janet did not live to see it, their town was on the verge of its "golden era."

The 1880s were exciting times in Micanopy. It was a good time to be alive in that area. The *Gainesville Bee* stated its opinion that "Micanopy, in comparison to the number of its inhabitants, if not now, will, in a half dozen years, be the richest place in the United States, simply from the product of her oranges, if from no other cause."

The *Micanopy Gazette* predicted that the orange business would "produce a race of rich men, who will rank with the plantation princes of the Old South; the Carp barons of Germany."

The *Florida Daily Times* of Jacksonville sent a reporter to visit the largest orange grove in Florida—on Orange Lake. Actually this was two groves owned by Harris and Bishop. Harris' portion had twenty–thousand bearing trees, with a capacity of increasing four–fold. The reporter said there were at least sixty–thousand trees budding or waiting to be budded on the one–hundred and eighty–five acres.

James liked to tell about the two Illinois school teachers who had visited in Florida in 1874 and bought thirty acres from Mr. Harris for one thousand dollars annually, as oranges held their price of one and a half cents to two cents each.

The McCredie brothers, all except John, had orange groves. Thomas had groves all over town and served on the Town Council.

"I'm a farmer," John said, tartly. "I don't know why you boys are fooling around with trees. One of these days the cold will come and clean you out. I can always re–plant after a frost."

John was doing well with his farm. He grew sugarcane and made fine syrup for the northern market. From his hogs came home–cured bacon, hams, and sausage. He shipped carloads of beans, squash, cucumbers, sweet corn, lettuce, peas, eggplants, and watermelons, all bought by the commission merchants from New York, Boston and Philadelphia while still in the field.

Julia was ahead in the baby race. She had another daughter, Mary Evelyn, on January 30th, 1881, and then to John's extreme delight, she bore him a son, John Hayes McCredie, on April 10th, 1882.

About a month later the main topic of conversation in Micanopy was Army gold–had it been found?

As the story was told, an Army quartermaster with gold coins for use in buying supplies and paying the soldiers during the Second Seminole Indian war, had been so pressed by the Indians near Micanopy that he hastily buried the money before he was caught and killed. Another version of the. Story was that the money was buried in a camp kettle and that it was the winnings of a gambler who hid it while the camp was under Indian attack.

At any rate, over the years the area had reported a number of mysterious occurrences—strangers visiting old residents, mysterious searching and diggings, sudden departures of the strangers; strangers asking about unknown ponds near houses long since deserted. One newspaper account said an old resident, still alive, had found a camp kettle like the one in the stories but denied, finding money in it.

"No one believed him," James told his wife, "because he suddenly had wealth where tie had nothing before."

What brought the old mystery to everyone's attention was a report on May 10th, 1882, that four men on horseback had been seen in Wacahootee Hammock, with some kind of instrument, riding up and down among the trees. These strangers were observed for some time before being approached by two local farmers. When overtaken, the men dismounted and revealed a number of pots they had dug up but would say nothing about the contents. The *Gainesville Bee* asked, "Did they find the money?"

"Sounds like newspaper talk to me," Julia said. "Just something to get everybody stirred up."

It was a pleasant June evening with swarms of fireflies turning the John McCredie farmyard into a kind of make believe fairy land. Surprisingly, there were few mosquitoes, which John attributed to the dry spring—no pockets of water around in hollow limbs and such places that would serve as breeding places for the troublesome insects.

John and Julia sat contentedly on their front porch, enjoying the evening and watching Annie Julia, eight, and Janet, six, scamper after the "lightnin' bugs" to put them in an empty pickle jar. Julia held two–month–old John Hayes McCredie on her lap while eighteen–month–old Mary Evelyn tumbled around the floor, worrying the life out of Old Rex, a cow dog of questionable background.

"John, you watch that child," Julia warned. "She's liable to go off this porch on her head."

"I'm watchin," John replied, with some irritation. Then, a moment later, he asked, "You hear somethin, Julia?"

"I hear them younguns," Julia said. "They've gone wild over them bugs."

John got up and went to the edge of the porch, his hands cupped behind his ears. "Sounds like cattle runnin, or horses," he said. Julia joined him, her sleeping son in her arms. "I hear it now," she said. "And look, there are lights moving along that line of trees."

"Take the children and go inside," John commanded. "Those are men on horseback, a lot of men, and they're coming fast."

John followed her inside and took his rifle from a rack over the fireplace. "Bar the door," he instructed Julia as he went back on the porch.

Soon the riders, twenty or more, reached the farmhouse and one approached the house, holding a lantern before him. "John McCredie," he called out. "Be you here?"

"I'm here," John said. "Who are you?"

"Amos Barber, Micanopy marshal," the man replied.

"What you doin' out here this time of night, marshal?" John wanted to know.

About that time another man called out, "I'm James. We need your help."

John went to the door and told Julia everything was all right. "It's Marshal Barber and brother James and some men from Micanopy," he told her.

The men dismounted and gathered around the porch while Barber explained their mission.

"We're riding into Hawthorne tonight to join with some other men at daylight to look for John Fullylove. He killed Hawthorne Marshal James Paschal this evenin, shot him three times."

"I'll be with you soon as I can git a sack of food and saddle my horse," John said.

Julia brought out a jug of whiskey and a pan of cold biscuits and some of her country butter. She knew the men had been riding hard and would enjoy some refreshments. They passed the jug among them and ate all the biscuits.

Later, as they rode out of the yard, Julia called to her husband, "You be careful, John McCredie."

"You be careful," John called back. "Bar the door. The're all kinds of mean folks hidin' out all around the prairie."

Julia did not need the warning, and she knew this John Fullylove by sight and reputation. She had seen him staggering down the street in Micanopy on a Saturday afternoon a couple of weeks earlier. He was a small man with a sallow complexion and a downcast look. At one time there had been a poster out for his arrest on a robbery charge. He was described as "weighing one–hundred–thirty pounds, very light hair, age twenty–four, with a scar near the shoulder bone where a pistol ball was removed."

John Fullylove was a troublemaker. He had been a terror throughout the Hawthorne, Gainesville and Micanopy area. He was known for heavy drinking, fighting with knives and pistol whipping weaker men.

Julia had never told John what he said to her in Micanopy the day she met him almost blind drunk in the street as she crossed to the post office.

"Howdy, Miz McCredie," he said. "You shore purty woman How bout meetin' me in the cemetery after sundown."

John would have killed him, she believed, so she had never mentioned the incident. The cemetery was known as a meeting place for some extramarital affairs.

Fullylove had been in the Micanopy jail many times, mostly for drunkenness. One night he had stumbled into a bull in the dark and became stuck between its horns on Ocala Street. The bull, startled and enraged, raked him against an oak tree several times before he fell free of the horns.

Thomas McCredie had heard Fullylove's screams and went to investigate the commotion. He found the man scratched and bleeding but so drunk he was not even aware of what had happened.

Amos Barber and his posse spent a fruitless two days on the trail of the killer but he seemed to have vanished into the dense forests between the Prairie and Orange Lake. John and James returned home in need of food and clean clothes. James told Betty it reminded him of the days he and John fought the Indians in South Florida.

It was the custom for all the McCredies to gather at John and Julia's farm at least one Saturday every month to enjoy their family fellowship, discuss Micanopy politics and eat heartily of the farm's bounty. John was generous with his hams, sausage and bacon and most Saturdays his brothers and sisters went home laden with meat and vegetables, much to Julia's dismay.

"They only come to get something," she told John often. "Your sister, Margaret, is the worst. You give her a pig every Christmas, an' if you forget, she's scoldin' you about 'her' pig."

John soothed her. "Stop yer frettin, Julia. We're family."

"It's family all right," she said, "but it only works one way. You don't ever get anything from them."

John let it pass.

A few weeks after the manhunt for Fullylove, the McCredies gathered at the farm for their usual all–day visit. They admired John's palm trees, newly planted around the front of the house. John loved his cabbage palms. He said they made his land look like Orange Springs where he had first settled in Florida. Besides, he liked the heart of the palm boiled as cabbage or cut up raw as a salad with lettuce and tomatoes.

"When these yard palms grow up, you gonna cut 'em down for the buds?" James asked.

"Anybody touches them cabbages will be in a heap of trouble," John said.

"I think he loves them ole palms better'n me," Julia chimed in. "He'll go way back in the hammock to get his palm hearts."

"You gonna come home one of these days," Thomas said, "an' find somebody's been here an' cut out all your cabbages an' the trees'll die."

"That day somebody's gonna get shot," John said grimly.

He had used palm logs to support the roof over his front porch, and Julia was always teasing him about "the Indian poles."

John's answer was always the same. "Palm logs don't rot. They'll be there long after you and me and everybody is dead."

While they were eating their noon meal, a hearty feast of field peas, crisp cornbread, turnip greens cooked with a ham hock, some of John's home–cured ham and red–eye gravy, old Sam Smith, a black man who had helped John with some plowing, came to get his pay.

He stood in the sun at the foot of the porch steps, hat in hand.

John called, out, "Sam, you set there on the porch while I get your money. Man, it's too hot out here in the sun."

"Nassuh, I'se fine," Sam replied. "Me and ole sun is friendly. He done burnt me bout as black as I can git," he laughed.

John went into his bedroom and soon returned to the dining area with his strongbox. He took the key out of a gourd vase and unlocked the box, a finely polished and sturdy pine box about eighteen inches long, ten inches wide and four inches deep. He took out Sam's money and gave it to him.

"Thank you, Massa John," Sam said. "Got to git into Micanopy this afternoon to git me some coffee an' bacon an' some snuff fer my ole woman."

"I'll be needin' you Monday morning," John said.

"Yassuh," Sam said. "I be here come daylight."

John returned to his dinner. James eyed the strongbox. "John, when you gonna put your money in a bank? It's not safe in there under your bed."

"How you know I keep it under my bed?" John wanted to know.

"I've seen you put it there," James said. "And so have half the people around here, I'll bet."

"I don't trust them banks, an' bankers either," John said. "It's better here with me."

The conversation moved to safer ground, the citrus business, as always.

"They said in town yesterday Lucius Montgomery is putting in a new grove on the Prairie," James said.

"True," John said. "He's planted two hundred twenty trees on forty acres not far from here."

Dr. Lucius Montgomery was possibly the town's richest resident. His home, two stories high, had an additional two–storied cupola, making it an imposing structure. The house and stable occupied four acres, surrounded by twenty–one acres of orange and lemon trees, including the famous Cicily lemon. Many of his citrus trees were thirteen years old and measured forty–one inches below the first fork.

John's oldest daughter, Annie Julia, was sitting on the edge of the porch, dangling her bare feet toward the sandy yard, listening to the citrus talk. "Papa," she asked, "how big is forty–one inches?"

John turned to his daughter, making a circle with his arms. "Bout this big, Punkin," he answered.

"Is that the biggest orange tree in the world?" she wanted to know.

"No, John Barr has one that measures six feet around. That's the biggest orange tree in Micanopy and there's one up at Fort Harley near Waldo that's nine feet around and thirty–seven feet tall." He laughed. "Maybe the one at Fort Harley is the biggest one in the world."

"John, where'd you hear that tall tale?" James asked. "Nine feet in circumference? And thirty–seven feet tall?"

"That's the gospel truth," John said indignantly. "That tree was damaged by fire a few years ago but today is as good as new. Bears more than ten–thousand oranges every year."

"That's two–hundred dollars a year from one tree," James said. "All we'd need would be a hundred trees like that and we could get rich."

"Dream on," said his older brother.

"You talk about oranges all the time," John continued. "The Micanopy area produces only fifteen–thousand crates of oranges a year and the vegetable farmers produced thirty–nine thousand crates of vegetables last year. Don't forget about the beans, peas, lettuce, tomatoes, cucumbers, cantaloupes and watermelons, as well as celery and squash."

"That's true," James admitted, "but the oranges bring three times as much cash as your vegetables. And Dr. Montgomery says the oranges bring a one–hundred percent profit. He's figured out that a box of oranges you sell for two dollars and a half cost you one dollar and a quarter. In the cost he includes the tax on the land, labor to cultivate the grove, picking, wrapping and boxing, hauling the fruit to the depot, freight charges, commission for selling, and one half of one percent to get the check converted to cash–and you know that two dollars and fifty cents per box is a minimum price."

And so the talk went. The following Friday, James asked Betty if she would like to go to Waldo with him. "Why do you want to go to Waldo?" she asked.

"To see an orange tree."

"James McCredie, you want to go all the way to Waldo to see an orange tree? What's wrong with the trees in our grove? Go take a look at them and save the trip and the money."

"This tree is different," James said. "It's the biggest in Florida."

"Oh, all right," Betty said. "I'll go with you to see your orange tree. We'll take the children out to John and Julia's."

They left on the morning train and arrived in Waldo in time for dinner at the Waldo House before taking a three–mile buggy drive out to the home of R. W. Campbell at Fort Harley. Campbell was the railroad agent at Waldo and offered to drive the Micanopy couple to see his greatest prize, the thirty–seven–foot orange tree that bore ten–thousand oranges most years.

The tree was impressive. "Never seen anything like that," James said admiringly. "What's the variety?"

"Parson Brown, and one of the sweetest I've ever tasted. Come back in November and taste the fruit."

Back at the Campbell farm they had a glass of fresh buttermilk and hot gingerbread and then were driven back to the Waldo House.

Before taking the train back to Micanopy the next day, Betty and James spent part of the morning exploring the town, which they had not seen in several years. Waldo, in 1884, had about five–hundred residents and was considered to be one of the up–and–coming towns in Alachua County. Most of the businesses were lined up along the railroad right of way. In addition to the Waldo House there was also the Sunnyside House, a carriage manufacturing company, blacksmith shop, wheelwright shop, cotton gin, grits mill, three sawmills, two schoolhouses, five churches, which included the Baptist, Presbyterian, Methodist, Episcopal and Congregational faiths, and a newspaper, the *Waldo Advertiser*, owned and edited by J. B. Johnston, formerly of the *Atlanta Constitution*.

Waldo also had a cigar manufacturing plant that employed from thirty to forty persons, and was headquarters for the Santa Fe Canal Company, whose chief engineer and superintendent was Ned E. Farrell, a man James admired for his grove activities. Not only did he have one thousand orange trees he had raised from seed, but he also had one hundred LeConte pear trees, one hundred peach trees, fifty Japanese plum trees, several varieties of grapes and twenty thousand more seedling citrus trees.

"Ned Farrell will be one of the richest men in this County one of these days," James told his wife.

There was a heavy downpour in the Micanopy area when their train pulled in shortly after noon so they had to wait until the following day to go to John and Julia's farm to get the children.

"We was beginning to worry," Julia said. "Expected you back yesterday and then decided the rain had kept you in town."

"I did some worrying myself," Betty replied. "Leaving you with all these younguns was a terrible thing to do, especially baby James. I couldn't sleep last night worrying about him. I told James I should have stayed home instead of gallivantin' all over the County to see an old orange tree."

James was only a few months old, having been born on March 18th, and he was the frailest of their children.

"James is fine," Julia assured her. "He's an easy baby to keep, sleeps most of the time."

"That's what worries me," Betty said. "Seems to me he sleeps too much, but, I suppose, he'll outgrow that."

On the way back home the McCredie children chattered away about their fun at the farm. "Annie Julia hurt her foot," volunteered James' Addie.

"What happened?" Betty asked her ten–year–old daughter, who was the same age as her cousin, Annie Julia.

"An ole spur," Addie said, shrugging her shoulders. "She got it in the cow pasture and Aunt Julia tried to dig it out with a needle."

"She'll be all right," Betty told Addie. "Spurs'll come to the top when the foot swells up and will get all angrified."

It didn't turn out that way. A few days later John came in his buggy to get Betty to go help with the children. "Julia's getting addled in her mind," he explained. "Somethin's wrong with Annie Julia. Her foot and leg are swollen all the way to her knee and we can't get her mouth open. She's bumin' up with fever. Dr. Montgomery's on his way out now."

All the way to the farm, Betty kept saying over and over to herself, "No, no, it can't be. Please, God, don't let it be lockjaw."

By the time they reached John's farm, however, Dr. Montgomery had already decided the child had the dreaded lockjaw.

"With her jaws locked, she can't eat," he said sadly. "If I had been called sooner, we coulda put a spoon in her mouth to keep her teeth apart so we could feed her through a quill. Now, I'm gonna have to break out one of her teeth."

"No, no, no," Julia wailed. "She will die."

John was pacing the floor. His eight–year–old, Janet, buried her head in his side. "Papa," she cried, "Mama says Annie Julia's goin' to die. Is she?"

John sat down and put her on his lap. He stroked her hair until her sobs ceased. "Annie'll be all right," he said. "Dr. Montgomery's goin' to help her."

Later, he took all the children into the yard while Dr. Montgomery pried and cut out one of Annie's front teeth, but wherever he went, he could hear the screams and agonized yells coming from his oldest daughter.

Chicken broth was fed into her system through a goose quill, but she died anyway, on August 14th. The poison in her blood from the disease killed her, not the lack of food. The pain from knocking out her tooth was not necessary. The evil was in her blood.

At the funeral in Micanopy, Betty said to herself, "What is to be will be. We'll see what tomorrow brings."

6

Yellow Fever

When Julia McCredie had her seventh child, a daughter, named Julia May, on September 23rd, 1885, the tongues began to wag.

At the Presbyterian Church quilting party on Wednesday afternoon following the birth, Mayme Sanders poked her friend Betty McCredie in the ribs and said, "That brother–in–law of yours is some man. Imagine, fathering a child and him almost sixty!"

"No such thing, Betty said stoutly. John's only fifty–six."

"Well, fifty–six or sixty, not much difference. He is gettin' to be an old man to be having children, don't you think?"

"Mayme," Betty said, a trifle angrily, "it's none of our business, you know. John wants more boys, and they'll have em too. Just like us. We want some more."

"You and James? Betty, you're the same age as Julia. You're thirty–four. You are both gettin' too old to be havin' babies. It'll ruin your health. You mark my words."

Betty laughed. "Oh, Mayme, stop worryin. We're both as strong as a pair of mules, Julia and me."

Betty was right about the babies. She had a boy, Norman Aubry, on August 11th, 1887, and Julia had another son, Walter Stewart, on February 5th, 1888.

The birth of little Walter Stewart was about the only happy event for the McCredies in 1888. The year seemed to cower under some kind of evil star. Spring was uncommonly hot and wet, a condition that bred millions of mosquitoes that plagued Micanopians all summer, a summer that seemed to have no end.

"If Mama were here," James said, "she'd be stompin' about, smokin' her clay pipe and swearin' she was going back to Scotland."

"I might be ready to go with her," Betty said. "These younguns and the heat have bout worn me out. And the fever in Jacksonville. Everybody's worried about that."

"We're safe here," James said. "You remember'71, the year we were married. Fifty people died in Gainesville of Yellow Fever, and we didn't have one case here."

"I remember," Betty said. "It's the filth in Gainesville. Everything goes into the streets. Filth brings disease. You have to fight your way through the buzzards to cross a street."

James laughed. "You sound just like Mama. You know it's not as bad as that."

James, John and David belonged to the Micanopy Guard, which was more of a social club than a military unit. They had barbecues and fish fries and marched in the parade on the Fourth of July.

On the third of September, John Hamilton, a long–time friend of the James McCredies, and captain of the Gainesville Guard, came to Micanopy by train to visit James and Betty. He arrived in time for dinner and after one of Betty's filling meals the two men sat on the porch smoking cigars.

Neither one spoke much. They had a kind of friendship that didn't require much conversation, but James was curious about Hamilton's visit

"What really brings you to Micanopy, John?" he asked. "I know you didn't come here just to see my ugly face."

"Quite right," John said. "You've got a face only your mother could love. Fact is, I need a favor."

"Just ask," James said.

"Don't be so willing. You been reading about them riots in Fernandina?"

"Yes."

"The Gainesville Guard has been asked to come up and help restore order. I'm short some men. How about you and John and David coming along?"

Betty had come out the front door just in time to hear the last part of the conversation.

"Come along where?" she asked John. "What's this all about?"

"John's Guard unit is going to Fernandina to help out in the riot," James explained. "And he wants me to come along. He' s short some men."

"Fernandina!" Betty exclaimed. "They've got the Yellow Jack up there. You men shouldn't go up there!"

"No, Mam," Hamilton said. "The public health folks in Fernandina say there's no Yellow Fever there. They've convinced Gainesville officials, otherwise we wouldn't be going."

Betty didn't like the idea of James going anywhere, with the fever raging in Jacksonville, but she knew that if he wanted to go and felt it was his duty to go, she couldn't stop him.

James agreed to accompany the Gainesville men, as did David, but John McCredie begged off, saying he had too much farm work to do, which was no doubt true.

On September 6th, the McCredies left Gainesville with their friends for Fernandina. A week later, the Ocala rifles also entrained for the riot–torn city.

In Fernandina, some of the Gainesville men were ordered to guard the home of the leader of the striking longshoremen. It was a rainy night and this particular detail sought shelter on the man's porch. Inside, his wife was ill with a fever believed to be Typhoid. By September 11th, the riot was under control enough for the Gainesville men to return home. As the train carrying them pulled into Gainesville that night, two of the Guard members, Elam A. Evans and M. Fitch Miller, were running fevers, and four more, W. N. Wilson, J. Hodges, J. Waugh and Jack Ammons, were feeling ill.

Evans and Miller died the next day, but the news was kept until Sunday night, September 18th. That evening the sermon at the First Methodist Church was interrupted so the congregation could hear the announcement that six members of the Guard had been confined to their beds, suffering from Yellow Fever, and that two had died.

The news was worse than a cry of "fire." Church members jumped from windows, crushed one another getting through the doors in their panic. A New York newspaper reported later that "All over town families were rushing to pack their clothes, provisions and cooking utensils–preparing to flee for their lives–trunks were tossed from the upper windows, women and children, were hustled into wagons half dressed and the consternation was scarcely describable."

In Ocala, there was general anxiety about the impending return of the Ocala Rifles, in view of news that the postmaster at Fernandina had died of Yellow Fever. The *Ocala Banner* explained that the solution arrived at was for the men to "Take a piney woods ventilation," a fancy way of saying that they would camp away from Ocala until they were considered free of infection.

The Rifles voluntarily agreed to camp at the "Sanderman Place" on Blue Springs Run, "so that assurance could be made doubly sure that no microbes through that crack organization would be imported into Ocala, to spread the pestilential epidemic of Yellow Fever," the newspaper reported.

Their sojourn at Blue Springs Run may have been somewhat bolstered, James said, by the fact Ocala was ringed with more than two hundred men armed with shotguns and instructed to allow no one to enter or leave the city without a health card saying he was free of the fever.

By September 19th, two–thirds of Gainesville's residents had fled the city, business activity had ceased, and on orders from the Surgeon–General of the United States, citizens could leave Gainesville via Live Oak until September 20th. Trainloads had already begun to reach Atlanta as early as September 18th. Some remained there and others went on to the mountains of North Carolina. All had health cards saying they were not carriers of the disease.

In Gainesville, the six homes where the fever had been, or was still present, were under quarantine, with yellow flags nailed to their gates, and guards on duty. Houses within a hundred yards were fumigated.

The city of Gainesville was also ringed with shotgun bearing volunteers.

In Micanopy, an emergency meeting of the town council was called and a decision made to set up eight guard stations covering all roads and trails leading into town. James and David were asked to fumigate their homes since they had been members of the Guard detail that went to Fernandina.

On Thursday morning, a day that began dark and sultry, Betty was up at daylight, as usual, to get the woodstove going, cook hot biscuits and a pot of grits, before frying eggs and home–cured ham for James, the children and three hired hands who were working the orange grove.

James didn't stir. Usually, he was up ahead of her to make a fire in the woodstove.

"James," she called, as she dressed, "I'm gonna need some more wood for the kitchen. You forgot to bring some in last night."

James mumbled, "Not now. I'm feelin' bad Later."

Betty, alarmed, felt his forehead. Is was hot and dry. With as many children as she had, she knew fever when she felt it.

"You stay in bed," she directed James. "I'm going to send for Doctor Montgomery."

James sat up. "No need for that. I'll be fine. Doc Montgomery will just come in here and dose me up with all kinds of stuff. Just wait awhile. If I've got fever, it'll go away."

To show Betty he was not really ill, James got up and dressed. "Maybe just a summer cold coming on," Betty thought as she went to the kitchen. James was never sick.

But by the next morning, he was burning up with fever, delirious at times and complained of aches throughout his body. Betty had been reading all about Yellow Fever symptoms in the *Ocala Banner*. These were the symptoms, but they were also the symptoms of diseases other than the dreadful Yellow Jack.

She sent one of the grove hands for Doctor Montgomery and he arrived within the hour. As he entered the bedroom, he stopped and sniffed the air, a frown on his face. He mumbled, almost to himself, “Saffron Devil. I can smell it.”

Without a word to his patient, Doctor Montgomery made a brief examination. Then, he sauntered over to the window and gazed into the yard where several Rhode Island Reds were lazily pecking at the ground.

“Nice fat hens you got out there,” he said quietly.

“Doc, we didn’t ask you to come out here to talk about chickens,” James said hoarsely. “What’s wrong? I never felt like this before.”

Doctor Lucius Montgomery, at age forty–five, was light on his feet. He spun around like a panther, ready to pounce. “It’s Yellow Fever,” he almost spat out. “And you do what I say, James McCredie, or you won’t ever gather another citrus crop.”

James already knew the answer, as did Betty, who had prayed all night that she was wrong as she lay alongside the tortured man. There was a peculiar smell about this deadly disease that Doctor Montgomery had detected the moment he entered the room. He had called it the “Saffron Devil,” a name that had come from the Louisiana bayous. They had a more horrible name for Yellow Fever in Cuba. There they called it “El Vomet Naro” or “Black Vomit,” because in the final stages of the disease, the patient would bleed internally and this blood mixed with the acid of the stomach to form a black substance that was thrown up when the victim became nauseated.

Doctor Montgomery turned to Betty. “Here’s what you must do,” he said. “Give him a large dose of Epsom Salts. His system must be cleaned out completely.”

“I prefer Glaubler salts, or sulphate of soda, owing to its specific action on the liver. Give it in a half tumbler of water or lemonade. If you don’t get action within two hours, repeat the dose.”

James interrupted. “I won’t take that stuff. I’m not some kind of horse or cow.”

Doctor Montgomery ignored his patient and continued to address Betty. “You then give him a vapor bath. Strip him and set him on a chair with a wooden seat and cover him with blankets, pinning them under his chin. Place his feet in a bucket of water as hot as he can stand. Next, put a lighted spirit lamp under the seat of the chair, or a small coal oil lamp. Be certain the blankets fit so tight no hot air or vapor escapes.”

"If I'm gonna be scalded to death," James said, "I might as well die here in bed of the fever."

Doctor Montgomery continued. "Make him a half pint of hot orange leaf tea. I prefer that but if he'll take it better, give him hot lemonade."

"How long do I do this?" Betty asked.

"In fifteen or twenty minutes that flush should leave his face and his pulse should soften. The perspiration should fairly roll off him. The purpose of all this is to produce free action of the skin and bowels."

"That gives him the best chance to fight this disease. If the flush returns to his face, repeat the procedure."

"There's another thing," Doctor Montgomery advised. "This house will be under quarantine and under guard. No one will be allowed to enter or leave. I want you to burn sulphur in smudge pots night and day to keep the children from getting the fever. And it won't hurt to soak their bed linens with camphor."

Betty followed Doctor Montgomery out of the room. When they were where James couldn't hear, she spoke, in a trembling voice. "Tell me everything. Does he have a chance?"

Doctor Montgomery shook his head slowly, in the affirmative. "I think so," he said, "but it will be the toughest thing you ever went through. Your job now is to survive yourself and keep your children from getting the fever. That's number one. If you can bring James through, that's number two."

He paused, a slight smile pushing at one comer of his mouth. He had seen a curly head appear around one corner of the door to the parlor and then quickly disappear.

"Speaking of the children," he said, "I'd better talk to all of them about what we have here."

They all gathered in the parlor.

"You should know," he told them, seriously, "your father has Yellow Fever. It's the only case in Micanopy right now. This house is under guard. You cannot go outside of your yard, and no visitors. No one will be allowed to come in. You must all stay away from your father—and mother. She must fight for your father's life. You older girls will have to take over and do everything. I'll come in every day."

For Mary Ella, sixteen and Addie, fifteen, this was the worst thing that had ever happened to them. No picnics, no hay rides, no taffy pulls. Then, Betty added the final blow. "All of you," she said, "must wear your asafetidy bags, day and night. You must not get this dreadful fever."

The asafetidy bags were small cotton bags, filled with a foul–smelling, yellow–brown powder–like substance that were worn on a string around the neck and were supposed to ward off all kinds of germs and evil spirits.

"But, Mama," Mary Ella spoke up. "you said you didn't believe in this kind of witch stuff— your very words. Didn't do Annie Julia no good. She died with one of them bags round her neck."

"I know," Betty said, rubbing her tired eyes, "but this time we have to do everything. Do as I say."

Then, the battle began. Days and nights turned into unending nightmares. Betty kept the room darkened so she could hardly tell when it was night and when it was day as she fought to keep the fever from going too high. If she got any sleep at all, is was on a quilt on the floor. James thrashed about in the bed so violently when the fever came on that she feared his flailing arms would injure her.

She re–lived the Civil War battles with him and had to place her hands over her ears as he screamed out warnings and orders to men he saw around him. Then, suddenly, he would collapse on his pillow and lie so still she feared he had died and crept to his side to see if the breath of life had fled.

One day his eyes opened and he searched the room until he saw her in a chair. "There's a storm coming," he said. "I hear thunder."

"No," she told him, "that's cannon. They've been firin' all morning."

James thought she had lost her mind from exhaustion. "Open the drapes," he said. "I want to see out."

She opened the drapes and from his bed he could see smoke drifting above the trees and realized the sound was cannon fire. Before he could speak, she explained. "They been bumin' tar and sulphur all over town since you been sick, an' firin' that old Civil War cannon. Some say the smoke and the noise will keep the fever away."

James grunted. "If smoke and cannon fire would of kept fever away, no one would of died from it during the war. That's all we had most of the time, smoke and cannon."

Betty realized he was bright–eyed and rational for the first time in two weeks. She felt his forehead. It was cool and moist to her touch. She hugged him and kissed him all over his face. “You’re well!” she cried. “You’re well! The fever’s gone.”

“I’d like some hot biscuits, some smoked sausage and some grits. I’m starved,” James said.

During most of his illness, he had been too sick to eat. She looked at his gaunt face and hollow eyes and decided food was the answer, lots of food. She opened the door and called Mary Ella. Her daughter came into the dining room at the far side and stopped. During James’ illness she had not been near her mother. At mealtimes, she left food for her parents near their door and then called Betty to say it was there.

“Git your daddy some biscuits, sausage and grits,” she said, “and lots of coffee. I believe he’s hungry enough to eat a polecat.”

“Oh, Mama!” Mary Ella said, and ran off to the kitchen to get the food and tell her brothers and sisters that their daddy was well again.

And that’s the way the dreaded Yellow Fever came to and went from the James McCredie house.

In a few weeks everything was back to normal and the McCredies planned a celebration at John's place on the second Saturday in September. It was a special occasion, not only because James had "come back from the dead," as Julia put it, but because the eldest son of Helen McCredie Marshall and her husband, Robert, had arrived by train from Leesburg the day before to visit his mother's brothers and sisters for the first time in several years. Helen McCredie Marshall, the eldest daughter of David and Janet, had died at Leesburg, Florida, in 1867 at age thirty–nine.

They held the dinner in the yard beneath the shade trees on tables fashioned with boards and sawhorses. Thomas being a town official and a deacon in the church was asked to say grace. This always caused the children to make wry faces at one another because Thomas was known for his long blessings at mealtime.

Mary Ella grew restless and raised her eyes to look down the lane just in time to see two men dart behind some trees. She was certain they had been watching the house. She was sitting next to her father and poked him in the ribs.

"Pa," she said, "I just saw two men hiding in the woods down the lane."

James eased away from the table, pretended to go into John's house but instead circled the house and approached the lane from a hidden direction. He was gone about five minutes and when he returned Thomas was just winding up.

James sat back down alongside his daughter. "I didn't see anybody," he whispered. "Are you sure you saw two men?"

Mary Ella nodded. "I saw em," she said.

James told his brother what Mary Ella had said, but John didn't seem to be alarmed. "If the're strangers around, they can't do anything without being seen. It's broad daylight."

So the meal continued until dessert time and Julia went inside to begin bringing out her famous lemon meringue pies.

Instead of coming out with the pies, however, she came out shouting, "John, the barn's on fire!"

"Got to get the horses and mules out!" John shouted, and everyone followed him to the barn. Despite the fact the building was burning furiously, they got the animals to safety, but were unable to save the bam. It burned to the ground.

Forty–five minutes later, they returned to the table to finish dinner with the lemon pie, but again, not one McCredie, not even one of the children, got a taste of dessert.

Julia discovered the door to her bedroom open and when she looked for John's strong box that was always under the bed, it was gone.

"I should a known that barn didn't set it self afire," John said savagely. "It was a trick to get us all away from the house. Somebody knew about that box under my bed."

"And they meant to kill us, too," Julia said bitterly, "If anyone had come back to this house, they would have been clubbed to death with this." She held up a stout piece of live oak limb she found near her bed.

"How much did you lose, John?" Thomas asked.

"Sixteen hundred dollars in cash and some checks, plus some of the family jewels that were brought from Scotland, and some papers. I'm going to town to get the marshal and his dogs. The hounds ought to be able to track them scoundrels."

Marshal Amos Barber came with his bloodhounds and they set off immediately on a trail through the pinewoods. The box was found with the checks and the papers still inside, but the money and jewels were missing. The lock had been broken from the box and it had been tossed into the wiregrass alongside the road. The men were on horseback, two of them, just as Mary Ella had said. Apparently, they had their horses tied a quarter of a mile behind John's house.

There was one peculiar thing about the way the hounds behaved, however. Three times they were put on the trail, and all three times they ended their tracking at the same house—the home of a man named Silas Marner Judkins, a newcomer to the Micanopy area from South Carolina. He had arrived six months earlier with a few pieces of furniture in a wagon pulled by one mule, an unkept–looking woman, driving, and a skinny boy of about ten on the seat with her. Judkins was asleep in the back of the wagon. At least, that's the way their arrival was described by old Mrs. Potter who heard the woman ask directions to the old Blackburn place, west of Micanopy.

Judkins insisted he had nothing to do with the barn burning or the robbery. "Yuh kin search my house," he said. "You won't find nuthin, an' that's a fact," he said.

"Why you think them hounds keep comin' heah?" the marshal kept asking.

"I don't put no faith in hounds," Judkins said. "Hounds'll do anything. I've had hounds. You kin fool hounds."

"I'll bet you know how, too," John said under his breath.

The robbery was big news in Micanopy and some citizens took their money from their personal secret places and took it to the bank in Gainesville, but not John. He put a new lock on his strong box and put it back under his bed.

"I don't trust banks," he reiterated.

A couple of months later, Julia drove their buggy into the farmyard after a visit in Micanopy. John was repairing the bam fence. She hurried to where he was working. "John," she called, "I've got some news for you."

John stopped his work and walked to her. "What's the Micanopy gossip today?" he wanted to know.

"It's not gossip. I saw it with my own eyes. That no–count Judkins has opened hisself a general store right on Cholokka Boulevard downtown. What do you think of that?"

John didn't walk, but ran to the barn for his horse.

Julia called after him. "Don't you do anything foolish."

When he rode out of the barn, he had his old Civil War pistol strapped to his side. Julia watched him ride out of the yard with great alarm. She knew John was not a violent man, but the theft of his money had been eating at his insides. He called back to ease her anxiety. "Don't worry, Julia, I'm going to get Amos Barber before I see Judkins."

Amos Barber told John he didn't think it would do any good to talk with Judkins because there was no proof that he had stolen John's money, but he did agree to accompany his friend to the new store. He didn't want a killing in his town if it could be prevented.

Judkins was all smiles when they entered his store. "Mornin, Marshal. Mornin, Mister Credy. Nice day."

Mrs. Judkins was partially hidden behind a new saddle, hanging from a rafter. There was no sunshine on her face, only meanness and hate.

"Don't you 'good morning' me," John said. "You stole my money and used it to set yourself up in business."

"Marshal, you shouldn't allow Mister Credy to talk to an honest businessman thet away," Judkins told Amos Barber. "Businessmen of this town pays yore wages."

John interrupted. "Judkins, you're a scoundrel. It takes money to start a store, an' you came into Micanopy with not much more'n the shirt on your back."

Judkins was still all smiles and good will oozed from every pore of his body, like a preacher at a chicken dinner. "Now, now, Mister Credy," he said soothingly, "that's why I had money. Saved it up. I'm a frugal man. Don't throw my money away on whiskey and sich."

John was getting angrier by the minute. He drew his pistol and pointed it at Judkins, whose eyes began to bulge and his mouth to quiver. "Marshal," he cried, "stop this crazy man. If'en he keeps threatenin' honest businessmen, next time he might git his house fired—and him in it."

"You're lower'n a snake," John said. "I ought to kill you right now."

"Put the gun up John," Amos said quietly. "Let's go."

John put his gun away and they started from the store. Amos turned and spoke to Judkins. "I'm going to be watchin' you, Judkins," he said. "You'd better not make any mistakes."

Judkins knew he had won for the time being. He resumed his air of confidence. "Yew make me any trouble, Marshal, an' I'll see you fired."

7

Citrus

James McCredie passed his fifty–third birthday on February 25th, 1890. He looked forward to the beginning of a new decade, particularly since Micanopy was thriving, as was the McCredie citrus business. In 1889 the family had pooled its resources and built Micanopy' s first packing house, the future looked bright, and everyone in the family appeared healthy.

"God willing, this should be a good ten years," he told Betty.

Despite all the prosperity and good feeling that pervaded the town, however, James began to drag around the house and had to drive himself to tend his grove and take care of house chores. By mid–spring, Betty had begun to notice his pale color and seeming lack of energy. One day she came home from town with a small bottle marked P.P.P. She handed it to James. "You take one teaspoon of this every morning and you'll begin to feel better in a week," she told him.

The girls were snickering in the background, waiting to see how their father would react to the medicine. He had not been ill a day since his Yellow Fever attack. He whirled around and glowered at them. "Is this some kind of conspiracy?" he asked. "What's this vile looking stuff?"

"You can read what it says, James McCredie. Prickly Ash, Poke Root and Potassium. It'll give you energy."

"Who says so?" James demanded. "Is this some of Lucius Montgomery's remedies?"

"I got it from Doc Mathews at the pharmacy. It's been in the paper. Everybody's talking about it. Lucy Smith says it made her Joe hug her everyday."

She gave her husband a quick look from beneath downcast eyes. "I haven't had many hugs lately."

James went to his wife and enfolded her in a big bear hug. "So, it's hugs you be wanting," he said laughing. Over her shoulder he saw the girls taking in the scene.

"Scat, scat," he told them, "or you'll be taking this Rand P, and P." Off they scattered in gales of laughter.

James did take the medicine—one dose. He told John later it tasted like something he wouldn't feed to a hog. From then on he poured a little of the vile mixture out each day.

By summer he was feeling fine, and then he received a letter from an old friend, Jack Beville, who lived at Denton's Springs, a few miles northwest of Gainesville. The letter was from Mr, and Mrs. Beville, inviting the McCredies to a birthday party they were giving for their son, Harper Beville, on August 12th.

Betty was excited. "We'll drive to the Brown House in Gainesville and spend the night and then go on to the Beville's the next day," she said.

When they arrived at the Beville farm they found relatives and guests numbering more than one–hundred and fifty. The spacious grounds had been laid with long tables, covered with great white tablecloths. The dinner began with all kinds of barbecued meats, fresh baked breads, a dozen dishes of summer vegetables, cooked with home–cured bacon and ham, rice, and gravy, mashed potatoes, big slices of sweet potatoes, cooked in wild honey and macaroni topped with imported cheese.

To complete the meal, there were mountains of cakes, ice cream and chilled watermelon.

A main attraction, of course, was the Spring, known throughout the area. After such a meal a tour of inspection was needed anyhow, so James and Betty went with some other couples to see what the Beville's had done with their Spring. They followed a winding path through the giant oaks down into a dim woodland dell. Betty had been down in Devil's Millhopper so she expected to find a pool of some kind that sent its waters underground into an unknown river.

Denton's Spring, however, was not as deep. After a short descent they came to the spring, flowing from the foot of the hill, amidst beds of ferns over a glistening sandy bottom, almost as white as sugar. The Bevilles had built a large pool of pine planks inside a large bathhouse. The flow from the spring was arranged so that it filled the pool to a certain level and then drained off to continue as a small creek across the pasture.

Harper Beville explained to the guests in his group: "This is a historic area. Exactly sixty–four years ago in 1826 the first election for a representative from this County was held on that hill above this spring." He pointed to the hill.

"There were sixty–eight votes cast and sixty of those went to Mr. James Dell, uncle of those staunch Democrats, J. B, and Maxey Dell. There were four other candidates who divided the other eight votes among them."

Harper continued, "That first election was held in the home of John Rawls. The year following, 1827, the first court was held in the County at Newnansville, then the County seat. The father of Kirby Smith was the first judge. Living across the road from Mr. Rawls was Joseph B. Lancaster, an ardent Whig. He named the place Spring Grove, a most appropriate name."

As they drove back to the Brown House to spend another night before going on to Micanopy in the daylight, Betty said to her husband, "It's been an interesting day. I'm glad we came. I get all choked up inside when I think of the people who were in this land before we came. It's so easy to think we are the only people who have ever lived here."

"Yes," James said slowly, "this truly is hallowed ground, every inch of it. I think often about the Indians, their forefathers and their children who lived here for hundreds of years. They buried loved ones here, but when we arrived we considered them to be only savages, no more than animals, without love for one another, without emotions, without feelings for their families." He paused, still in thought. "It's not strange they fought like demons to keep the white families out. This is beautiful country, bountiful, a good place to live."

Betty asked, “What would you and your brothers and sisters have done if hordes of foreigners had come ashore in Scotland and began taking the land?”

“We too would have fought like demons from Hell,” James replied.

Before leaving Gainesville for home the next day James stopped by T. E. Culverhouse, home of fine liquors, wines and beer for a half–barrel of his favorite Scotch whiskey, H. W. McBrayer. He told Betty this was to be his Christmas stock.

Betty sniffed. “It’ll never see St. Nicholas.”

James laughed. “We’ll see,” he said.

On the way home he complained about the price. “Old Culverhouse has raised his price. A half–barrel was four dollars and a half. Now it’s five dollars.”

“You could have got Kentucky Coon,” Betty said. “It’s only three dollars.”

“You know I don’t like bourbon,” James said. “That’s a drink for women and squaws.”

“Your Mam a liked it,” Betty said in defense of bourbon. “And I like a touch of it in Christmas nog.”

James grinned. “I said it was a drink for women and squaws.”

The summer passed and soon it was fruit picking time, the busy season for the packing house. Micanopy got a new newspaper, the *Micanopy Courier*, edited and published by a newcomer, D. E. Thompson. In his first issue the new editor reported that citrus packing houses in the area were “working one–hundred and twenty–five hours and thirty teams.” The daily output from Micanopy alone, he said, was more than one–thousand boxes each day.

By early December the work with the fruit had slowed so the talk turned to Simonson’s Opera House and the grand opening on December 12th of the renovated theater. The theater had been completely lighted with gas. The “sun” or central reflector, six feet in diameter, had been fitted with thirty–five gas jets at a cost of one–hundred and fifty dollars.

Twenty footlights with brass shields lined the stage and ten overhead stage lights, each with ten burners, could be turned on either from the stage or from the side wings.

The *Micanopy Courier* reported that the Gainesville Opera House was the "Equal if not the superior of any other opera house in the State."

"Opening night is this Friday," Betty told James as she put the newspaper on the table after reading James the details. "The play will be 'Little Coquette' and the paper says there will be nothing in it that would embarrass the most fastidious. I think we should all go."

James snorted. "Nothing to embarrass the most fastidious." He snorted again. "What kind of talk is that? Sounds dull. I like my stage shows to be spicy."

"He likes his stage shows spicy." Betty mimicked her husband. "And just how many spicy shows has my man of the world seen?"

"Well, let's see, there was that time in Glasgow. No, that was in New York in 1854. Well, actually, none, but if I did see one I'd want it to be spicy," he ended triumphantly.

"James McCredie, you know good and well if you so much as saw a woman lift her skirt above an ankle, on the street or on the stage, you'd hide your face in your hat and run," she laughed. "I know you."

They all went to the Opera House to see, "Little Coquette," which turned out to be lively but not spicy.

In April of 1891, Betty told James that she was pregnant.

"You can't be," he almost shouted. "We're too old. You're mistaken."

"Doc Montgomery says it's true," Betty said "I saw him this morning."

"That old scoundrel!" James said. "You know he drinks too much these days. You'd better see another doctor."

"No," Betty said. "I like Doc Montgomery fine. He's always taken good care of me—and he saved your life."

Doc Montgomery was right. She was pregnant and before sunup on January 7th of 1892 she gave birth to a rosy–cheeked little girl. In all of Betty's other pregnancies she and James had chosen boy and girl names long before the births. This time it was different. Nothing was ever said about a name for the child.

After Doc Montgomery left that morning and while the girls were caring for their mother, James came into their bedroom with a book in his hand. He handed it to Betty.

"Why, it's 'Lorna Doone', the book you brought all the way from Scotland," she said.

"Read the last paragraph on the last page," he said.

Betty turned to the last page and read aloud:

"Of Lorna, of my life–long darling, of my more and more loved wife, I will not talk; for it is not seemly that a man should exalt his pride. Year by year her beauty grows, with the growth of goodness, kindness, and true happiness—above all with loving. For change, she makes a joke of this, and plays with it, and laughs at it; and then when my slow nature marvels, back she comes to the earnest thing. And if I wish to pay her out for something very dreadful—as may happen once or twice, when we become too gladsome–I bring her to forgotten sadness, and to me for cure of it, by the two words 'Lorna Doone'."

Betty looked at her husband questioningly. "What does it mean?" she asked.

Mary Ella, now twenty–one, and Addie, eighteen, had listened to the reading.

"That's a beautiful thing for a man to say about his wife," Mary Ella said. She sighed. "I hope some man, whoever he may be, will say that about me some day."

Betty looked at the passage again. "I see this book has been marked over and over, that same passage, like your Mama's Bible," she said. "Did you do that, James?" She had whispered the question softly.

James shuffled on his feet. "I always wanted to say that to you," he said. "I memorized those words. I almost wore em out."

He pointed to the tiny red bundle lying alongside Betty. "I know this will be the last one," he said. "I want her to be called Lorna Doone—Lorna Doone McCredie."

"Betty had tears in her eyes as she called her husband to her side. He knelt beside the bed and she took his head between her hands and pulled it down to the pillow beside her. Mary Ella and Addie tiptoed from the room."

"I've never seen Daddy like that," Mary Ella told her sister. "I want a husband just like him."

Lorna Doone was a healthy child and "grew like a weed," as her mother put it, but there was one difference in her approach to childhood. She and her father were inseparable when he was in the house or yard. He carried her on his shoulder and she nestled in his arms as he sipped his whiskey after supper.

"He's spoilin' her rotten," Betty told her daughters.

They had just finished cleaning the kitchen and after hanging up their aprons were seeking James and the baby in the living room. "He didn't act this way with either one of you girls, or the boys either," Betty said.

"Well, Lorna's sure gonna feel loved," Mary Ella said.

Betty looked sharply at her eldest daughter. "You don't feel loved?" she asked.

"Oh, Mama," Mary Ella said, "I didn't mean anything by that. Of course I feel loved. People are loved and feel loved in different ways. I can tell the way Papa looks at us, he loves us."

"See what I mean," Betty whispered to the girls. They had entered the living room and there was James by a roaring pine knot fire, his jug of whiskey on the floor by his chair and Lorna Doone curled up in his arms, her hair like black silk spread across his chest and her dark eyelashes against pink cheeks as she slept. She had just turned two. James was no longer rocking and was breathing easily as he also slept.

"That pair," Betty sighed. "I'd better wake him up. He's liable to get up, half asleep, and dump Lorna into the fire."

Addie laughed. "Mama, you think of the worst things," she said. "Daddy's not close enough for that. Sides, he's got her so tight, she'd jest get up with him."

"I can picture that," Mary Ella said, "daddy walking around with his eyes shut and that baby in his arms like one of them kangaroos with a youngun in a pouch."

But that's the way it went, day after day, father and daughter, inseparable.

"I hope nothin' bad ever happens to that child," Betty said. "It'd kill your father."

Nothing happened to little Lorna, however, and besides there were other matters to trouble the McCredies in 1894. In fact all of Micanopy, Alachua and Marion Counties, and all of Florida were troubled—those in the orange and lemon growing business, in particular.

A meeting had been called for January 23rd in Ocala at the Ocala House to discuss ways and means to fight citrus competition from the Mediterranean area.

James and his brothers, whose livelihood, except John's, depended on a profit from their groves, agreed that a protective tariff was the only answer.

"Them Dagos gonna put you out of business," John told his brothers.

The Ocala meeting was held and those attending said the citrus situation was serious enough to warrant a general call going out to all citrus growers to meet in Ocala on February 6th to get organized and press for action. In the meantime a petition was framed to be sent to the United States Senate after being sent to orange growers for their signatures.

The petition called for a protective tariff of one dollar per box to be placed on all citrus being shipped into the country. The petitioners pointed out that the cost to Florida growers to put a box of oranges on the market in New York City was a dollar and a half while the Mediterranean growers could do the same for a dollar and a quarter.

They explained that they paid from one dollar per day for unskilled labor to three dollars per day for skilled labor while the foreigners paid thirty–seven cents.

The petition said, "We have invested in this industry nearly thirty–million dollars and now produce from three to five–million boxes of fruit annually."

"Our fruit begins to come to market in August and the last shipments are made in April. Thus, with Florida and California oranges, the market of the United States can be fully supplied year round."

The meeting in Ocala on February 6th was well attended by growers from surrounding Counties and had to be held in the courthouse. All the early speakers, Dudley Adams of Orange County and General Bullock, advocated a protective tariff. Then the fireworks began.

Mr. W. P. Haisley rose to give his views. He didn't want anything to do with a protective tariff.

"That woke em all up," James told John later. "I liked that fellow," he said. "I believe I'll change my mind about a protective tariff."

Haisley was a feisty little man with a loud voice. He suspected this whole thing was a Republican trick and reiterated that the Florida orange industry had to take its chances with the other interests of the nation.

"I don't fear outside competition," he said. "I've visited groves in California, Arizona and Mexico and I feel confident Florida can hold her own against them. I've grown oranges since 1875—never made much money out of them because the transportation companies been gettin' the lion's share—stealin' me blind I don't ship any more. I sell my fruit on the trees or let it rot."

He paused to mop his face. "Y'all do like me and you'll git something for your fruit. Let's git together fellers. We can lick this thing. Make them transportation companies bid for our business—and git a new bid each year. If we give the entire fruit crop to a single bidder, we'll git the price down to twenty–five cents a box—an' I tell you, that's all it's worth."

Mr. F. C. Buffum, a Marion County grower, proposed that the growers use their power to push freight rates down. "If the transporters won't meet with us, we've got enough growers in Florida, if they'll work together, to buy our own steamships and build our own railroads. We can lay down a box of fruit in New York for twenty–five cents."

Amid all the enthusiasm for union and cooperation, a committee of fifteen was appointed to labor "through the night if necessary" to effect rules and regulations for an organization.

Labor through the night they did and recommended an organization of Florida producers and shippers that would represent all the growers and the vegetable men in Florida. A committee of four: General Bullock, F. C. Buffum, S. H. Gaitskill and W. M. Bennett, was appointed to "issue a stirring address to the fruit and vegetable growers of the state to come together and effect local organizations."

"I'm afraid the gunpowder is damp and won't explode, just talk," John told his brothers on the way back to Micanopy. "These growers will never get together."

"I agree with Bill Haisley," James said. "I'm not worried about competition from the Mediterranean even if their labor is cheaper. Our fruit is better and I believe the northern markets will pay our prices to get better fruit. They tell me that foreign citrus is puffy and diseased and there's fear for the health of the folks who eat it."

"I read in the paper some of the shipments are condemned on the New York wharves and ordered destroyed," Thomas said.

"That's true," John added. "And I don't know about this labor thing. Who pays a dollar to three dollars a day. I don't."

James asked, "What are you paying, John?"

"Fifty to seventy–five cents a day, plus food when they need it, an occasional doctor bill, some old clothes, and in some cases a place to live. What more do they need?"

"Self respect," James said.

"Self respect? What do you mean by that?"

"All those things you give the hands are hand outs, charity. How can they have self respect if they have to depend on Charity," James said.

John was astonished. "James, you've worked the local field hands. You know them as well as I do. If you paid them five dollars a day they'd still need this 'charity' as you call it."

"It's a poor system," James argued. "You can't develop good citizens and honesty that way."

"They're honest," John said, "but they do need help. I didn't know we had some kind of socialist in the family." There the matter rested.

About the middle of October, the James McCredie family had just come out of the Micanopy Presbyterian Church on a crisp Sunday morning when Mary Ella whispered to her mother, "Mama, Will Cooper wants to drive me home in his buggy. Will you ask Papa?"

"Ask him yourself, or tell Will to," Betty answered. "He won't bite."

"Will's scared. Ask him, Mama, please."

"Oh, all right," Betty said. Mary Ella was twenty–three and had never had a steady beau, which had been a source of some concern to her mother. She thought to herself. "She could do a lot worse than Jim Cooper's grandson." James L. Cooper had been running a pharmacy in Micanopy since the 1850s.

James was agreeable. "But I want her home for dinner. You know Sunday dinner is special. Tell her to invite Will."

That started the courtship. Will became a regular for Sunday dinners and in November he asked James for his daughter's hand. In view of her husband's Protectiveness of Lorna, Betty didn't know how the request would be handled, but again, James was agreeable. His only stipulation was that the couple be married in the Micanopy Presbyterian Church.

Later, he told Betty, "I hope all of our children can be married in the Presbyterian Church: John and I helped build it in 1870 and I feel it's part of this family."

Betty had a sparkle in her eyes. "How come we weren't married in that church if you were so fond of it?"

"You know the answer to that as well as I do," James said. "Your father was so set against me as a son–in–law, we had to elope."

"You don't want any of our children to elope, then?" Betty asked.

"No," James replied. "I'm not that kind of a father."

Betty smiled. "We'll just see what tomorrow brings."

"You say that all the time. Tomorrow brings what it brings and there's nothin' we can do to change it."

"That's what I mean," Betty said "And maybe one of our children will elope just like we did."

There the matter rested.

Actually, the Micanopy Presbyterian Church was also a part of Betty McCredie, since her father, Jacob Winecoff, had been one of the original trustees when the church was built in 1870, along with Dr. Lucius Montgomery and James Simonton. She and Julia and other ladies of the church were in the little white building on Cholokka Boulevard early on the morning of December 20th, decorating for the wedding of Mary Ella and Will Cooper, which was scheduled for high noon.

The church was packed for the wedding, each of the heart pine pews holding five persons on each side of the aisle. The weather was warm for December and by the time the bride came down the aisle friends and relatives were fanning vigorously with palmetto fans in pockets on the back of each pew. James had been worrying about the unseasonably hot weather. "The sap's still up in the grove and all we need is a sudden freeze to put us out of the orange business," he told Betty.

"Forget about that for now," she said. "We've got a daughter to marry off."

The wedding went as planned and the couple left in Will's buggy, pots and pans and all kinds of colored ribbons trailing behind. They boarded the train at two o'clock for Gainesville, where they planned to spend the night before going on to St. Augustine for a two–week honeymoon at the new Ponce de Leon Hotel.

As the train pulled away from the Micanopy depot, Betty turned to James and said, "I want to go home." He could see she was about to fall apart. In the buggy she burst into tears. "This will be our first Christmas without her," she sobbed.

James put his arm about her. "We haven't lost Mary Ella," he said. "She will be gone two weeks and then they'll be back to stay with us until Will can build his own home."

"It'll never be the same," Betty cried.

The time passed slowly and Christmas 1894 was less than merry. James fussed and fumed about the weather remaining so warm. The Jacksonville weather station had arranged a flag and whistle signal system to warn the downstate grove owners of weather changes, but James said it was too complicated.

"You can't be at the station to watch every train that goes through to check the color of the flags," he complained. "And sometimes you can hear the whistle and sometimes you can't. Depends on the way the wind's blowing."

The warning for a cold wave was three short blasts.

Two days after Christmas, by nightfall the temperature was in the forties. Betty said the only whistle she heard had been one short blast, which signified lower temperatures on the way. Because of the warm weather, trees were in full foliage. Most of the fruit had been picked.

James' grove, like others in Micanopy, was spotted with piles of pine knots, ready to be fired in case of severe cold. At 9:30 p.m., he and Betty retired, believing the temperature would go no lower than freezing by morning, but when James checked the thermometer at 6 a.m. on December 28th, the reading was fourteen degrees.

When it was light enough for him to see his way around the grove behind the house, he found a tree of navel oranges that was about half filled with fruit. An orange he picked felt fresh and cool with frost and when he sliced it open the meat was filled with ice crystals. He ate it, thoroughly enjoying the cold, sweetness of the orange. This was citrus at its best, he thought. He picked a dozen to take into the house for breakfast.

"We'll probably lose the leaves and the fruit still on the trees, but I don't think the trees are damaged," he told Betty when he returned to the house.

James proved to be correct in his diagnosis of the citrus damage. Most growers lost their leaves and fruit, except for the fruit they were able to pick and market immediately. The labor supply was limited and only a few growers were able to do this, except for those, like the McCredies, with large families, that could be called in for such an emergency.

By the time Mary Ella and Will returned from their honeymoon, the weather was mild again and attention was turned to the task of getting the young couple settled, and attending the round of social events that followed.

By the first of February, everyone had relaxed, believing the winter was over, old Mother Nature having thrown her worst punch in late December. Groves had entered a new growing season with sap up in the trees and the leaf buds shooting out into tiny twigs. Citrus growers were being quoted in the newspapers about the great success of the 1894"45 season. Figures for the year indicated that Florida had shipped about six–million boxes of fruit, despite the brief December cold wave.

On February 3rd, Lorna Doone awoke with fever and red spots on her face. Doctor Montgomery came immediately, took one look and said, "Measles." After a brief examination of the child, he nodded, "It's measles all right. Keep her in a darkened room and I'll bring back some medicine later today." James was like some kind of caged animal, in and out of the room where Lorna, now aged three, was lying in her crib, hand–crafted by her father.

"James, for pity sakes, stop worrying about that child," Betty begged. "Have you ever had the measles?" she asked. James nodded in the negative. "Then, you'd better stay out of here. I don't want another sick one on my hands."

Her words went unheeded. James continued to watch over his ill daughter.

On February 7th, every train through Micanopy was flying the cold weather flags and blowing three short blasts at appropriate intervals, but no one could believe the report. The day was bright and warm until noon, and then the thermometer began to drop. By nightfall it read forty degrees, the same as on December 27th, 1894.

James was too concerned about Lorna to fire his grove. "We may lose the budding leaves," he said, "but they'll grow back."

At bedtime that night Betty got out a pile of extra quilts for the beds. She told Will and Mary Ella, "It's going to be cold before morning."

During the late evening hours on February 7th, a steady rain beat against the tin roof of the McCredie home. After midnight, the rain turned to sleet and bits of ice large enough to arouse Betty and James with its raucous rattling over their heads. "I'll light a lamp," Betty told her husband.

Together they stared into the darkness from their bedroom window. The house shook and trembled from wintry blasts and they could see the white bits of snow and sleet sticking to the window pane and beginning to pile up on the windowsill.

James' face was grave. "I fear for the grove," he said, "but there is nothing we can do tonight. Let's try to get some sleep." Betty awoke one more time before daybreak, "Because of the silence," she told James. The wind had ceased and there was no sound on the roof. "It was like someone had put a big blanket over the house so we could all sleep in peace," she said.

When she awoke in the morning, James was already up and had fires popping and sputtering in all the fireplaces. The windows in their bedroom were coated with white so Betty could not see through into the yard. When she went into the living room she knew why the house had grown so quiet during the night. The "blanket" she said had been thrown over the house was snow that was still falling.

Soon Will Cooper, Mary Ella and all the McCredie children were in the yard, throwing snow at one another and marveling at its softness. They had never seen anything like it in their lives.

"God is having chicken for supper," Mary Ella told her younger sister. "Silly," Addie told her, "God doesn't eat supper. Why did you say such a thing?"

"Cause the servants in the kitchen are plucking the supper chickens right now. At least that's what it looks like."

James took little Lorna to the bay window in the living room and let her see the snow. She pressed her nose against the glass and Addie said later she looked from the outside just like some little old, flat–nosed midget, sad of eye and forlorn.

The temperature that morning was fourteen degrees and continued below freezing throughout the day. James paced the floor as his orange and grapefruit trees split wide open with sounds like rifle shots. The sap that had come up in the trees after the December freeze had come and gone was now freezing and causing the trunks of the trees to burst open.

By the end of the day it was clearly apparent that the James McCredie citrus grove had been wiped out. James sat staring into the fire all afternoon. Betty knew he was suffering. The grove was his dream. He had told her many times of his entry into Florida by way of the St. Johns and Ocklawaha Rivers and how on seeing the lushness and green of the citrus groves he had vowed to build his own citrus empire. Now, an unseasonable, vicious cold wave had shattered that dream.

The enormity of the disaster became all too clear in the days that followed. Snow had extended south in Florida as far as Ft. Myers. News reports told of ice on the St. Johns river, strong enough to support a man, that extended into the river as far as eight feet in some places. Hunters seeking game in the wooded areas and fields of Alachua and Marion Counties told of finding farm homes deserted, some with food still on the tables. The occupants had simply walked away with only the clothes on their backs, and never returned. Others sold out for what they could get and returned to their homeland in Europe or a northern state.

The Sunday following the freeze Micanopy ministers told their members that Florida had been visited by this "terrible disaster" because of the sins of the people. Later the editor of the *Bradford County Telegraph* in Starke, Florida, quoted one of his ministers who said he did not believe the freeze had visited Florida because of the sins of the people. He said he had been led to believe that hell was hot not cold. The editor of the paper commented. "Anyway you look at it, it's H—, isn't it?"

The size of the disaster became apparent when the fall and winter shipping season arrived for Florida's once golden crop. The figures for 1894"45 were six million boxes but those for 1895"56 were only seventy–five–thousand boxes.

James told Betty he was through with citrus. "Too risky," he said tersely. "I can make a living carpentering." That was in March. By April he was in his grove with a crew cutting down the dead trees and pulling stumps with a pair of mules.

Like most Micanopians, he had decided to replant his beloved citrus. "I know it'll take five years to get fruit again," he told John.

"What are you going to eat on during those five years?" John asked. "A hammer and a saw," James replied. "I can still build a pretty good house."

During the remainder of 1895, James replanted his grove and at the same time took carpenter jobs when they were available. When there was no work he spent his days at John's farm, helping in the fields.

He returned home one day in late August after a tiring day in John's hayfields. Betty met him at the back door after he had stabled his horse. "Old Mose is here," she said. "He won't tell me what's on his mind."

"Where is he?" James asked.

"He's down in the grove just sittin' under that old pecan tree you left when you first planted fruit."

Old Mose was really Moses Brown, a deacon in the African Methodist Church, a small log building located on Lake Tuscawilla about a mile from the McCredie farm.

Mose Brown was a respected farmer with a large family which lived from the products of his small farm. His lettuce, beans, tomatoes and cucumbers were usually the best in the area and the first to reach the markets in the spring.

When James reached the pecan tree, Old Mose was standing, hat in hand. "What can I do for you?" James asked his neighbor. Mose's boundary line was not more than a hundred yards from the McCredie grove.

Old Mose shifted from one foot to the other, his eyes directed at the top of a distant pine tree.

It was obvious something weighed heavily on his mind and he did not know quite how to approach the subject.

James tried to help him out. "Moses, if you need some help, just say so," he said. Mose finally said, "Nawsuh, I don't needs help. It's yoh boys. They's cause some trouble down at the church."

"Trouble at your church?" James asked. "What kind of trouble?"

"You jes ast them. They's good boys, an' I don't mean to trouble you none, but you ast dem about they's doins' at the church." With that he shuffled off toward his farm.

James went back to the house and called his sons, Fred, twenty: Tip, eighteen: Jake, sixteen: James eleven and Norman, eight.

James went directly to the point. "I been talking to Old Mose," he said. "He told me to ask you boys about some trouble at his church. What do you know about that?"

All was quiet. The boys seemed interested in something on the floor. James pointed to Fred. "You're the oldest, Fred. I want to know what's been going on."

"Nothin', Pa," Fred said. "We was jest havin' some fun."

"What kind of fun?"

"Me an Tip and Jake took some sheets and went down to the church last Sunday night. All they got is some candles for light so we marched round the church, moanin' and groanin' and then we went in the door and started down the aisle. You'd a laughed yourself to death. Them folks went out the windows and almost took the back door off the hinges. They was screamin' and hollerin' like some kind of demon was after em."

"I don't see anything funny about that," James said. "Those folks were in their church worshipping the same as we do in ours. You've never seen me really angry, but I'm angry right now. I know you've heard Preacher Smith talk about hell fire, but you are going to find out what hell fire really is, firsthand."

He turned to James and Norman. “You two boys can go,” he said. “I understand you didn’t have anything to do with this.”

He turned back to the other three boys, who were still staring at the floor. “Now, here’s what you’re going to do. You’re going to see Old Mose and make arrangements to appear before the congregation next Sunday and apologize for what you did. And I want you, Fred, to report to me after you have met with them church folks.”

Fred finally looked up. “But, Pa it was all in fun. All the boys in town like to have fun with the colored people.”

“Not my boys,” James said, and left the room.

Later, Old Mose told him the boys came to the church and told the members of the congregation they were sorry. “I told you they was good boys,” he said to James.

Despite the freeze, Micanopy had a good year in 1895. Vegetables were replanted and the truck crops in the area were plentiful and brought good prices. John’s farm was particularly productive. His brothers lost everything they had in the freeze but he made money.

“I been telling you boys you’d better get into some real farming,” he told his brothers. “If I was you, I’d never plant another citrus tree.” But they planted more trees than ever.

In the fall, all the McCredies gathered at John’s farm for a cane grinding. It was an annual affair. In fact, John supplied all his brothers and sisters with vegetables and everything produced on his farm. He was generous with everything he had, even though Julia told him he was foolish “to give away everything he had.”

The cane grinding got a little out of hand because of the power of the “skimmings” which had been left to ferment in a barrel. The “skimmings” or “cane buck” in the bottom of the barrel was powerful stuff. The trouble began when Julia McCredie, John’s wife, asked Maggie Shuford, her sister–in–law, to share some cloth scraps with her so she could make a quilt. Maggie, who was known to be as tight fisted a Scottish lady as ever came from the old country, replied that she had no scraps she could spare.

This really got Julia’s goat. Every Christmas John gave his sister a pig and if the pig was not forthcoming on time Maggie would always say, “John, where’s my pig?”

This year, however, Julia was so riled up because her sister–in–law refused her some scraps of cloth for a quilt that she ran over to the barrel of cane juice, turned it over and ordered everyone to go home.

"All you come out here for is to get something," she screamed. "You never come to see us except when you want something."

That broke up the party. Later John told his wife that his sister would never get another pig for Christmas. And he kept his word.

As they drove home, Betty told her husband, "I never saw anything like that. I wonder if we'll ever have another cane grinding?"

James laughed. "Julia'll be over it before morning. Soon as that cane buck wears off."

Later in the fall, James and Betty and little Lorna drove their buggy out to "Coon Hill" to the W. C. Smith farm to get their Christmas supply of guava jelly. The Smith farm was located in an area called "Tacoma," nearly three miles northwest of Micanopy on Levy Lake. The community had been settled by Wilmot Austin Smith, from New York State, in 1877. The reputation of the W. C. Smith guava jelly had spread far and wide. W. C. Smith, a son of the pioneer settler of the area, had a contract with the Pullman Company under which he provided small jars of his jelly, labeled "Tacoma Brand," which were served in the dining cars of trains coming into Florida from the north and east and, later on the Flagler's Florida East Coast Railroad that ran down the East Coast of Florida.

The jelly was available in several of the general stores in Micanopy, but the McCredies liked to visit the Smith farm and see the jelly being made. In growing his guavas, Smith had mastered the problems of drought and cold weather. He grew the small trees inside wooden enclosures that had removable roofs. In the winter he heated the areas with small stoves and during dry spells he irrigated the areas with water stored in tanks that were kept filled from windmills.

Smith bought sugar by the barrel and cooked his guava mixture in copper boilers but he never revealed his recipe. Betty had discussed the secret with Martha Smith, his wife, but she just shrugged her shoulders and said, "I don't know what he puts in it. He won't even tell me."

Betty was sure the recipe contained more than just guava juice and sugar. "It's got a rare flavor that makes it different than any guava jelly I've ever tasted," she told James on the way to the Smith farm. "The jelly Addie made and sent us from Umatilla last year had a different taste, not as sweet and it had a stronger, wild taste." Addie had married Richard Fillmore Rice in July of 1892 and moved to Umatilla where she and her husband were in the hotel business.

In late 1894 the Gainesville, Rocky Point and Micanopy Railroad had begun a drive to acquire right–of–way lands for a railroad into Micanopy from Gainesville and James had sold the line a sixty–foot strip through the heart of his property for a hundred and twenty–five dollars. Other Micanopians did the same to get the twelve miles of railroad from Gainesville to Micanopy. The effort to obtain the railroad had been going on for ten years with little success.

After the freeze, James told his brothers, "We don't need the railroad now. There are no oranges to ship."

"That's short–sighted," said John. "You forget that vegetable crops from this area must go out in refrigerated cars, and the value of those crops is far more than your citrus. We need the railroad."

"The railroad charter's been sold to the Gainesville and Gulf people," Thomas added, "and they seem to mean business. I think we'll soon have a new railroad."

Thomas was right. The railroad was built in 1895 and operated under the name Gainesville & Gulf. Between 1883 and 1895, Micanopy had been served by a spur track from the main line of the Florida Southern Railroad. When Florida Southern extended its Line from Gainesville to Tampa, it would have passed through Micanopy, except that a few citizens made such a fuss about the noise and dirty smoke created by a train that the town ended by refusing to grant Florida Southern a right of way.

The only option left for the shippers was a three and a quarter mile spur line on which the trains entered Micanopy from the east and on leaving had to back all the way to the main line, where a freight depot had been built and came to be called "Micanopy Junction."

Eventually, Micanopy had a fine passenger depot on the western end of the spur line. That depot was modern with loading platforms, waiting rooms and telegraph and ticket offices.

The arrival of the Gainesville and Gulf Railroad in 1895 was considered to be a good business omen and was cause for a large celebration. Special trains, gaily decorated with bunting and flags, ran between the two towns all day carrying city and town officials. Speeches and a barbecue in each town and fireworks in the evening added to the general merriment.

In Marion County, the citrus tragedy was offset somewhat by the largest timber contract ever let in all of Florida. Mr. W. N. Smith of Saginaw, Michigan, had made a million dollar contract with the Wilson Cypress Lumber Company to get out about two hundred million feet of cypress logs, for which Mr. Smith would receive five dollars a thousand feet. It was estimated that along the Ocklawaha River and Silver Springs Run there were more than two–hundred and fifty–million feet of cypress.

"I can get a dollar a day over there helping to get out those logs," James told Betty. "I'd be home on weekends."

This was in September of 1895. Betty shook her head. "No. I want you here. We can make out. Besides, Mary Ella is carrying our first grandchild. She told me today."

"How can you keep such a secret," James exclaimed. "Why didn't you tell me?"

"I just did," Betty smiled. "I have a feeling 1896 will be a fine year."

What "tomorrow brought" in 1896 was trouble–bad trouble. Dr. Lucius Montgomery had said that Mary Ella's baby would come into the world around the middle of May but by late March it was evident that the birth could be complicated. Doctor Montgomery was worried about Mary Ella and told Betty and James about his fears.

"She's weak and running a fever," he told them. "I can't seem to stop her decline. Force her to eat more and get her out in the open. She must regain her strength."

By the first of May, Mary Ella was bed–ridden, ran fever most of the days and complained of a burning pain when she used the chamber pot. Doctor Montgomery was deeply concerned about his patient.

"It's her kidneys," he told the parents. "They're about gone. It's going to be a race to get the baby into the world before she's too far gone."

Betty grasped him by the arm.

"Lucius Montgomery," she said, "are you tellin' us that she's about to die before that child can be born?"

Lucius Montgomery nodded glumly.

"Oh my God," Betty cried. "Mary Ella's our first born You can't let her die. Isn't there something we can do, and what about the child?"

Doctor Montgomery's face was still glum. "I'll do everything I can to save them both, but you'll have to do your part. Keep her hopeful—and fighting."

The McCredies rallied around the stricken family. Prayers were said in the Micanopy churches since Mary Ella was one of the most liked young married women in town.

"Prayers won't do any good," James said. "Our Lord Jesus doesn't work that way. He gave us healing powers within ourselves and until we unlock those secrets people will die."

"James McCredie, how can you say such a thing," Betty said indignantly. "With all the prayers being said, there's a power in the wind that will work wonders. You'll see."

"No," James said sadly, "We don't know enough yet about how to save our loved ones, but in time we'll have the knowledge."

In the end Betty came to believe as did her mother–in–law, who said, "What is to be will be and the hand of man cannot change God's design for us."

Mary Ella continued to fight until she went into labor on May 22nd and delivered her child, a healthy boy, then she gasped her last breath as her life's blood poured from her birth canal while her young husband wept quietly in one comer of the darkened room and James and Betty knelt at the foot of the bed, clutched in one another's arms. Doctor Montgomery labored to stop the blood but to no avail.

Despite the fact that store–bought coffins were available at J. L. Patton & Co, in Micanopy, James worked through the night to fashion a sturdy cypress box for his daughter and Betty lined it with satin padded with cotton. "Mary Ella favored pink," she said softly. "If the regular order of things had taken place," she told James, "Mary Ella would of been laying me out in the course of her life. It shouldn't happen this way." She covered her face with her gingham apron and fled into the house.

"Poor Lass," James said "She paid dearly for a grandchild."

James brought two sawhorses into the parlor from his work shed and draped them with black velvet. The coffin, tapered at the head and foot with newly polished brass handles, shone like pecan wood in the candle light of the semi–darkened room. Little Lorna Doone didn't understand why but she imitated the rest of the family as they walked softly in the house and whispered to one another.

The next day, Mary Ella was laid to rest in the McCredie plot in the Micanopy Cemetery near David and Janet. The cemetery dated back to 1826.

Will Cooper remained at the home of his mother and father–in–law and Betty added the new baby William to her responsibilities, as if the grandchild were a new baby of her own.

Following Mary Ella's death, James became more protective than ever of Lorna Doone. His Addie had married and moved away, Mary Ella was now gone and he seemed in mortal fear of losing his youngest daughter. She went everywhere he went except when he worked at carpentering.

"I'm beginning to feel sorry for Lorna," Betty told Julia. "When she gets to courting and marrying age, I fear James won't let a boy near her."

Julia laughed. "Don't you fret none about that. Girls in love can handle fathers. You didn't let your father keep you away from James."

"That's true," Betty agreed, "but you don't know James." "I've never seen a father like him. I'll have to help her out when the time comes, even if James turns against me."

She sighed. "I wouldn't like that."

The days went quickly and soon 1896 turned to '97, then '98. James' grove was beginning to look green again. "I believe we'll get fruit, maybe enough to ship before the century goes out," he told John.

"There's another bad freeze predicted for this winter," John said. "If that comes you can tell your fruit goodbye. Better get into truck crops like I been tellin' you."

"No, these bad freezes don't come back that soon."

James was wrong. The winter was a bad one with some hard freezes before Christmas and he had to fire his citrus to keep down the damage. After the new year the weather moderated and James told Betty, "We'll have an early spring. I feel it in my bones."

Betty laughed. “Don’t put too much faith in bones. You said yourself your bones are beginning to get old. Maybe they don’t predict the weather so good anymore.”

In February there was a repeat of 1895. During the afternoon of the 12th a cold rain began to fall. By 8:30 p.m. the rain had turned to sleet that rattled on the roofs and porches. *The Gainesville Sun* published a play–by–play description of how this “unusual” weather came to that city.

“This (the sleet) lasted until ten thirty, when it began to snow. At first the flakes were fine, but in a very few moments the flakes had become large and were falling thick and fast.”

“There were a number of people in the office of the Brown House who witnessed the sight as the snow was falling from under the electric light. So thick were the large flakes descending that the large globe of the bright street lamp was completely hidden from view. The wind was blowing strong, and the snow was sent flying through the air in every direction. Most people had retired for the night but not a few arose and witnessed the sight of the snow falling so thick and fast in what was once termed the ‘Land of Flowers and Perpetual Sunshine.’”

“The storm ceased about 2:30 a.m. and during the short time it lasted the fall was about an inch and a half, allowing for that which had fallen and melted after it struck the damp ground.”

“In the morning everything was white, and, with the icicles hanging from the eaves of the buildings, gave the country the appearance of a landscape where winter abounds in earnest for several months of the year. The biting void which prevailed did not serve to draw from any of the material features of the wintry picture.”

“The ground where sleet had fallen, and where the wind had relieved it of snow, was covered with ice, and it was with difficulty that people walked upon the street.”

“Most of them were never accustomed to walking upon ice, and were as awkward, as the saying goes, ‘as a hog on ice’.”

James had determined during the afternoon that he was going to fight to save his returning grove. Old Moses came over with his entire family to help. Betty and James and all the children still at home hauled pine knots and piled them throughout the grove. By the time the thermometer stood at freezing they had hot fires going. They worked through the night, and on into the next day.

In Pensacola the newspapers reported an official low of six and eight tenths degrees, and said some thermometers "on the Hill" had registered one degree below zero. Jacksonville reported a low often degrees.

They saved the grove, but James knew with a heavy heart that he would not have citrus to ship before the turn of the century.

When the danger was over, Betty asked, "What are you going to do now?"

"Keep working with the grove. It's my life."

"But," Betty argued, "they're saying that we're in a new weather cycle. This can happen year after year, for the next ten years maybe."

Lorna Doone grew up under the watchful eye of her father. When she entered school in 1899, he insisted on taking her to the Schoolhouse in his buggy and sat there in the lane until the bell rang and the children were inside.

The other children walked to school. James explained that Lorna was too young to walk "such a distance," although he justified the walking for his other children by saying they were older and stronger and "needed the exercise."

In fact, the Schoolhouse was less than a mile from the McCredie home.

"You're going to make that child the laughing stock of the school," Betty told James. "No one rides to school. She'll be teased about being 'daddy's Utile baby'."

Betty was right. Lorna put a stop to the rides one day by telling her father she was "tired of riding."

The truth was that she had been called "the Princess who rides in her pumpkin coach."

One cold day in November, Lorna's brother Norman, arrived at the school just before lunch time so breathless he could barley talk. He had run all the way from the McCredie house to the school. The teacher looked at his flushed face and excited eyes and exclaimed, "Why Norman, what are you doing here? You're supposed to be in bed with a fever."

"Our house, it's burning up!" Norman gasped. "I come to fetch Lorna."

That ended school for the day. Miss Williams dismissed all the children and took Lorna and Norman home in her buggy.

As they entered the lane they could see smoke and hear the shouts and the crackling of the pine boards, rich in rosin and pine tar. Most of Micanopy was there and folks kept dashing into the burning building to get pieces of furniture, pictures, bedding and anything that could be carried out. Just about everything the James McCredies owned was piled up in the yard.

Bucket brigades had been formed to carry water from the well to the burning house but it was like trying to put out a woods fire with thimbles of water. By mid–afternoon, Betty's pride and joy, the home James had built for her, the place where all her children had been born, was a pile of charred timbers and ashes.

Only the day before she complained to James about the roaches. "The horrible little beasts," she called them. "If only we could kill them all!"

James looked at the remains of his home and then at Betty, sitting on a cowhide chair from their front porch. "You got your wish," he told her. "We got rid of the roaches."

She looked up at his singed hair and blackened face and the reality of the situation was too much for her. She burst into tears. "James, what will we do?" she asked. "The cold took our grove and now fire has destroyed our home. There's nothing left."

James put his arms around her. "Come, now, Lass," he said. "I'll build you another house, as fancy as you like. "He grinned wryly." The best house in the County."

"I don't want another house, fancy or not." Betty sobbed. "This house had memories. I want one just like it."

"That's what you'll have, then," James said. "Another house just like the old one—and that's what he built, with John's help and the help of his sons. They moved in early in the new century."

8

Lorna Doone

During the building of the house, James became aware for the first time that John was getting old. His older brother had difficulty climbing the ladder to the roof when it came time to put on the sheets of tin.

"You better let me an' the boys do this," he told John. "Mean' you been through too much for me to lose you on a rooftop."

"Hah," John retorted, "I kin work on as high a roof as you any time you say, little brother," and went on pounding nails.

James told Betty his fears that night. "He's really got no business on that slippery tin that far off the ground."

"I'm afraid for both of you," Betty said. "He's going on seventy–two and you're no spring chicken. You both should stay on the ground. I'm surprised Julia hasn't laid down the law for him."

"She's got her hands full trying to get him to stop drinkin' so much," James said. "That's the other problem. He came to the job the other mornin' half drunk and without sleep. Been up practically all night drinkin' with his bunch down at Buck's place in town."

"Can't you do something about that?" Betty asked.

James laughed. "You know better'n that He still looks on me as his kid brother. Besides, he doesn't think he drinks much, no more'n a good Scotch highlander ought to drink."

"You Scottish Highlandets!" Betty said. "You're all alike. You like your jug by the fire in the evenin' same as John."

"I can still take care of you," James said, moving from his side of the bed and taking Betty in his arms. That ended further conversation.

The house was finished, and, thanks to John, it had all kinds of pretty carving along the eaves, up and down the stairways and around the fireplaces, but it took a mild heart attack and Doctor Montgomery's stern warning to make John stop his drinking.

"I don't know why he'd listen to old Doc Montgomery bout drinkin' too much," Julia said. "That old man don't practice his own medicine. He's the scandal of Micanopy an' all Marion and Alachua Counties."

It was true that Doctor Montgomery was one of John's drinking companions and there were times when the old doctor would come tearing down main street on a Saturday night, as naked as a jay bird, riding his bay bareback and firing a horse pistol in each hand. When he had used up all his bullets, the marshal and some of the town boys would close in on him, put a coat around him and carry him off to jail to remain until he was sober enough for them to take him home.

This frequent event was a source of considerable pain and conversation at the ladies' meetings at the Presbyterian Church, and the church officers were under considerable pressure to haul the offender before them and, if necessary, expel him from the church. There was one problem, however, Doctor Montgomery was a member of the Session, a founding member at that, an Elder and a heavy contributor to the financial support of the church, so the town, the ladies and the church members bore their burden with great resolution, spoke of it in whispers and tried to pretend to outsiders that there was no problem at all.

Be that as it may, John McCredie stopped his drinking, to Julia's delight, and the relief of other members of the family, but it was clear to all that he was not a happy, contented man. He went through the motions of farming and his crops turned out well but there seemed to be no joy in his life.

James asked him one day, “Are you sorry you came to Florida? Would you have been more content in the old country?”

John looked at his brother with searching eyes. “What makes you think I’m not content here?”

“Well, I dunno. You seem to be in a kind of shell, like a turtle that has pulled his head in—for good.”

John looked at the ground, which was not his way. He always looked a man in the eye when he spoke. “It’s just…” He stopped.

“Just what?” James asked, when John didn’t go on. “Is it Julia? You and Julia having problems?”

John looked up and smiled. “Me and Julia are fine. She’s the best thing in my life. I just hope I go before she does. I don’t think I would want to live, have the heart to go on, if she died before me. No, no it’s not Julia.”

“What then?”

John laughed and clapped his brother on the back. “Just feeling my age, I reckon.” And that was all he would say.

Julia had another explanation.

“He thinks he’s not goin’ to live much longer, and he sits around thinking of the failures in his life, the loss of some of our children, theft of his money, things like that. He lets a lot of the past weigh too heavily on his mind.”

“What can we do?” James asked her.

“Remind him of his fine family, his skill as a carpenter and cabinet maker and all the fine buildings he has in Micanopy and all over Alachua and Marion Counties. Remind him of his successes.”

One Saturday, John hitched up a two–wheeled cart to go into Micanopy for some supplies. Julia called out, “John stop at Mathers and get me a bottle of wine.”

While it was true that John had stopped drinking, Julia had been told by her doctor that a little wine at night would help her sleep better. John waved to her and drove on down the lane to the main road into town. Sundown came and he had not returned, but Julia was not concerned. She knew he would be along any minute. It had happened before, but when bedtime came and he had not shown up, she became alarmed. She called to her eldest son. "John, you and Walter hitch up the buggy. We've got to go look for your father. I know something has happened to him."

After instructing Walter to remain with her youngest son, Hugh Hawthorne, Julia climbed in the wagon with her lantern. About a quarter of a mile from the house, where the road made a sharp turn, they saw the horse and cart just off the road, but the cart was empty. Julia felt faint and clutched at her breast. Her heart was beating violently, like a frightened bird trying to escape from a cage. "I knew something had happened," she told her son. "I'm afraid he's dead."

"We don't know that," John said "Calm down and I'll look around."

She watched as the lantern moved along the road, spreading a circle of yellow light in the dark woods. Soon John called out, "I've found him. He's alive!"

Julia drove the buggy to the spot where John stood with his lantern. There she saw her husband, lying on the ground at the side of the curve. The smell of whiskey was strong in the night air.

"He's all right," John said. "He had too much to drink in town and when the buggy rounded that curve, he fell out. I'll get him in the buggy."

"No you don't," Julia said. "Leave him right there. Let's go back to the house."

John protested, but Julia's fear had turned to cold anger. At the house she gave her son a quilt. "You go back and cover him with this, and bring his cart and put his horse in the barn," she said.

Soon after daylight the next morning, while Julia was cooking breakfast, she saw her husband come into the yard, the quilt wrapped around his shoulders. He looked bad. One side of his face was bloody where he had struck a root when he hit the ground and his clothing was torn and spotted with blood. The smell of whiskey was still strong around him.

When he entered the kitchen, Julia went on with her work without looking at him, or speaking. After a minute or two of silence, John spoke, "Well, I guess I done it last night," he said.

Julia turned around. "John, I want to know just one thing. Did you start drinking again because I asked you to bring me that bottle of wine?"

Her husband shook his head. "No," he said, "I just stood it about as long as I could. I had one drink, and that led to another and another."

Julia walked over and took John by the shoulders and looked him in the eye. "I don't have many years left to live," she told him. "And I want to live them in peace."

From that day on John McCredie never took another drink of anything alcoholic for the remainder of his life.

At one of the McCredie family gatherings at John and Julia's farm, Julia told James and Betty that John worried too much for his own good—and hers. "He sets in that cowhide rocker on the porch and worries about his palm trees an' the fact he's seventy–two and has no grandchildren," she said.

"He keeps asking, 'Who's gonna take care of them palm trees when I'm gone, 'and,' Who's gonna carry on my family line if I don't get any grandchildren'."

"James, you know how he's babied them palm trees. He likes to look at them waving in the wind with their palm cabbages at the top, an' he wouldn't eat one for the world. He'll walk all through the woods to find a palm cabbage for supper when he's got a yard full of them."

"If he cut one of the cabbages in the yard, it'd kill the tree," James said.

"I know that," Julia said, "an I guess he'd rather cut off his right arm."

Margaret Elizabeth, John's third daughter, born at Lady Lake, Florida, on January 22nd, 1879, got a head start on the grandchild problem when she ran away and married Claude Newberry on August 24th, 1903, but her first child was born in Ensley, Alabama, in April of 1906. That brought on new problems. John wanted to see his granddaughter, Margaret Helen, "before he died," he said, but there was no money for the long train trip to Alabama and the newly–married couple had no money for the trip to Florida.

"They might just as well be living in Scotland," John said.

And then, he would begin to cry.

Julia said they could go to Alabama. John had plenty of money in his cash box. And there was land aplenty to sell if he'd just make up his mind. "Truth of the matter," she said, "is he don't want to leave this place. He's about to aggravate me to death."

Mid–1907, Julia moved John into Ocala where he could get immediate medical attention. The farm was rented—and that was like cutting John's heart out. "He won't last long," James told Betty. "That farm was more than just a home. It was his life. It was his dream. I can remember back in Scotland when we were boys, workin' on some rich man's farm, practically as slaves, John would sift a handful of soil through his fingers and tell me, 'I'm gonna have land like this some day—as far as my eyes kin see'."

James stopped and Betty could see his eyes moistened with his own tears. She put her hand on his arm and he continued, "Julia says he isn't right in the head, but his mind is clear as a June morning. He's got a broke heart, that's what"

All through December, John kept telling Julia he wanted to go home.

"You're home here," she told him. "This is our home now."

"I want to see the farm one more time," he pleaded, and toward Christmas she agreed to take him. They rode the train to Micanopy and borrowed one of James' buggies to drive out to their old place on the prairie. That was a mistake.

As they drove up to the gate, John took one look and began to cry and swear at the same time. The fence was down in places, the gate was sagging, and the neatly swept front–yard with the flowers that Julia had nurtured was no more. Weeds had taken charge. And then, the worst blow, "By damn, they've killed my palm trees," John cried.

The palm trees were dead, killed when the heart of palm had been chopped from their crowns.

Julia just turned the buggy around and hurried back to Micanopy. John cried and cursed the renters of his property all the way back.

Despite his depression, John's appetite was always good. He ate a hearty supper on the night of January 28th, 1908, and then retired to the living room where he could sit by the fire and read his newspaper. But when Julia came into the room he was pressing on his right side and his face was contorted with pain.

"What's the matter, John?" she asked.

"It's nothing," he replied. "Just some indigestion. Ate too much, I reckon."

Those were his last words.

When the news reached Micanopy, the report was that he had died of "acute indigestion," but James knew better. "It was his heart," he told Betty, and then he hurried out the kitchen door to walk in his orange grove. She watched him as he walked, shading his eyes against the rising sun. She knew he was hurting, and there was nothing she could do to help.

Between the turn of the century and John McCredie's death in 1908, many changes occurred that cast long shadows across Alachua and Marion Counties, shadows that gave only a hint of what the future held for the areas, as well as all Florida.

In 1903, the Florida State Legislature passed laws that brought a form of prohibition to the Counties. The sale of alcoholic beverages had to be licensed and all unlicensed sales were illegal, subject to fine and imprisonment for the seller. In Gainesville, the first arrest of this kind was of a barber, caught selling a bottle of gin in an alley behind his barber shop on Union Street. An Alachua County ordinance provided an award of fifty dollars for any person assisting in the arrest and conviction of anyone caught selling whiskey illegally.

In Micanopy, Mayor J. H. Prater presided at a citizens' meeting at the Baptist Church to allow citizens to express their sentiments about enforcement of the liquor laws in Precinct Ten. A committee was appointed to draft a strong resolution supporting the authorities. The committee was chaired by Dr. Lucius Montgomery with members Dr. Watkins and the Rev. Mr. Milne. This was on June 16th, 1903.

If you find Dr. Montgomery's connection with such a committee surprising, you need to know that after he fell off his horse on a Saturday night, nearly killing himself, he denounced John Barleycorn as "an instrument of the devil," and became a staid and sober citizen, a leader in the prohibition movement.

"He's going to dry up this entire County so I can't take a drop of toddy by the fire of an evenin' in my old age," James complained.

"And a good thing, too," Betty said.

Dr. Montgomery's committee submitted a resolution that added an additional twenty–five dollars to the award for the arrest and conviction of the illegal whiskey sellers. The resolution was adopted unanimously.

"I'll bet old Lucius is gonna pay that extra twenty–five dollars out of his own pocket," James concluded.

Without doubt Dr. Lucius Montgomery was Micanopy's most colorful, wealthy and leading citizen. In 1883, Charles H. (Carl) Webber, a journalist who gave his northern address as Salem, Massachusetts, and his southern address as Gainesville, Florida, had written:

"Dr. Montgomery's residence is doubtless the finest in town. It is two stories high, with a two–story cupola, and is built in the finest style of architecture, with every convenience for pleasure and comfort. The house is surrounded with orange groves. The doctor is one of the most enterprising men of Micanopy. He has several groves in the County. He came to Florida from St. Louis in 1868, and purchased land in Orange County, fronting on the St. Johns River. During the next two years he went prospecting all over South Florida. Of all places he found Alachua County to be the best in quality of soil, purity of water and healthfulness. The adaptability of this section being so fine for orange growing and agricultural purposes, he sold out his possessions in Orange County and settled at Micanopy."

James and John McCredie admired the Montgomery residence since they had helped build it.

Dr. Montgomery was the first grower in the Micanopy area to ship a carload of citrus fruit after the great freezes of 1895 and 1899. That was in

1901. As a farmer, he had many interests. Adjoining his home was a cotton gin and a grist mill, both run by steam power. He had cattle and five hundred head of poultry, so healthy that the dreaded cholera had struck his flock only twice in fifteen years. From his dairy herd came some of the richest butter in the area. At Kirkwood, near Levy Lake, he had eight hundred acres of orange trees and forty acres planted to oranges on Alachua Lake and another large grove northeast of Micanopy, out John McCredie's way.

Best of all, as far as Dr. Montgomery was concerned, his son, H. L. Montgomery, a student in Atlanta at the Atlanta Medical College, would graduate in 1904 and return to Micanopy to practice with his father. That would leave the doctor more time for his other pursuits, farming, citrus growing and politics.

As a physician, Dr. Montgomery was known throughout medical circles in Florida and elsewhere, primarily through his handbook on practical steps to take in all kinds of illnesses and afflictions, including medications that would speed recovery.

In 1903 electric power had become a major concern. Two men, W. N. Camp, owner of Payne's Prairie, and James M. Graham, and "other capitalists," the *Gainesville Sun* reported, conceived the idea of building a dam around Alachua Lake so that a controlled flow of water into Alachua Sink could be used to provide water power that would develop one–thousand horsepower to generate enough electricity to light the city of Gainesville.

"What an idea!" James McCredie told his wife. "Why, wires could be run into Micanopy and give us all electric lights."

"I don't understand this thing," Betty said. "Where would the water power come from? I thought you had to have a waterfall to make power by water."

"That's what they plan to do, make a waterfall," James explained. "As the water from the lake pours over the rim of the sink it will fall more than seventy–five feet and turn wheels to make electricity."

The entire plan was elaborate. Alachua Sink would be made into a resort with clubhouses and a pavilion and an electric railway was planned to go over the entire city and provide a belt line service to the resort area.

The dam was built, but despite all the expert engineering advice that the project would be successful, no electric power was ever generated at Alachua Sink.

Citrus culture in the Micanopy area continued to produce fruit but never to the extent known before the great freezes. The industry began to move farther south in the state, seeking a climate more favorable to the cold–vulnerable oranges, lemons and grapefruit. With the exception of a few men like James McCredie, farmers turned to truck crops and refrigerated carloads of vegetables moved from sidings along the Gainesville and Gulf Railroad in an unending stream during late spring and early summer each year.

The Gainesville and Gulf Railroad was built by V. J. Herlong along a forty–eight–mile right of way from Samson City in the north to Fairfield to the south, through miles of rich farmland known for its celery, beans, squash, tomatoes, cucumbers, eggplants, field peas, lettuce, sweet corn, cantaloupes and watermelons. The majority of the railroad's stock, seven–hundred and fifty shares, was acquired by John J. Barr of Micanopy in 1903 at a cost of twenty–five–thousand dollars, and V. J. Herlong retired from the railroad business. Later the railroad was called the T, and J., for Tampa and Jacksonville, although the road never went to either of those cities.

The McCredies rode the Gainesville and Gulf on occasion from Micanopy into Gainesville, a distance of nearly twenty miles around the western edge of Payne's Prairie. The journey took an hour and ten minutes, according to the schedule, but with stops to drop off and pickup freight cars, the trip took longer.

"You'll have time to pick some blackberries at some of the stops," James told a friend about to take the journey.

The stops between Gainesville and Micanopy bore names like Minnie Hill, Cannon's Crossing, Rocky Point, Wacahoota, Flewellen, Clyatt's Station, Kirkwood, Elmore, Tacoma, Taylor's at Lake Wauburg and then Micanopy.

Passengers often rode in a boxcar with wooden benches for seats, in later years. The early trains consisted of one or two passenger coaches on the end of a string of boxcars.

James and Betty occasionally rode the Gainesville and Gulf out to Kirkwood to visit the Abner and Susie Emerson family, long–time friends, but in late February of 1905, they drove a buggy out to meet R. B. Dean of Anderson, South Carolina, a seventy–year–old relative of Susie Emerson who was visiting at the farm for a few weeks to escape the colder weather in South Carolina.

"You must stay for supper," Susie exclaimed when they arrived. "We'll have some fresh trout. Roy took Mr. Dean to the Underhill Place on Levy Lake. He always brings back a good mess of fish when he goes there."

During the afternoon Abner and James inspected the newly planted acres along the lake while Betty and Susie peeled potatoes for potato salad, made plans for the next meeting of the Presbyterian church women and set the table for supper. About 5 o'clock, Susie began to watch the lane leading to the house for signs of her son, Roy, and their guest. "They'd better be getting back here," she said. "There's fish to clean and fry."

At 6 o'clock, when James and Abner came in, she showed her concern. "Somethin's happened," she said. "Roy always worries me when he goes out in a boat. Neither one of them kin swim."

"Now, that's downright foolish talk," Abner told his wife. "That lake ain't deep enough to drown anyone but a midget, but me and James will drive over that way and see what's holdin' them up."

At the lake they found the cypress rowboat full of water but still floating near the shore. The Emerson horse and wagon was tied to a tree.

There was no sign of Roy or Mr. Dean.

Abner put his head in his hands. He was shaking all over. "James, I'm afraid Susie was right. I believe something awful has happened," he said. "We'd better go for help."

"I believe we'd better," James agreed.

By 8 o'clock, more than a dozen farmers with lanterns and more boats in their wagons had arrived to drag the lake with chains and logging hooks. Betty remained with Susie and tried to convince her that the men were somewhere around the lake shore and would be found alive and well.

"Abner said the lake was not deep enough to drown a full–grown man," she told Susie. "You remember that?"

"I remember," Susie said, "but Abner's wrong. The lake has a lot of deep holes."

The bodies were found around midnight in about six feet of water, not more than a few yards from shore.

"There's a broke fishin' pole in the boat," one of the farmers said. "Looks like Mr. Dean was tryin' to land a big fish that broke his pole and he fell in.

That might have thrown Roy in too, or Roy might have jumped overboard to help Mr. Dean. I dunno. It's plumb senseless."

The drowning was more than the loss of a beloved son and a relative for the Emersons. Roy, at twenty years of age, was a major helper for Abner on the farm.

After his brother John's death, James McCredie had two obsessions, a belief that his own death was not far away and a fear that his darling Lorna Doone would marry some no count scallywag, perhaps even a Yankee. James had no dislike for Yankees but he didn't want his daughter to marry one. Concerning his impending death, Betty scoffed at the idea. "James McCredie, you're gettin' to be an old worry wart," she said. "You 're as healthy and strong as a full–grown ox. I don't want to hear any more talk about you passing away."

James held out his right hand. "See that lifeline," he said. "It's all broken, don't go nowhere. You know what that Gypsy fortune teller told me last summer. She said I'd have a short life."

Betty put her arms around her husband and looked him straight in the eyes. "If you believe the Gypsies you're sure addled in the brain. Now, I love you and you' re gonna stay right here on this good earth as long as I'm around. You hear that?" She kissed him and then went to the kitchen to cook breakfast.

She had few of her children to feed. Fred had married Maude Johnson in 1901 and moved to Umatilla where the couple ran a large boarding house. Thomas, called "Tip," had moved to Jacksonville where he was working for a furniture store owner and was writing letters home about the beauty and virtues of a Kate Bowden. James, called "Jim," was in the furniture business in Tampa and serious about a girl named Ada Floyd. Only sons Jake and Norman were at home. Jake showed all the signs of being a bachelor but Norman was making frequent trips to Bamberg, South Carolina, to see a Maude Davis.

That left Lorna Doone, age sixteen, fun loving, popular, a dark–haired beauty who had the attention of every gay young blade in the County. "Not a one of em worth the powder it'd take to blow em up," James said. "I'm gonna have to keep her shut up in her room or keep a loaded shotgun to drive em away. All any of em can do is pluck on a banjo an' look at her like a dying calf."

"Has it been so long ago you don't remember how you looked at me?" Betty teased him.

"That was different," James mumbled.

Then came Micanopy's big day as its citizens hosted the opening day of the 1908 political campaign with an all–day speaking and barbecue on the shores of Lake Tuscawilla. Businesses and schools closed as more than fifteen hundred gathered from Alachua and surrounding Counties to hear gubernatorial candidates. Gen. Albert W. Gilchrist and Frank Stockton, and candidates for the U.S. Senate, Governor N. B. Broward and Duncan U. Fletcher. Frank Stockton was not present, but Dr. Lucius Montgomery spoke for him, denouncing General Gilchrist as being a "whiskey man."

The speaking halted at noon for dinner of barbecued beef, pork and mutton and quantities of turkey and chicken as well as basket dinners prepared by the Micanopy ladies. All the barbecued meat was prepared by Micanopy's Uncle Joe Shannon who was known throughout the County for his barbecues, prepared with his secret sauces.

All the McCredies were on hand although James paid scant attention to the speakers as he kept a sharp eye on Lorna. Even so he missed what turned out to be, for his family, the most important event of the day.

Lorna was assisting her mother and other Micanopy ladies in handing out the dinner baskets when she saw him.

She had a feeling that someone was watching her and when she looked around her eyes locked on his. She suddenly felt a little dizzy, but she was aware that he had a round, gentle face, jet black eyes that were as soft and smiling as a young doe. His face was tanned from constant exposure to the outdoors. She assumed that he was a farm boy.

Lorna dropped her eyes before his gaze and he noted with pleasure the touch of pink that mounted from her throat to her high cheek bones. "Could she be part Indian?" he wondered, but he was convinced she was the loveliest creature he had ever seen.

During the rest of the dinner, Lorna glanced at the young man every now and then, when she thought she could catch him unawares, but each time she found his gaze fastened on her. She began to feel silly and a bit angry. "Who does he think he is?" she said to herself, "looking at me like that? Am I some kind of cow?"

She pointed him out to a number of her girl friends. No one knew him. "Can't be from around here," they all said.

The afternoon speaking began at 2 o'clock so Lorna took advantage of the commotion to escape her father's watchful eye. She began to look for the young man to confront him and demand to know why he stared at her so. She found him sitting with his back to the crowd under a large oak tree, his eyes gazing across the lake. Although Lorna was a shy person her curiosity and some other force she didn't understand drove her to walk up to the dreamy–eyed man and say, bluntly, "Why were you staring at me all during dinner?"

The young man stumbled to his feet, almost falling in the lake. He looked so startled and confused Lorna began to laugh. "I do believe you're embarrassed," she said.

Now that she felt in command of the situation and had this stranger at a disadvantage, she was no longer angry.

"I'm Lorna McCredie," she said. "What's your name?"

He could only look at her, his face flaming red, like a little boy caught stealing a puff on a home made cigarette of rabbit tobacco behind the bam.

"You can talk, can't you?" she asked, "or, maybe you were thinking so hard about your girl friend you didn't realize you were staring at me. Is that it?"

"I was looking at you," he said finally. "You're the most beautiful girl I ever saw. I've been sitting here daydreaming about you."

Now, it was Lorna's turn to be off guard. Her only recourse was to run. "Well, I never," she said, and ran off toward the safety of the crowd.

"Wait, come back," he called after her, but she kept running. It was not until she reached her family's side that she realized she had not learned his name.

James looked at her suspiciously. "What have you been up to?" he wanted to know.

"Nothing," she said, "just walking around."

"You don't get red–faced and out of breath from just walking around. Some boy after you?"

"No, Sir, I was just skipping along."

About this time the Honorable Christopher Matheson, Gainesville's mayor, announced that the trains for Gainesville would be departing soon and the Gainesville delegation of about two–hundred persons would have to leave for the station. And so the incident was over, but Lorna was haunted by the memory of this person she began to think of as "her mystery man."

She had a feeling all week that something had changed in her life. She knew she wanted to see him again and regretted that she had run away. She was not usually so cowardly. She thought, "Maybe he'll come lookin' for me, the way he was makin' eyes my way." She was right about that.

The following Sunday afternoon she and Norman were sitting on the front porch, letting their dinner settle and enjoying a perfect May day. The jasmine on the trellis at the end of the porch was in full bloom and the clear air was heavy with perfume. The air overhead was a blue dome without a cloud and the day was so bright it shone like a diamond. Then, she saw him.

He came swinging up the lane in a little buggy drawn by a Morgan horse that stepped along as proud as if it were in a Christmas parade. The driver was wearing a dark, tight–fitting suit and a straw hat, the suit probably was a hand–me–down since it fit so poorly, Lorna thought, but her heart was beating wildly just the same, as though he had come in shining armor on a huge white horse.

"Who could that be?" Norman thought out loud.

"Just a boy I met at the barbecue," Lorna told him.

"What's his name?" Norman asked.

"I didn't get his name?"

"You don't even know his name and he's calling on you. Papa'll skin you alive."

By this time the young man in the ill–fitting suit had hitched his rig to the gate post and was walking up to the porch, his hat in hand.

He smiled. "Remember me?"

"Yes," Lorna said, "but I never did get your name."

"I know," he said. "You ran away so fast I didn't get a chance to tell you." "I'm Paul Jones. Live out on the Gainesville road near Wacahoota."

Norman came forward, holding out his hand. "I'm Norman McCredie, Lorna's brother. So, she ran away, eh. Doesn't sound like her. She usually runs after boys."

"Oh, you," Lorna said, slapping at her brother. "Ignore him, Paul. He never tells the truth."

During all this the McCredie dogs were disturbed by the stranger and were running up and down in their pen, barking and taking on so that James and Betty came into the front yard to see what was going on. When Lorna saw them her heart sank. She didn't know what her father would do. She was not long in finding out.

"Who is this young m an?" he asked coldly.

"Daddy, Mama, this is Paul Jones. He lives out Wacahoota way. I met him at the barbecue."

Paul came forward to shake hands but James' hand was not extended for a handshake. "It's such a nice day," Paul said. "I came to see if Lorna could go for a drive."

"No, she can't," James said curtly. "If you want to talk to her you can do it right here. We don't know anything about you."

Betty turned and walked toward the porch. When she reached the front door, she called her husband. "Mr. McCredie, I need you inside for a moment."

This startled James, Norman and Lorna. They had never heard her call her husband "Mr. McCredie." They knew she was angry.

James immediately went inside and Lorna apologized to Paul for her father's actions. "Don't be upset with him," she said. "He still thinks I'm his little girl, the last one at home, and he's that way with all the boys who come calling."

Norman said he was going to saddle his horse and take a ride down to the lake. Lorna invited Paul to sit with her in the swing beneath the grape arbor.

When they were alone, Paul asked, "Lot of boys come calling on you?"

"Some," she said, as if she really meant a lot, "but Daddy has run most of them off."

"You like any of them specially?" he wanted to know.

"Maybe," she replied, teasing him.

"Will you tell me I have a chance," he pleaded.

"Maybe," she said, but her eyes said, "Yes."

"I'd like to call on you regular," Paul said. "Will that be all right?"

"It's all right with me, but you'll have to ask Papa about that," Lorna said.

"Oh no," Paul said. "I don't want to go through that again. He's unfriendly."

"He's really a dear," Lorna said. "Don't worry, I can handle him."

They talked for an hour or more and Lorna learned that Paul lived in Gainesville during the week with Judge George Mason and Mrs. Mason, his grandparents, while he took classes at the University of Florida. Summers and weekends he spent on the farm with his parents, Mr, and Mrs. Mitchel Jones at Wacahoota. He was taking a business course and planned to go into business in Gainesville when he finished school.

It seemed to both of them that they had just begun to get acquainted when James appeared at the door.

"Lorna, you'll have to come in now. That young man had better go on home."

As Paul was leaving, Lorna took his hand and whispered, "Come back any time. Don't let Papa stop you. I want you to come back."

"I'll be back," Paul said, and left.

The day after Paul Jones called on Lorna at the McCredie home, James asked his daughter to walk with him in the orange grove behind the house.

She suspected from the stem look on his face that she was the cause of his discontent. He spoke abruptly.

"I don't want you seeing that Jones boy again."

"But, why, Papa? He's a nice boy. I like him. I like him a lot."

James saw the tinge of red creeping up her soft throat to her cheeks as she repeated, "I like him a lot."

"I knew it," he said to himself. "She's in love with him. This must stop now."

He answered his daughter. "He'll never amount to anything. He's got a weak face, just a dreamer." This was just his excuse. What he was really thinking was that she was too young to be getting serious with any boy, and besides he was an old man and needed her youth and vitality around him. "Just a few more years," he thought, "my final years."

Lorna stopped and faced her father. Her mouth was set in a determined, thin line. "Just like her mother," James thought.

"There's nothing wrong with dreaming, Papa," she said. "Mama's told me all about your dreams. This orange grove. You dreamed about all this." She pointed to the rows of orange and grapefruit trees, their healthy leaves shining in the morning sun.

James felt on the defensive. "That's different," he said lamely.

"What's different about it?" Lorna wanted to know. "Are you the only man who can dream? Paul has different dreams. He wants to be a business man. That's why he's in college."

"That's another thing," James said. "College, that's for dandies. He ought to be on the farm helpin' his folks make a living. They're poor enough."

Lorna began to wonder about something. Could her father be so set against Paul Jones because his family was poor. Had he forgotten his own past. She had to know.

"Papa," she said, "I don't believe I'm hearing you. I must be talking to somebody else. Are you upset because Paul is poor, because you don't think he's good enough for me? Is that it?"

Now James was red in the face. "You don't argue with me, Lass," he said. "He's a bumpkin, clothes don't fit He's not the kind of man I have in mind for you."

Lorna was near tears. She turned and ran for the house. James started to order her to come back, but thought better of it and decided to let her go.

"She's going to her mother," he thought. "I'm goin' to have to fight both of them."

James was right, and it was a bitter fight, the only hard words between Betty and James in their married life. It ended in compromise. Lorna could see Paul only at the McCredie house, and only in the day time. That meant Sunday afternoons.

No one was satisfied with the arrangement, particularly Betty. She discussed at length with Julia her husband's behavior. "I wish John were alive," Julia said. "James always listened to him."

Telephone service arrived in Micanopy in July of 1908 and later that year Lorna applied for a job as a telephone operator. What she had in mind was using the job in some way to see Paul when she was not under the thumb of her father, but she feared James would ruin her scheming by not letting her take the job. To her surprise he was enthusiastic about her going to work. "Take the job," he said. "Do you good, and you'll learn something. Of late you've been right peaked, an' you're not eating enough."

The job worked out fine after Lorna discovered she could keep a line open to the Jones farm and chat with Paul when she wasn't busy with her switchboard duties. There were risks, however. She never knew who was listening in and what she was doing was against the telephone company rules.

The strange courtship continued in this way until well into 1910. Paul came to the house on Sunday afternoons and they talked in whispers in the swing. During the week they visited by telephone. They didn't dare sit close together in the swing, let alone try to kiss. Lorna tried in many ways to be alone with her beau. She would ask Paul to go with her into the orange grove, but James was too alert. "Where are you going?" he would ask.

"Just to the orange grove," Lorna would say. "I want to send some oranges to Paul's mother."

"No need," her father would reply. "I have some in the house. I'll fix a bag."

Or she might offer to show Paul a new horse. "I'll go with you," James would say. "That horse is too frisky. You might get hurt."

Finally, Lorna, now eighteen, had reached the breaking point. She went to her mother.

"Mama, I need your help. You've got to help me. I don't know how much longer Paul will want to come see me. All the other girls go riding with their boy friends when they're of a mind to. It's not fair. Can't you do something with Papa?"

Betty put her arms around her daughter. "I'll think of something," she said.

A few nights later she slipped into Lorna's bedroom after Lorna had gone to bed and whispered to her, "Your cousin Edna is having a party Saturday night. Just some girl friends. She wants you to come and spend the night."

"But, Mama," Lorna said, "Paul can't come to a girls' party."

"Don't be a goose," her mother replied, and left the room.

This arrangement worked fine. Lorna went to Edna's house, that was her Uncle Thomas' daughter, and Paul arrived there in his buggy to take her for a ride. They visited with other couples, sipped sodas at the drugstore and, best of all, on moonlight nights snuggled close together under a lap robe, the reins loose over the dashboard while the horse took a sandy road it well knew to a special oak tree on Lake Tuscawilla where Lorna had first spoken to Paul.

In May of 1911, James' brother, Thomas, met him at the Micanopy Banking Company one day and greeted his brother, "When's the wedding going to be?"

James looked puzzled. "You know something I don't know?" he asked.

"Lorna," Thomas said. "Edna and Mabel have been talking about her and Paul Jones getting married. She meets him at our house all the time. Seems like a fine boy."

"They meet at your house?" James exploded.

Thomas was shocked and visibly taken aback. "Why yes," he said. "Don't tell me you didn't know."

Without answering, James turned and hurried from the bank. "Guess I put my foot in it," Thomas said to himself.

When he arrived home, James went into the orange grove to think. Betty saw him pacing back and forth, from one row of trees to another. Finally, she went to see what was troubling him.

"It's Lorna," James told her. "She's been seeing that Jones boy behind our backs. When she goes to Thomas' for a party, she meets him there. I feel sick inside. You know how I love that child. And she's done this to us."

Betty faced him. "You're wrong about two things, honey," she said gently. "Not behind our backs, but behind your back. And she's deeply in love. Love is a force you can't lock up—and you've tried to do that. The second thing is, she's no longer a child."

James appeared crushed. "You've known," he whispered, almost to himself, "and you've kept this from me. You've never kept anything from me before."

"I'm sorry," Betty said, "but you were making a prisoner of her. She deserves the chance to have a normal social life. You never acted this way with Mary Ella or with Addie. Why only Lorna?"

"I don't think you could ever understand," James replied. "She's special because she's the spittin' image of you. I can look at her and re–live how you looked when I first met you. There's something else. I was of a mind not to tell you but maybe now's the time. Lucius says my heart is bad. I can't get the old devil to tell me how long I've got but I know somethin's happening. I can't hear the clock ticking anymore, and I get these pains here." He touched the middle of his chest.

"James McCredie, I don't know what I'm gonna do with you," Betty exclaimed "You're worse'n an old woman. Bad heart my foot That's gas in your belly. Old Lucius is a doomsayer. He's gittin' too old to be goin' round telling folks they gonna die."

She paused, and then went on, "Another thing, you're not the only one who has been hurt when our children left home. Our Jim has always been my favorite. Lord knows I tried not to have a favorite son but Jim is you all over. He's got your eyes, your hair, your bearing. I cried all night when he went to Tampa to live. I worry about him all the time because he's so frail––not like you in that."

James took her hand and led her back toward the house. "I'll make it up to Lorna."

That evening when Lorna came home, James followed her to her room. Lorna's heart sank. She feared the worst, but her father put his arms around her and told her he had been a poor father and she could have her Paul. "Bring him here, have parties. This old house has been a tomb of late and I want you to enjoy your home. You haven't played the piano in months."

On June 2nd, Lorna left the house with a traveling bag she told her mother she was taking to Edna's for her cousin to use on a trip to Ocala. The next morning James met her on the porch as she was leaving for the telephone office. She had on her newest hat with a large white egret plume, her best lavender silk dress with a saucy little bustle. He commented, "Lorna, you're sure pretty this mornin'. If I didn't know better, I'd be sure you were meeting Paul."

Lorna laughed and went on her way, but instead of going to the telephone office, she went to the depot, and there was Paul, half hidden behind some baggage. It was obvious he was nervous and trying to be inconspicuous. Her heart was singing as she reached him. "Do you have the tickets?" she whispered.

That was the beginning of an eventful day. They took the train to Ocala, were married at noon in the parsonage of the First Presbyterian Church. They took the early afternoon train back to Micanopy.

"When are we going to tell them?" Paul asked his bride when they arrived at the Micanopy depot.

"Let's wait awhile," Lorna said. "The time must be right I don't know how Papa is going to take this. You stay away until I call you. We don't want anybody, getting suspicious."

"Don't wait too long," Paul said. "I might come climbing in your window."

Lorna pulled him to her behind a pile of cotton bales, awaiting shipment, and they embraced in a long kiss. "Take a tater and wait," she teased him as she skipped off toward home.

Ten days later the McCredie telephone rang and Norman answered. It was Julia in Ocala. "Oh, it's you Norman," she said. "I want to speak to your mother."

"Mama, it's Aunt Julia," Norman called, and Betty came to the telephone.

Julia was bubbling over. "It's so romantic," she said. "I know you and James must be in a tizzy. That little witch, running off to Ocala to get married, right here in my town, and she didn't let me in on her secret. When did you find out?"

"Find out what? Julia, whatever in the world are you talking about?" Betty asked, suspecting that her sister–in–law had been drinking too much wine for her "condition."

"Oh, Betty, don't be a ninny. You know what I'm talking about—Lorna's marriage to Paul here in Ocala Saturday a week ago. Now, don't tell me you don't know."

Betty was too surprised to speak.

"Could this be true?" she thought.

Then she remembered Lorna leaving that Saturday with a suitcase.

"Betty, are you there?" Julia asked. There was no answer.

"Oh lordy me," she said. "You really didn't know."

Betty had regained her composure. "No, I didn't know and I'm not sure I believe you," she said "How could Lorna be married? She's been home every night—you say it was June 3rd? She hasn't been away from this house a night since then."

"She's married all right," Julia said. "Married by the Presbyterian minister in the parsonage. Heard it from Lizzie Williams who heard it from the minister's wife, who was a witness."

"I'll talk to you later," Betty said. "I've got to talk to Lorna before James hears this."

"I'm sure you do," Julia said, as she hung up the telephone.

When Lorna came home from the telephone office, Betty met her at the door. James was hoeing in his garden. She took her daughter by the arm. "I want to talk to you in my room," she said.

Betty closed the door and turned to Lorna "Lorna is it true?" Lorna put her arms around her mother, her head on her mother's breast and her long black hair a tangled mass hiding her face as she wept softly.

"It's true, Mama. I wanted to tell you, but I was scared of Papa."

"Lorna, Lorna," Betty said, stroking her daughter's hair. "You'll have to tell him now before he hears it downtown. You know he loves you better'n all the rest. You and Paul should have come to us and we would have had the wedding right here in your home."

"There's somethin' else, Mama," Lorna said. "Paul's going to business school in Jacksonville and we're leaving Monday to live there."

Betty moved away from her daughter and sat in her rocking chair. "This is too much for one day," she said.

"Don't tell Papa yet," Lorna pleaded. "Paul is coming in on Saturday and we'll tell him together."

About that time the bedroom door opened and there stood James. "Caught you red–handed," he said, grinning. "I know you're up to something. Never seen two people who looked more guilty in my whole life."

He crossed the room and placed his hands on Lorna's shoulder. "Now, Lass, you wouldn't be telling your mother about your marriage to that poor Wacahoota farmer, would you?"

The two women stared at James in disbelief.

"James McCredie," Betty gasped, "you knew about this and didn't tell me. Why I ought to take a switch to you."

"Little bird told me," he said and started to leave the room.

Lorna ran to him and held him in the doorway, hugging him tightly.

"Oh, Papa," she said, "I love you more than anybody in the world."

"Well, not quite," James smiled.

After that there were more hugs and kisses and then plans made for a party on Saturday to announce the marriage to friends and all the McCredies.

On Saturday, Lorna learned how her father found out about the Ocala elopement. Paul had told him. After the couple had returned from Ocala, Paul couldn't sleep. His days and nights were a kind of never–never land. Finally, a nervous wreck, he had called James and made arrangements to meet him in downtown Micanopy.

"I can't stand it any longer," he told Lorna's father. "I feel like I've done you and Mrs. McCredie a grave injustice," he said, and then related how he and Lorna had slipped down to Ocala on the morning train and were married.

"You can beat me, do anything you wish," he sighed, "but I want you to know that I love Lorna very much and I'll spend all my days trying to make her happy."

"Well, now young man," James said sternly, "I ought to horsewhip you all up and down this street, but I have something worse in mind for you. I sentence you to life imprisonment, and may God have mercy on your soul."

His face had a scowl that would have frightened the bravest of military men. "What's he mean by that," Paul thought. "Is he turning me over to the marshal? Can he do that? I know Lorna is of age."

James was enjoying his moment of triumph, but the look on Paul's face was too much for him. He burst into laughter and put his arms around the shoulders of his new son–in–law and said, "I sentence you to life imprisonment in the arms of my youngest daughter and if she is as much like her mother as I think she is, you'll never want to escape. Welcome to the McCredie family."

Of course, when Lorna learned about all this, especially the fact that Paul had not told her about his meeting with her father, she was furious.

"That was a mean trick," she told him. "You let me suffer for a whole week, while your mind was at ease. How could you do that?"

"It was your father's idea," he said. "He made me promise not to say a word. He wanted to see how long it would be before you told them."

Lorna grabbed him by the ear and twisted. "Promise me that's the last secret you'll ever keep from me," she commanded, "or next time I'll pinch you where it'll hurt more."

Monday, June 19th was the worst day in Betty's life, or so she thought. That day Lorna and Paul left on the early morning train for Gainesville and then Jacksonville, where they planned to live while Paul was in business school. James tried to make a happy occasion out of the departure, but Betty knew he was only trying to hide his own anguish. She saw that when they returned home. He spent the remainder of the day walking in the orange grove. The weeks passed, with Betty and James alone in their big house for the first time in their lives. Betty had not touched Lorna's room since her marriage. Every time she went near it she felt like someone had turned out a light in her life. James never went near his daughter's room and never mentioned her.

"This will never do," Betty told herself. "It's like a sickness."

She told James at supper, "There's a big Fourth of July celebration in Gainesville next week. Let's go. It's time we had some fun."

"I dunno," James said. "I've got these chest pains again. I don't believe I can stand the trip."

Betty was angry. "He just wants to stay home and wallow in his misery," she thought.

"Chest pains, my foot," she said. "You get out there and weed the garden in the hot sun. There's nothing wrong with your heart. I'm going to Gainesville and you're going with me."

"Don't blame me if something bad happens," James said glumly.

"Nothing's gonna happen to either one of us," Betty told him.

July Fourth was on a Tuesday, a gorgeous day so they decided to drive up in the buggy, leave the rig at the livery stable and spend the night at the Arlington House. They left at daybreak to be on hand for the opening parade at 9:30. The road was filled with buggies, carriages and wagons as most of Micanopy and surrounding communities were emptied as couples and families headed for the big celebration. Micanopy had elected not to have a Fourth of July event that year.

You could hear laughter and folks chattering up and down the road and the squeaking of wheels in the sandy ruts. The sweet smell of the pines blended with the sharp odor of sweaty harnesses as the cool morning began to warm up with the rising of the sun. Occasionally, the vehicles aroused a covey of quail and they exploded in a loud whoosh from the grass into the trees. Betty told herself it was good to be alive. She looked at James and she was happy to see that he had apparently entered into the spirit of such a fine day.

But, a few minutes before 9 o'clock something happened.

As the line of vehicles approached Gainesville, suddenly the earth began to shake and the trees along the road danced Crazily, weaving and swaying like they had been taken over by some kind of evil force. Then the air was filled with a devastating roar like all the demons in hell had been let loose upon the earth. Betty grabbed her husband who was having great difficulty controlling his two horses.

People were screaming all up and down the line. Horses went out of control and some of the buggies were dragged into the woods and crushed against trees as the animals seemed to go out of their minds.

"It's the end of the world," a woman screamed in a wagon back down the road. "Look," she said, pointing at the sky.

What they saw was a huge ball of fire hurtling through the heavens at an unbelievable speed. It came out of the southwest and went over Gainesville toward the northeast. Betty clung to James gasping to her husband, "What is it? What should we do?"

Some folks had jumped from their vehicles and were kneeling in the sand, asking God to spare their lives.

And then there was a man shouting like the voice of doom. "Hit's the Judgment Day," he yelled. "The Devil's in that ball of fire and he's come to take us all to hell, but he ain't gonna get me."

Then a shot was fired and a woman screamed, "Silas, you fool, you done killed yerself. Oh Lordy, Lordy!"

By this time the ball of fire was gone, the rumbling had ceased and the ground was as firm as ever.

"What was it, James?" Betty asked in a trembling voice. "A meteor, I think," James replied, "but I never seen one like that."

There was crying and wailing from the wagon to the rear. "I'd better go see what happened back there," James said. "Sounded like someone shot himself. Must have gone out of his mind."

He returned in a few minutes. "Would you believe that was Silas Marner Judkins? Shot himself in the right temple. John Simonton's driving Mrs. Judkins on to Gainesville to find an undertaker."

9

1913

The mystery of the fireball was solved on July 5th when it was learned that a meteor had passed over Melrose and buried itself in a cornfield northwest of town. Ministers all over north Florida used the coming of the fiery mass from the sky to warn their church members that its presence was a sign that if their wickedness did not cease, the next fireball would be bigger, big enough to destroy the earth and all those on it.

For awhile excursion trains delivered loads of curious citizens to Melrose, where enterprising farmers had vehicles waiting to take them to the cornfield, but this activity gradually stopped after the visitors returned home and reported all they saw was a big hole in the ground.

In mid August, Lorna arrived from Jacksonville for a brief visit with her parents, and tell them her news. James and Betty met her at the train and she rushed into their arms, hugging both at the same time. Her eyes were shining and her face glowing with health and happiness.

As they parted to climb into the McCredie buggy for the drive home, Betty took a good look at her smiling daughter and then said, abruptly, "You're pregnant!"

"Oh, Mama, how did you know?"

"Child," Betty said, "it's in your eyes, your face. I can tell."

Lorna pretended to pout. "You spoiled my surprise. I wanted to tell you about the baby."

James gave his daughter a hug. "You can tell me all about it. I didn't guess. Sometimes I think your mother is a witch. Let's go home."

On the way to the McCredie home they discussed names for the baby. "If it's a boy, we're gonna call him Paul," Lorna said.

"John Paul Jones, Jr.?" James asked. "What a thing to do to a boy. They'll all call him Junior."

"We'll call him Paul," Lorna said. "We don't want him called Junior." "If it's a girl, she'll be named after Mama, Mary Elizabeth."

There was a long silence and then James said, abruptly, "When you going to name one for me?"

Lorna looked at her father in surprise. "Why, Papa, you have a son and a grandson named after you."

"So I have," James said, and there the subject was dropped.

Later Lorna discussed the matter with her mother. "I do believe Papa was hurt because I am not naming our first baby, it's just got to be a boy, for him. I wouldn't hurt him for the world, but he named one of his sons James and Paul wants our first boy named for him."

"Don't worry about it, Lorna," Betty said. "Your father has been acting strangely lately. He thinks he's going to die soon. Try to cheer him up. Tell him how well he looks—and he does look well, healthy as an ox, and eats like one too."

Lorna's week in Micanopy passed quickly but she did find time to see all the changes in the town and visit her friends in the stores. There was the J. E. Thrasher & Son, general merchants: S. B. Smith's meat market: N.B. Mott, general merchant: W. A. Carlton, variety store: W. C. Barnett, drug store, a gentleman who loved Lorna like his own daughter and greeted her with a hug: O. L. Feaster & Sons, general merchants: Crawford & Company, drugs and groceries: J. W. May & Co., drugs and groceries: S.R. Chitty, general store and baker; the Micanopy Banking Company with a capital of fifteen thousand dollars. J. W. Barr was president and J.D. Watkins cashier, both good friends.

Lorna noticed that E. C. Chitty & Sons, general merchants and furniture dealers, were at their same old address. She passed by the office of Doctors Montgomery and Montgomery but the door was locked. Miss Maud Haviaird, millinery expert, tried to get her to buy a new hat. Work was progressing on the new hamper and crate factory for Willis & Jones who had cotton gins and grist and feed mills. The Melton Lumber Company was in full operation and its whistle sent the whole town off to eat dinner at noon.

"The town's growing," James told her, "but we need more good farmers, truck and orange growers, people with money to invest here."

In 1911, Micanopy had seven churches, two schools including a junior high school with three teachers, two hotels, two railroads and some hard–surfaced streets.

"Beats what was here when we came in 1856," James told his daughter. He sighed, "But I miss the old times. I miss John and the good times at his farm, an' I miss you, Lass."

Lorna wondered when he would stop calling her "Lass." Then she remembered he still called her mother the same thing.

Before the end of the year, Lorna and Paul had moved to Gainesville and Paul was in business with his brother–in–law, Norman McCredie. They had opened a "quick–lunch" restaurant across North Main Street from the Atlantic Coast Line Railroad station. Norman had married Maude Davis of McIntosh and they had two children, a boy, Claude Aubrey, and a girl, Mary Ella.

The restaurant was almost Lorna's undoing. During the final weeks of her pregnancy, she craved strange foods, particularly dill pickles. One night, Paul had to go to the restaurant at midnight to get her some pickles and at 2 o'clock in the morning she began to scream in pain. Paul was white and trembling with fear as she told him she was dying and dug into his back with her fingernails so that he felt tiny streams of blood trickling toward his midsection.

"Let me go," he pleaded, "so I can get Doctor Hodges."

"No, no," she cried. "I'll die here all alone. Call Mama."

"Your mother can't get here in time to help," Paul told her. "I'm going for the doctor." He almost flung her from him to get away. He felt like a monster as he left the room with Lorna calling after him, "Oh, Paul, I'm dying. I won't be alive when you get back. Oh my poor baby!"

Doctor Hodges lived less than five blocks from their apartment and Paul ran all the way. Dr. Hodges in his nightshirt and robe followed him back. They found Lorna tossing and moaning from pain.

After examining her swollen abdomen and listening to the tiny heartbeat of her unborn child, Hodges asked, "Lorna, when did you eat last?" Paul answered. "She had some dill pickles around midnight."

"Lorna, how many pickles did you eat?" Hodges wanted to know.

"Just one," she murmured.

"Are you sure?"

"Maybe two."

Paul spoke up. "I brought five large ones from the restaurant, and they're all gone."

Hodges shook his head. "Five large dill pickles this time of night. No wonder you're in pain. You have acute indigestion."

He motioned for Paul to follow him out of the room. "I'll give her something for pain and to relax her muscles but this is serious. With the pressure of the baby and now the gas from her stomach, anything can happen."

Hodges spent the remainder of the night in a rocking chair, but by morning Lorna's pains had eased and she was out of danger.

On March 1st, Paul turned the restaurant over to Norman and took Lorna home to Micanopy to have her baby. Despite Betty's warning that he would have a stroke, James built a tiny cradle for "little Paul." Betty was so certain the infant would be a boy that she padded the cradle with cotton and blue satin.

He came right on time on March 3rd at 8 p.m. Betty brought him in and placed him in Lorna's arms. "Here's your little Junior," she told her daughter.

Through her weariness, Lorna scolded her mother. "Don't say that. He's not a Junior. Just call him Paul."

Betty thought to herself, "There's going to be a problem here. If he's not to be a Junior, he's bound to be 'Little Paul'."

And that's the way it turned out.

During the birthing, James and Paul walked through the orange grove, up and down the rows, each deep in his own thoughts.

Paul was thinking how he was going to make a successful businessman out of his son. In his vision he saw a big, healthy man with deep brown eyes, an ever flashing smile, mild mannered, courteous and kind to his parents.

James had other visions, draped in crepe, from the superstitions of his highland home. The naming of a child in Scotland was a serious matter, and the name could bring good or bad fortune to the child or the family or both. He remembered how his father had laughed at the idea that naming a child after one who had died would condemn the second child to death. And yet, the second William of David and Janet McCredie had died in Ocala shortly after the family had arrived in Florida. On the other hand, the second Margaret had lived and prospered.

He smiled inwardly. "Well, she hadn't prospered in one way. She no longer got a pig for Christmas."

There was another superstition that bothered him, although he considered himself an enlightened, twentieth century man. After all it was 1912. But, in Scotland, if an ordinary man tried to set up a family dynasty by naming his son John Paul Jones, Jr., for example, and that son named a son, John Paul Jones III, etc., he was courting disaster. James had defied that superstition and named one of his sons James McCredie II and the son had named his first son James McCredie III.

Would God look upon this kind of thing as a vanity of man that had to stop?

He never lived to find the answer.

On February 5th of 1913, Lorna returned to Micanopy to have her second son, Richard Irvin.

On February 14th, Betty was up at daylight, as usual, fired up the big kitchen range with fatwood, made buttermilk biscuits and put on a pot of grits. She could hear James stirring in the bedroom. She went to the henhouse for fresh eggs and sliced some smoked bacon. They both liked a big breakfast even though Doctor Montgomery had warned them to keep their weight down.

"You can eat your way into the grave," he said.

1913

James came in. "Lass, you must be the best cook in all the world. That bacon smells like heaven."

"It's just bacon," Betty replied, "same as always, but you might just go to heaven if you eat too much. At least, that's what old Doctor Montgomery keeps saying."

"The old scallywag," James retorted. "He's always trying to take away somebody's pleasure. Don't see him going hungry. He's gittin' fat as a hog." He laughed. "Besides, Heaven's not where I'm going."

They both ate heartily. As they got up from the table, Betty noticed her husband stagger slightly. "Jim, you all right?" she asked. She hardly ever called him "Jim."

"Sure," he replied. "Just a bit of dizziness. I need some exercise, and the garden needs hoeing."

"Get your hat," Betty told him, "and don't stay out too long. That sun's gonna get right hot before 9 o'clock."

He got his hat and went out.

Betty cleaned up the kitchen, but she couldn't get her husband out of her mind. There had been a look on his face she had never seen before. At 7 o'clock she decided to check on him.

At the far end of the garden she saw him on the ground, his hoe under him.

Doctor Montgomery came as quickly as he could from his home and office a half mile down the lane.

"There's nothing I can do here," he told Betty. "I'm sorry. He's dead. Paralysis."

"James will like it here," Betty McCredie thought as they lowered his store–bought casket into the ground at the old Micanopy Cemetery.

A slight smile curled her lips beneath her black veil as she wondered how he felt in the new–fangled casket. He had made many handsome caskets for friends and family members in the old days and she felt like his Scottish blood would rebel at being encased in anything more than a plain cypress box. This one had expensive silver handles, a see–through glass opening at the head and was tapered at both ends. "Throwing away good money," he would have fumed

She had thought about putting a small bottle of whiskey near his right hand to help him on his journey but decided against it when she thought about the winds of gossip that would blow across the town if her gift were discovered.

James was fond of the old cemetery. It was less than a mile from his home and he had remarked many times how peaceful each day began and ended there. He regularly visited the McCredie lot to tend the graves of his mother and father.

Giant oaks, draped in grey moss, almost shut out the sun and the blue sky, but on this March afternoon the gentle rustle of the breeze and the sweet singing of a mockingbird in the distance added a festive touch to the somber occasion. "Thank you, bird," Betty thought.

It was comforting to know that there was still something alive and well in her world that had ended so suddenly. Since James' death she had refused to think about anything but she knew the time would come when she would be forced to face a future without "her Jim." In the meanwhile, she just accepted everything around her, sons, daughters, grandchildren and friends as part of the natural flow of life.

There had been one moment, however, as the family sat around the casket during the night when she had grown cold and sat trembling until Lorna brought her a shawl for her shoulders.

Julia nodded her head. "I've been feeling a strange chill all day," she said. "It's some kind of omen. Mark my words, there will be two more deaths."

"Hush, Mama," said her daughter, Mary Evelyn. "You musn't say things like that."

"It's true," Julia said. "Bad things come in threes. This is a bad year, 1913. It's a bad year for the McCredies. You mark my words!"

Less than a month later, on April 14th, Betty received word that her son, James, had died of lung fever in Tampa. The death had not come as a complete shock because Jim, had been a frail boy, and for months prior to his death had been bed–ridden off and on. Nevertheless, she could not help but think of Julia's warning. Was there another death to come?

Betty decided it was time for her to look to the future. She knew she could not handle the chores of running the citrus grove, but how would she live?

"Come with me to Ocala," Julia urged. "We can just be two old women rattlin' around in a big house together. Maybe we can catch us some new husbands."

"That's not for me," Betty said. "Nobody could do after James." She smiled, "Besides, it's too much trouble to train em."

Julia's house was the last place she wanted to go. She couldn't take her sister–in–law's lifestyle.

By July, Betty had made it known that what she really wanted to do was go to Gainesville and live with Lorna and Paul and her two grandchildren, but she couldn't bring herself to add another burden to that family, just getting started in life.

The family members gathered and arrived at a solution. Thomas, told his mother, "You sell the old home place to Lorna and let her sell it and use the money for your needs. She won't have to give you any money, except maybe a dollar or two to make it binding. You can apply for government pensions for both the Indian War and the War Between the States and have a monthly income as well."

And so it was agreed.

On August 27th, before anything had been done about the house, Betty learned that her brother–in–law, David McCredie, age seventy–four, had just died. "Lord, in Heaven," she thought, "Julia was right. That's three McCredies dead in 1913!"

These were lonely days and nights in the old McCredie house. Even Betty had grown to regard it as the "old McCredie house," and not the home she had known for so many years. She caught herself looking into the grove behind the house, expecting to see James walking between the rows of trees, heavily laden with young fruit. The grove had been his life and his love and he spent many hours there, examining the ripening fruit and carefully observing the trees for insect damage and disease.

"I've got to get out of here," she thought. "It's time to end this chapter and begin a new one."

She spent a lot of time sitting in her favorite rocking chair on the front porch, from where she could see down the lane toward Micanopy's downtown area. Despite her sixty–two years, her hair was still dark, with a few strands of grey, and her dark eyes still sparkled with the luster of her youth. Her relatives and friends said often of her, "She carries her age well."

One day, as she sat on the porch, smiling to herself while she remembered the day she had first sighted her husband–to–be, a two–seater buggy, drawn by a matched pair of magnificent percherons, drew up at the front gate. She recognized Doctor Lucius Montgomery. He was in his seventieth year but she noted that he jumped from the buggy, as spry as a man of thirty. He was dressed as usual in a tight–fitting suit, tailored in New York to hold in his aging figure that should have been sagging at the waist. She suspected he was wearing some kind of corset–like arrangement to trim up his figure.

He came up the steps, his gold watch chain gleaming across his stomach, his stove–pipe hat in his hand. "Mornin', Miss Betty," he said. He had always called her "Miss Betty" and Lorna was always "Miss Lorna."

"Thought you might like to go for a drive," he said. "You been keepin' too close to home. Ain't right for a purty lady like you to grieve so much. It's a mighty fine morning."

"Oh, my Lord," Betty thought to herself. "He's come a courting. Look at him, all dandied up. What am I going to say?"

Doctor Montgomery must have read her thoughts.

"Just wanted to cheer you up," he said, smiling. "We've been friends for more than forty years. James would approve."

She felt a little guilty for her thoughts, but she did have an excuse for refusing his kindness. "I do appreciate your thoughtfulness, Lucius," she said, "but I'm waitin' on John Hamilton, James' friend, to arrive. He's going to be doing some carpenter work in Micanopy an' he'll be staying here with me for a few days."

"Bachelor, ain't he?" Doctor Montgomery said, rolling his eyes around.

Betty suspected that she had been right about Lucius' intentions. "He's a bachelor all right," she said, "an' he'll probably stay that way until he dies. Besides I'm not lookin' for another man."

Doctor Montgomery prepared to leave. "You'll change your mind about that," he said. "You're too young and purty for the men to leave you alone. It's nature's way. I'll be back." He bowed slightly and left.

Betty could imagine how the tongues would wag if she were seen riding in a fancy buggy with Doctor Montgomery. She remembered as if it were yesterday the big scandal that swirled around the doctor in 1889. Micanopy had never known anything like it before or since.

Rumors flew all over the County that he was holding men in bondage, that he was selling whiskey illegally, that he was involved in an adulterous relationship with an orphan female clerk in one of his stores and that he had approached one of his female patients who was a member of the Micanopy Presbyterian Church in an effort to obtain her favors. On one occasion he was said to have used force on the female patient so that she left his office and never returned to get medicine he had prescribed for her.

The result of all the rumors was that the Presbyterian Church appointed a prosecutor and others to prepare a case against Dr. Montgomery in a full–fledged church trial. Among those asked to assist in the prosecution was Thomas McCredie, Betty's brother–in–law.

Although the church tried to keep the trial within the church family, Dr. Montgomery, outraged by the whole affair, had it all aired in the *Gainesville Record* as an advertisement, for which he paid on June 20th, 1889. Another newspaper, *The Lake View* of Micanopy ran a completely false story that Dr. Montgomery had been so ashamed he had committed suicide.

Actually, the accusations and counter–accusations flew back and forth as letters in the newspapers for weeks ahead of the church trial and during all of these encounters in print Dr. Montgomery met The Reverend James

M. Shearer, pastor of the Presbyterian Church, on main street in downtown Micanopy one day with the intention of Cowhiding the minister. They ended up clawing and scratching at one another as they rolled on the ground until Montgomery asked the preacher to let him up, which he did. Montgomery then struck at Shearer with his whip. He bragged about Cowhiding Shearer but Shearer said the whip never touched him.

A peace warrant was sworn against Montgomery to prevent a repetition of the Cowhiding incident, and later an attempt was made to have Doctor Montgomery arrested for assault and battery against the minister. The case was thrown out of court, however, on the grounds that the whip "was not a lethal weapon."

The church court found him guilty of all charges and took away his church membership as well as stripping him of his position as a church elder.

The "Micanopy Affair," as the newspapers called it, does not appear in any of the town's history but it shocked the townspeople to the core and created a divided community that took years to heal. There were many substantial citizens who believed that Doctor Montgomery was unjustly accused and unjustly punished. Others, also outstanding citizens, were just as certain that the good doctor got what he deserved.

Thomas McCredie, who was privy to all the details, believed the Presbyterian Church had done what it had to do. Betty and James, remembering Lucius Montgomery's skill in curing James' Yellow Fever, his long friendship with all the McCredies, his services to the family as a physician and his conduct as an outstanding citizen of the town, the County and the state, withheld judgment.

Although Betty McCredie did not even dream of it, the day Lucius Montgomery left her front porch, the year 1913 still had some tragic events waiting in the wings for the McCredie family.

Early that year, Norman McCredie's wife, Maude Davis McCredie, had left her twenty–three–year–old husband and gone home to McIntosh with her two children to live with her mother, who ran a boarding house. This had happened before James died and caused him great torment.

The separation had caused such a rift between the Davis and McCredie families that James was not able to see his two grandchildren, a boy and a girl, both of whom he adored. The separation had been caused by Norman's excessive drinking and abuse of his wife.

James did a lot of walking in the citrus grove over this family problem. "I could horsewhip that youngun," he said over and over to Betty. "How can he make that sweet wife and those children suffer so."

Lorna was in the middle of the problem. Norman was her favorite brother. He had hacked off one of her fingers with a hatchet one time while cutting "kindlin'," and James had patched her up by sticking the piece of finger back on with a wad of cob–web, and it worked! She never had any trouble with that finger the rest of her life. Also, Norman was in the restaurant business in Gainesville with Paul, and she saw him every day and had tried to get him to stop drinking. He had a half interest in the Hotel Graham Cafe, which the restaurant had been named.

Norman was hot–tempered and became mean when he drank, but despite this he was one of the most popular young men in the County. After the separation, Maude finally filed for divorce, although she told a girl friend that she would always love Norman. He had threatened to kill her if she obtained a divorce and had threatened her brother, Claude Davis.

Norman deliberately set about to carry out his threats against his wife. First, in order to give her a false sense of security, he sent a telegram to Claude Davis, saying he would see them all again some day but in the meantime he was leaving the country. Then, on November 11th he asked Paul for the afternoon off to attend the night performance of the Sautelle Circus, then playing in Gainesville.

He was not heard from again until Friday when he appeared suddenly at the Davis boarding house, went inside and attempted to drag his wife out the front door. His mother–in–law tugged on her daughter's arm, trying to prevent his taking Maude with him. Failing to get her farther than the porch, he pulled a pistol and shot her in the back of the head. She fell to the floor and thinking he had killed her he then shot himself in the head and died instantly.

An empty whiskey bottle in his coat pocket and a note that read, "I'm on the train, going to McIntosh to kill my wife because I love her so much I cannot bear to lose her. Please, God, someone take care of our babies."

Maude Davis was only dazed by the flesh wound inflicted by the thirty–two caliber bullet and recovered fully. On Saturday, November 15th, Norman was buried in the McCredie plot in Micanopy.

"I told you it would be a bad year," Julia told Betty at the cemetery, "and there's another month to go."

Betty put her hand over her eyes and walked away without replying. She had suffered deeply from Norman's death, and especially the way it happened. Her heart went out to her daughter–in–law and the two grandchildren, but she knew she would never see any of them again—and that was the worst blow.

The rift between the Davis and McCredie families would be too wide to cross ever now, she thought.

On December 27th, 1913, William McCredie, David's only living son, died. That made five McCredie deaths in 1913.

By this time Betty was living in Gainesville with Lorna and Paul. She sold the old home place to Lorna who then sold the property to H. L. Merry and E. B. Howell. The fifty–one acres, including the two–story, Queen Anne house, fifty acres of orange and grapefruit trees, and household goods brought one–thousand dollars.

The question was how to get her household goods to Gainesville and then where to put them? Paul and Lorna lived in a small apartment. Lorna's father–in–law, Mitchell Jones, agreed to meet Betty in Micanopy with his wagon and team of mules and take one Wagonload to Gainesville. The rest of the furniture would be left for the new owners.

The day came when Betty boarded the train in Gainesville for Micanopy to meet Mitchell. She was heavy of heart. She wondered if all her life had been pointed toward this sad ending. She got her harpsichord in the wagon, some silverware, family pictures and bedding. That was all.

As the wagon pulled out of the yard into the lane, she looked back at the house, the house that held most of her memories and she felt she could not hold back the tears. Then, she remembered Janet McCredie. She turned to Mitchell, and with bright eyes, said, "We'll see what tomorrow brings!"